LOYAL WOLF

LINDA O. JOHNSTON

MILLS & BOON

Published in Great Britain 2014
by Mills & Boon, an imprint of Harlequin (UK) Limited,
Eton House, 18-24 Paradise Road, Richmond, Surrey, TW9 1SR

© 2014 Linda O. Johnston

ISBN: 978-0-263-91402-3

89-0814

Harlequin (UK) Limited's policy is to use papers that are natural, renewable and recyclable products and made from wood grown in sustainable forests. The logging and manufacturing processes conform to the legal environmental regulations of the country of origin.

Printed and bound in Spain
by Blackprint CPI, Barcelona

Linda O. Johnston loves to write. While honing her writing skills, she worked in advertising and public relations, then became a lawyer...and enjoyed writing contracts. Linda's first published fiction appeared in Ellery Queen's Mystery Magazine and won a Robert L. Fish Memorial Award for Best First Mystery Short Story of the Year. Linda now spends most of her time creating memorable tales of paranormal romance, romantic suspense and mystery. Visit www.lindaojohnston.com.

Loyal Wolf is dedicated to shapeshifters and the readers who love them. And also to my husband, Fred, who, though not a writer, is an excellent sounding board for plot issues.

Chapter 1

Deputy Sheriff Kathlene Baylor steered down the narrow, tree-lined lane toward the entrance to Clifford Cabins, a rustic motel a few miles out of town. She was driving her personal car, a silver SUV, rather than an official Clifford County, Montana, Sheriff's Department vehicle, despite being in uniform. It was late afternoon, and she was off duty. If she'd had time to go home and change, she would have.

But she was too eager for the pending meeting to incur any further delay.

This outing was definitely not an official activity, though. In fact, it was just the opposite. Even though it should look, to anyone who might be paying attention to her, as if she was just dashing off to go meet up with an old friend.

Not quite.

Kathlene always considered herself a by-the-book, dedicated law-enforcement officer. But that was before.

Now she was too concerned about what was going on in Clifford County to do nothing, even though her boss, Sheriff Melton Frawley, was certain that she was wrong.

That she was "worrying her pretty little head about nothing," was the way he put it.

She sniffed at the very thought of the way the whole department was encouraged by Melton to return to old, antiquated ways, when women weren't skilled and respected officers of the law, but handy cooks and cleaners who also entertained their men in bed.

She would have complained, claimed discrimination to the County Counsel, the City Attorney of Cliffordsville, or anyone else who would listen. Problem was, no one with any clout cared.

Well, maybe she had no clout, but she wasn't about to just sit there and let her county be overrun by anarchists.

She slowed down when she saw a small deer darting through the underbrush toward the road. Good move, she thought as the animal stopped, then leaped back into the woods. She wasn't a hunter but there were a lot of them around. Some legitimate.

The others were the ones who worried her.

At least their encampment was a few more miles down this road. And that deer—plus, much more important, the humans around here—might survive if what she believed was true, and the people she was going to see helped her do something about it.

There. She had reached the sign identifying the winding drive to the Clifford Cabins. She turned and headed toward them.

She'd received a call. Help had arrived.

She only hoped they would really figure out what was going on—and the situation was thereafter fixed appropriately.

A knock sounded on the cabin door. Right on time, Lieutenant Jock Larabey thought.

"Want me to get it?" His aide, Staff Sergeant Ralf Nunnoz, glanced toward Jock. Like his superior officer, he was dressed casually, with no indication that either one of them was in the military, let alone part of Alpha Force. Ralf had on well-worn jeans with a Seattle Seahawks T-shirt, since they were supposed to have driven from Washington State to drop in and see Jock's supposed long-term friend Kathlene Baylor before heading for Yellowstone National Park. Ralf's hair was short, of course, as was Jock's, but there was no other indication of their background.

"You're sure Click is hidden well?" Jock asked. He didn't want his cover dog seen, particularly this early in the assignment.

All Alpha Force shapeshifting members had cover dogs that resembled them in their changed forms, and Click looked a lot like a wolf, which was ideal. Jock was a werewolf.

"He's locked in the cabin next door with some beef jerky treats to keep him occupied for now." Even though Kathlene had reserved this cabin on their behalf, Jock had Ralf book another one next door in case they needed additional space. And cover. Like now.

"Good. Then let her in."

Ralf approached the wide wooden door attached to the cabin's fake log walls and opened it. "Jock?" said a woman's voice in a low, husky tone.

"You must be Jock's friend Kathlene," Ralf said more loudly, obviously in case there was anyone outside eavesdropping. "Come in. I'm his good friend Ralf Nunnoz."

"Good to meet you, Ralf." The female voice was louder now, too. Higher in tone, as well, in her apparent embarrassment.

The woman who had to be Kathlene Baylor, deputy sheriff of the local Montana county and seeker of Alpha

Force help, walked in the door, looked around and approached Jock.

Not that she truly knew what Alpha Force was about. Jock was certain of that.

"Hi," she said, sounding relieved now as Ralf shut the door behind her. "Jock? I'm Kathlene."

"Good to see you, buddy," he said, donning their cover as if it was who they all truly were. He strode over to the woman and, ignoring her unappealing law-enforcement uniform, gave her a big hug.

She was tall, though not as tall as he was. She was slender. And those curves—his body reacted immediately as if their cover was that they were long-separated lovers instead of friends.

Hell, if he had known her in the past they would have been more than friends. He'd have had sex with her as fast as he could have seduced her.

Then.

But not now. They had a joint mission to accomplish. One that, if she was correct about what was going on around here, definitely needed Alpha Force's unique touch to straighten it out. And if Kathlene found out the truth about him, he felt sure that making love with him would be the last thing she would ever want.

Unless his seduction could convince her otherwise…

She backed up. Quickly. Her face was flushed. She was one good-looking woman, despite how severely her dark hair was pulled back from those reddened cheeks. That face didn't need adornment. It was smooth, with sexy, full lips and sparkling eyes that peered out from beneath black brows that helped to frame them.

Her gray uniform wasn't the sexiest thing he had ever seen a woman wear—and yet Kathlene filled it out in all the right places. A definitely appealing bustline—as he had felt pressed against him. A small waist.

Of course the holster she wore at her hip didn't exactly turn him on, but it went with the rest of her gear. He wondered where her weapon was, figured she'd locked it up since she wasn't currently on duty, or so he assumed.

But admiring her—or not—wasn't why Ralf and he had come.

Right now he needed to get this woman's description of what was going on here.

And then Alpha Force could get to work.

Jock Larabey. Her old college buddy. Or so the rest of the world should believe.

The guy did look military, muscles bulging from beneath his snug University of Montana T-shirt. It appeared that he had indeed come here prepared to play the cover-story role they had decided on. They were supposed to have gone to the U of M, Missoula campus, at the same time and become friends there.

That was, in fact, the part of the state where she had grown up. And then had her life turned utterly upside down, when her parents—

No. She wouldn't think about that now. It was why she hadn't actually remained friends with people she had known back then, but she didn't tell anyone that.

And at the moment, she had something a lot more pressing to think about. But she hadn't expected someone as hot-looking as this man, with his wide shoulders, chiseled face and sexy hint of pale brown facial hair. His piercing hazel eyes surveyed her as if assessing whether she, too, was all she was cracked up to be. She forced herself to smile and was rewarded with a grin that suggested he had been assessing more than that about her.

And that hug? Appropriate for the situation, sure, but it had set her insides very inappropriately on fire.

She had to back away from those kinds of thoughts. Cool off. Or at least try to.

"We need to talk, Kathlene," Jock said.

She glanced toward the door. It was closed, and the other man, Ralf, stood nearby. They could, in fact, talk now.

"I know what the story is that you described to get Alpha Force's interest," Jock continued, "but I want to hear it directly from you."

"Of course."

This could take a while. She glanced around for someplace to sit. This cabin was as rustic in here as it was outside. Near one wall there were a couple of narrow beds with green plaid blankets, pale green sheets and pillows with matching covers.

Beds? Her mind again darted to that hug and the feel of his body against her. She quickly looked away.

In one corner was a kitchenette, and beside it a small table with two chairs. Should she sit there with Jock to go over the situation? Safer than anywhere near the beds, of course.

But what about Ralf?

Good thing he was still around. That also helped Kathlene focus on what was important, and not how her libido had been stoked.

Ralf stood near Jock, arms crossed, watching her. He was shorter than Jock and not quite as muscular, but he, too, looked strong. The gray in his black hair was surprising since he didn't look older than mid-thirties, only a few years older than Kathlene. Ralf's facial features were wide and suggested, like his last name, a Hispanic background.

Like Jock, his casual outfit didn't even hint that he was currently in the military and on assignment.

Jock must have caught her indecision. He gestured with one muscular arm toward the table. "You and I can sit there, and Ralf will hang out near us."

Ralf strode toward the nearest wall and leaned against it, arms crossed over his chest. It appeared that he was used to taking orders from Jock. All Kathlene had been told about them was that they were members of a covert military unit called Alpha Force, her "friend" Jock was a lieutenant, and he would be accompanied by a noncommissioned officer.

She only hoped that the two of them could at least provide whatever juice was needed to bring in more help if needed.

And she expected it would be.

For now she, like Ralf, followed the sort-of instructions that Jock gave and sat at the table.

And decided how best to begin this conversation.

Jock sent Ralf to the kitchen area to grab bottles of water for all of them. Until he rejoined them, this would be a good time to learn Kathlene's background.

Like, did she believe in shapeshifters?

He laughed internally at the thought. That was a question that would never get asked.

As she spoke, she told him she had always lived in Montana, moving from Missoula after college.

Despite their cover story, Jock had never been in Montana before. He had grown up in Wisconsin, another state where there were more rural areas than city life. Where wilderness was the primary topography.

That was where his family had settled long ago. The remoteness helped to hide what they were. But what he was had made him gravitate toward the U.S. Military as soon as he first heard of Alpha Force.

Ralf returned and placed a bottle of water on the smooth but unpolished wooden table before each of them.

"Here's to our success in resolving the Clifford County situation," Jock said, raising his bottle.

"I'll drink to that," Kathlene said. Ralf joined them in their alcohol-free toast. The look on Kathlene's face nevertheless appeared strained, as if she doubted they in fact would be successful.

If so, he intended to surprise her. In many ways.

Right now it was time to really get down to business. And talk.

And make sure he ignored how much lust he felt for this lovely, obviously determined woman.

Kathlene started their conversation after downing a drink of water. "I chose this motel for you to stay in," she said, "because the former ranch where the people I believe are anarchists are gathering isn't far from here."

"Yes, the anarchists," Jock said. "Why we're here. I'd like you to tell us why you think that's who they are. I've looked at the file that was started on this matter before Alpha Force was called in, but as I said I want your version."

"Of course." She seemed to hesitate, but only for a second. And there was nothing at all hesitant in the strong, sure glare of her blue eyes. "I could be wrong about the whole thing but I don't think so. The number of people at the apparent conclave, all men as far as I can tell, keep increasing. They stay mostly to themselves but when I've headed in the direction of the formerly abandoned ranch where they live, I've sometimes heard gunshots."

"It's late summer," Ralf said from behind them. "Isn't it hunting season for something?"

"The season for large game like elk, moose and all tends to start in late September. But when any members of this group have come into town, they seem to make it a point of saying they've been holding target practice to be ready when the season starts."

"That target practice could also be with the intent of hunting more than wildlife," Jock said.

Like people?

That was the crux of their involvement here. They would find out about what these hunters, or whatever they were, were up to.

And stop them if necessary.

Perhaps in the form of an animal they otherwise would hunt.

A wolf.

Jock glanced at Ralf, who nodded. He undoubtedly knew exactly what Jock was thinking.

The sudden glance between Jock and Ralf stoked Kathlene's curiosity. This man wasn't a fan of hunting? His look of displeasure actually pleased Kathlene. She might have gone into law enforcement, but her intent was to save as many lives as possible, human and animal.

Especially human. That was the reason she had become a deputy sheriff. She knew more than most people what it was like to lose loved ones to unanticipated and unnecessary violence.

"What about wolves?" Ralf asked. "Are they fair game?"

"Yes, sometimes," Kathlene said. "I'm not sure what the season for them is this year."

"Oh," Jock said.

Kathlene couldn't quite figure out what his tone meant—irony? Anger? A challenge of some kind?

But she had been saving her biggest concern for last.

"It's not only multiple rounds of gunshots I've heard near that old ranch area," she said. "And I think this is what actually got the military's attention. There have been explosions, too. Small ones, but more than just shots being fired."

Her boss, the sheriff, had only shaken his head when she'd mentioned them. Told her she had one hell of a female imagination.

In essence, told her to bug off and maybe respond to some phone calls from senior citizens who called the cops claiming they heard things because they wanted some attention.

Like she supposedly was doing despite her lesser age.

"Interesting," Jock said. He asked her questions—cogent ones that indicated he actually believed her, which made her feel a lot better than it should.

But she managed to explain her own patrol duties—both assigned by the department and assumed by herself because of her concern about the growing number of apparent hunters hanging out at the old ranch that had been unused for years but apparently had been purchased recently by a relative of one of the men now living there, according to public records. Or at least it had been purchased by someone with the last name Tisal, but not Nate Tisal, the guy who apparently was in charge of the group.

"If anything, they could be terrorists and not also anarchists," she said, "but when I've spoken with any of them, which is rare, their comments suggest that they hate any kind of authority, not only local."

"If they're either," Jock said, "we need to confirm it and shut them down before anyone's hurt."

"Definitely," Kathlene said. "One thing I'm particularly concerned about is that there have been threats made against at least some of the Clifford County Commissioners. A friend of mine who's a commissioner told me about some anonymous emails with sources that couldn't be traced, as well as actual letters mailed to the County Administration Building from other parts of the country. They apparently tell the commission to back off from enacting some laws currently under consideration that would help enforce state regulations to protect wildlife and require the arrest of poachers. The sheriff said he's got some officers looking into it but nothing's been found so far. It's not certain that the anarchists are to blame, of course—but with the timing and all, that's my suspicion."

"Got it," Jock said. "We'll look into that, too. Right now, though, let's go over our cover story."

"Yeah," Ralf said. He'd been leaning against the cabin wall beside the table sipping water. "Jock's your old buddy, and we're both insurance salesmen from Seattle, which is where Jock supposedly lives these days, too. Don't we look like insurance salesmen?" He mugged a little toward Kathlene and she laughed.

"'Course we do," Jock said. "Risk and liability and all that kind of stuff, right?"

"Right," Ralf responded. "And high premiums, too."

Both men laughed this time. Great. They apparently had a good working relationship. But Kathlene hadn't figured out what Alpha Force was and why it was considered a particularly special military team.

Good thing she had made friends in college with Bill Grantham, whose dad had been an army colonel then. Now he was a general working at the Pentagon. Kathlene, frustrated and not knowing what else to do, had wound up explaining her concerns to Bill about what was going on in Clifford County. General Grantham had listened, then suggested sending in help to scope out their validity. The result had been the deployment here of members of this covert unit. But why Alpha Force? What was Alpha Force all about? Kathlene had no idea…yet. But she would definitely learn.

"You'll need to explain insurance to me one of these days," she made herself joke. Then she got serious. "And also about what your special unit's all about and how you'll be dealing with the situation here."

"Sure," Jock responded. "Once we've done our recon and we see what we're actually up against."

But why was it that Kathlene had the sense that the last thing that hot, amusing, obviously determined Jock Larabey wanted to do was to let her know what Alpha Force was really about?

"I'll give you my schedule," she told them. "I'll want to be with you as much as possible."

"No need," Jock said. "We'll handle it."

She glanced at him. He was sharing a look with Ralf that clearly excluded her. What weren't they saying?

"My participation, helping out? That's part of the plan," she said coolly.

"Not exactly."

"Yes, exactly."

He just glared at her, but only for a moment before moving on as if she hadn't spoken. "Now, as I started to say, we're here from Seattle, which is where we ostensibly live. Right now we're here visiting my old buddy Kathlene on our way to tour Yellowstone once we've done some sightseeing and real camping around here. We love this area, though, and will explore it for fun—or that's what it'll look like. But we'll do some nosing around to find out more about it. That will include where you indicate your anarchists are living."

"Fine," she said. "I unfortunately don't have vacation time I can take right now but I'll visit you a lot here at the cabin, camp out with you on nights when I don't have to report for duty early the next day. And—"

"No, not necessary. We'll hang out in town with you some of the time, get together for lunch or dinner in public, that kind of thing. We're the ones here undercover, and we'll handle all the covert investigation stuff. No need for you to get involved."

Kathlene felt herself rise to a half stand. Her shoulders were tense. Her whole body was stiff, in fact.

Was this man telling her, as her boss, the sheriff, did, that women had no place in down and dirty law-enforcement matters—maybe just pushing paper or bringing coffee?

If that was what he wasn't saying—but meant—Jock Larabey was going to learn that exactly the opposite was true.

Especially with her.

Chapter 2

Kathlene decided not to push the point with this man. Not yet. Instead, she suggested that she give them a quick tour of Cliffordsville.

Even though they must have driven through the town to get here, she could give them a different perspective on it, both as a resident and a peace officer.

Not to mention being the person who thought the town—and possibly way beyond—needed help.

"Sounds like a good idea," Jock said, and Ralf agreed.

They concurred that Kathlene should drive them. Her chauffeuring them around would help substantiate their cover of Jock being an old friend of hers.

"Kathlene and I are going to talk a little bit first," Jock told Ralf as they reached her car. "Why don't you meet us at the front gate to this place? You won't mind stopping there for a minute, will you, Kathlene?"

The cabin-filled motel area was surrounded by a decorative wooden fence, with a gate near the office that was almost always open. "No, that's fine," Kathlene said, although she wondered what was really going on after the two men exchanged looks that appeared to hold a brief, silent conversation. Some Alpha Force business that they weren't going to tell her about?

If so, that was okay—for now. But it made her even more determined to learn what they really were about.

She looked in the rearview mirror after backing her vehicle out of its space in front of the row of cabins where these men were staying. Only a few other cars were around, including a black, nondescript sedan which, considering its proximity to their cabin, was the one she assumed they had come in.

She glanced again into the mirror after aiming her SUV toward the entrance and saw that Ralf still stood there, apparently waiting for her to leave the area before doing whatever he and Jock had communicated about.

That only piqued her curiosity all the more.

"So how long have you lived in Cliffordsville?" Jock asked as she drove slowly toward the parking area near the entrance.

"About six years," she said, glancing toward the hot-looking man who was getting her to think about sex a whole lot more than she had in ages. Well, she could think about it all she wanted. But the only action around here would be the impending demise of the anarchist group if it presented the kind of threat she believed it did.

"Did you live in Missoula before you went to college there?"

"Yes." She knew her voice sounded curt with that answer, but he was now edging too close to topics she refused to discuss. Like her childhood and background. Sex? Hah. She was now being turned off by this man thanks to his chosen topic of conversation.

They passed three other rows of identical cabins before reaching the much larger one that served as the reception area and offices. She pulled into a space nearest the exit gate and parked.

To preclude Jock's continuing her interrogation, she decided it was time for one of her own. "So tell me about Alpha Force," she said.

His craggy, handsome face seemed to shutter, but only for an instant. Then he smiled. "I'm sure you've been told that we're a covert military group, and we can't discuss our methodology with anyone, either other military personnel or civilians."

"But in a situation like this, where I know you've been picked out particularly because of whatever it is you do to look into what's going on here—"

"So did you always know you wanted to go into law enforcement?" His tone was smooth, but his expression was both wry and warning.

He wasn't going to tell her anything.

Well, she wasn't going to tell him anything, either, unless she was sure it would help her cause.

Another car pulled through the gate and parked close to the office. Kathlene pretended to study it.

That was when she saw Ralf approaching on foot from the direction from which they'd driven.

Good. This conversation was clearly over.

Ralf was now ensconced in the backseat. Although Kathlene turned the car toward town as they exited the motel's entrance driveway, she told Jock she would drive them farther along this road on their return—past the entry to the formerly abandoned ranch where the people she believed to be anarchists now lived and multiplied.

"That's where we'll do whatever recon we decide on later," she said. "But I figured I'd get you started by showing you the town and innocently drive past the area on our return to your motel room."

"Thanks," Jock said. "That'll work. And I'd like you to tell us everything you know and suspect so Ralf and I will be able to do our job here."

She heard between the lines. They thought they were going to exclude her.

They weren't.

Right now, as promised, she headed toward town.

As she drove down Main Street, she chatted about Cliffordsville, the shops they passed, the nature of the place before the anarchists had started appearing. They drove along a well-stocked commercial area, with stores ranging from name-brand casual clothes to a men's suit outlet to a variety of restaurants from fast-food to nice, sit-down dining.

Main Street was pretty much a straight line, with a few traffic lights to allow drivers to pull onto it from the myriad side streets, some of which were also commercial, and others led to residential areas.

They didn't drive far enough down it to reach the County Administration Building, City Hall and the Sheriff's Department. The official part of town sat on the outskirts of the business area.

Kathlene liked Cliffordsville. A lot. She had made it her home.

Unlike Missoula, where she had grown up, it held only good memories for her—at least before.

Nothing controversial.

Not till recently, at least.

But her mind veered in different directions from all she was talking about. She was determining how she was going to take a stand and make it clear to Jock that she would participate in the investigation. Period.

"Where do you live?" Jock asked out of the blue. They

had just turned down a side street so she could show them some of the closest residential areas—but she hadn't intended to show them her house.

A jolt rocked through her body nonetheless. She knew he wasn't asking to come home with her, yet the idea suddenly heated up her insides as if he had suggested they engage in some down and dirty sex.

Damn. She'd already convinced herself not to feel turned on by this man—hadn't she? She wanted them to be comrades in arms, conspirators in figuring out what was really going on in that odd and growing encampment outside town.

She knew what would turn her off. Fast.

"I own a house in the same general direction we just turned," she told him as casually as she could muster. "It's in a small residential neighborhood within the city limits, though. The cabins where you're staying are in an area considered to be outside town, although still within Clifford County, which means they're within the sheriff's department's jurisdiction." She paused. "As I said before, I'll be spending time with you at your cabin. That'll help us look like the old friends we're supposed to be. I'll also accompany you if you go camping. That way, I'll be able to help in your surveillance."

There. The gauntlet had been thrown down once more, but this time she had given a cursory reason why she should be with them at least part of the time as they worked.

Jock said nothing. But as Kathlene reached Main Street again and stopped for a traffic light, she looked over at him.

He seemed to be staring out the windshield, but his large hands were fisted in his lap. What was he thinking?

She had a feeling she wouldn't like it. But she was dying to know.

* * *

The woman was trying to drive him nuts—and not just because she was so hot that he didn't really want to keep his hands off her. But he would. Sex would only complicate things even further.

She had to keep her nose out of what Ralf and he were doing. Hell, Jock knew she had no idea about the facts.

First of all, when he did his surveillance of the supposed anarchists' camp, he wouldn't look like he did at the moment.

No. He would look a lot more like his cover dog, Click. The dog Ralf had gone to check on in the cabin next door before they left their motel.

Click must have been fine, or Ralf would have stayed behind. Or at least said something.

Jock glanced quickly into the backseat. Ralf remained there, of course. Looking all nice and neutral—and interested. But staying out of the conversation.

A good thing? Maybe. But it might be better if his aide participated. Even took over for him. Ralf was good at being discreet, keeping things calm.

Keeping Jock in line, both in human and in wolf form.

At the moment, Jock knew he had to make his position clear with Kathlene. Not give her all the facts. But even though she had been the one to trigger Alpha Force's involvement by taking her concerns to the right government contacts, now she had to stay back and let him do what was necessary—and only with Ralf's help, not hers.

He thought more about Ralf and what he should do. What he should say.

And how their commanding officer, Major Drew Connell—the man who had approved Jock's enlistment into the military and into Alpha Force, the man who had first created the very special elixir that gave Alpha Force's shifting members such an edge over other shapeshifters, other *people*—would handle this.

Discretion is the key, he reminded himself.

He let himself respond to Kathlene's challenge at last.

"I appreciate your offer to help out," he lied, but he did manage to keep his tone calm and level. "The thing is, you may not know it, but Alpha Force's position is that, once we accept a mission, we work alone, without outside help." Another lie, but it made sense, especially now.

"That may work sometimes," Kathlene said, her tone as flat as his, "but not here. Not now. I need to stay involved because I *am* involved."

"But you could get hurt!" Damn. He hadn't meant to blast that out that way. It was what was on his mind, though.

Always. Especially in a situation like this.

"I won't," she countered, her voice raised as much as his. He wanted to grab her and shake some sense into her. But he couldn't. Not with her driving.

Besides, he found Deputy Kathlene Baylor so attractive, so sexy, that touching her again for any reason would be a huge mistake. All he would want to do, despite all his common sense, would be to get her under the covers.

And then what would happen to the mission she had gotten him into?

His attraction to her was a huge part of the problem, though. He couldn't help comparing this lovely, determined woman with Jill, his high school sweetheart.

Jill, a shapeshifter like him.

Jill, who had gone into law enforcement like Kathlene.

And who had been killed during her first year on the job, not while shifted but while in human form on a dangerous assignment.

Would Jill have survived if she'd been a man? If she

had been in wolf form? Unlikely, of course, and he knew that even wondering about it allowed him no closure, especially after all this time.

But one thing Jock was sure of. He didn't like it at all when women he felt attracted to got into perilous circumstances. If he happened to be there, he'd save them.

There was no way of his being certain he could be with them at the crucial time, though. He knew what a dinosaur he might be—yet, thanks to what had happened to Jill, he couldn't help thinking it was a lot more foolish of women, even trained ones, to put themselves into hazardous situations than it was for men.

Because they were not physically as strong, they were more likely to get killed.

"Jock?" Her challenging tone shrieked irritation. She was waiting for his further response.

He still said nothing. He wasn't about to explain his beliefs to her—or his rationale for them.

"Jock, tell you what. I appreciate your protective attitude." She sounded anything but appreciative, yet she continued. "But I'll prove to you that I can take care of myself. I'm a skilled law-enforcement officer. I've been trained in everything from accuracy in shooting guns of nearly all types to hand-to-hand combat. I'm challenging you, Jock. We'll start when we get back to the cabin. If I can pin you to the floor in a hand-to-hand fight, then you'll let me be there when you do your surveillance and more."

Silly? Foolish? Absurd to the max? All of the above. But the challenge had been impulsive, a way to show him who she was and what she really was made of.

And now? Well, she had no choice. She could do it. She *would* do it.

Notwithstanding her inability to fully read Jock's expression when he looked at her so incredulously.

There seemed to be an angry set to his brow.

A heated look in his blue eyes that suggested her words had turned him on.

Since it was now early evening, she went through a fast-food drive-in lane and they all got their meals, which they ate in the car. Fine with her. She was on a mission of sorts and didn't want any further interruptions just now.

Next, she did as she had planned from the moment they had set out on this drive. She made a left turn at one of the traffic lights, then drove them onto the narrowing lane they had come from before.

This time, though, she went beyond where the cabin motel lay, heading down the road even farther.

There was a sparse number of homes along it, some tiny, others large, mostly in good condition, but a few were run-down cottages that had been there forever. All were set in the midst of large stands of trees, some with branches carved back to avoid blocking the road and others somewhat in the way.

Eventually, she reached the turnoff she had been looking for, a very narrow, nondescript driveway. No one could tell from this better-traveled drag what lay beyond.

She knew. She had visited it, several times. And had seen the huge chain-link fence that had been built in the middle of nowhere.

Farther down the drive, the guard at the gate had not let her through, claiming that it was private property and everything was fine there. No need for law enforcement's interference...er, help.

"That's the way to the enclave in question." She slowed and pointed in that direction.

"All the way out here?" Ralf leaned forward so his head

was between the front seats. "Guess that could make some-one suspicious in itself."

Was he questioning her thought processes? Kathlene would have expected that more from Jock—although she really didn't know Ralf any better than she knew her sup-posed friend from the past.

"But it looks innocent enough," Jock observed.

Okay. No surprise. He was questioning her, too.

"From here, yes," she acknowledged. "Farther along… well, I'm sure you'll see for yourselves soon." *With me along*, she thought, but didn't voice it just then.

Now, though, it was time to go back.

She found the turnoff she was looking for a mile down the road, then maneuvered her SUV to return in the direc-tion from which they'd come.

Once again, they drove along the narrow road with coni-fers looming overhead—lodgepole pines, junipers, cedars, firs. Every once in a while the blue sky showed through, but the roadway was mostly shaded.

Kathlene knew it would be unpleasant to come here at night, and she hadn't done so…yet. But she suspected she would. Maybe with these Alpha Force men.

Soon they again reached the area where the motel cab-ins lay. Kathlene smiled grimly to herself, wondering what awaited her here this time.

Was she really going to fight Jock?

Hell, yes, if that was the only way to get him to coop-erate.

She had done extremely well as a rookie, training to be-come a deputy sheriff. She had outfought all of the other would-be deputies, male and female.

Sheriff Frawley had yet to acknowledge her skills—even though she still engaged in training exercises with other deputies more experienced than she was.

Would surprising Jock, toppling him, be enough to convince him?

Even if it didn't, it would certainly improve her frustrated state of mind.

Although, considering how sexy she found the muscular guy staring at the narrow, barely paved road in front of them, it was bound to cause her another kind of frustration.

Jock hadn't actually responded to her dare. But the moment they reached the large cabin at the front of the development that contained the offices, he jumped out.

After one cold stare and shake of his head, he turned away from Kathlene.

Fine with her. She waited until Ralf got out of the backseat. Would he try to talk her out of her challenge?

She'd gathered, from the way the two men interacted, that Jock was probably the superior-ranking military officer, with Ralf perhaps reporting to him.

That was something else she wanted to know, in addition to what Alpha Force was really about.

How could these men, members of this particular unit, help to figure out what was going on here better than other cops or military members?

Well, if she won their fight, Jock would owe her. He'd have to let her help in their investigation.

And he'd also have to tell her more, including about Alpha Force.

But would he?

He damn well better.

They'd gone back to the cabin. All three of them.

"So…thanks for showing us around, Kathlene," Jock said, finally glancing at her. She'd been helpful, but now it was time for her to go. "We'll get more of the lay of the land tomorrow morning on our own. What's your schedule? Can we meet you for lunch? That'll fit with our cover story."

"Yes," she said curtly. "It will. And I'll be glad to meet you then. But my next day off is Friday, the day after tomorrow. We'll get together in between, too, when I can. You'll keep me apprised in between by phone or meeting, let me know what you learn. I'll join up with you as much as I can."

She looked so attractive as she snarled at him, her hair still pulled back from that gorgeous face.

But she was still trying to take control of a situation that *he* controlled.

Wasn't going to happen.

"We'll keep you apprised," he agreed mildly. "Let us know what time you can take off for lunch tomorrow. And we'll let you know every step we've taken." After we take it. But he didn't say that aloud.

She obviously figured it out, though. "No, like I said, I'm going to be part of this. You remember my challenge?"

"Now look, Kathlene," Ralf said. "We know you were joking, but—"

"I wasn't," she responded curtly, still staring at Jock.

"Of course I remember it," he retorted. "But Ralf's right. It was—"

"Then let's get started," she interrupted. "You win and I'll comply with what you've said. *I* win, and I'm dead center in the middle of the operation. Got it?"

"Yes, but—"

He was shocked. Amused. And taken by surprise as the lovely, slim woman removed her sheriff's department jacket, belt with its holster and radio, and dropped them on the floor.

And then she approached him fast, hands out, and grabbed him by the arms.

Chapter 3

Jock Larabey's body felt just as muscular as it looked. Kathlene wasn't surprised by that. In fact, she'd felt it before, when they'd hugged.

She'd only hoped to take *him* by surprise, here in the middle of the cabin's main room on its polished wood floor, between the beds and sitting area she had checked out previously. She had to get him to take her seriously, and defeating him like one of the guys should help.

"Hey!" Ralf shouted, and out of the corner of her eye Kathlene saw him approaching, his hands out, too, as if he intended to pull her away.

She wouldn't let him. But fighting two muscular men at once?

That could be a problem.

She was gratified, therefore, to hear Jock snap out, "Stay back, Ralf. In fact, get out of here. I've got this covered."

He didn't, of course, but fortunately Ralf backed off and stormed out of the cabin. Good.

But why had Jock done that? So Ralf wouldn't see his humiliation? Doubtful. He had to believe he would win.

She'd inhaled as she moved and, now even more aware

of her breathing and what was around her, she smelled the sweet combo of aromas of whatever had been used to clean this space for the next occupants.

But she quickly threw all of that out of her consciousness. She had to focus on what she was doing.

At the same time as she had grabbed Jock, she'd twisted her body, her legs around his, to trip him and take him down.

It was like trying to pull down a sturdy steel pipe.

"Hey!" he yelled, but he didn't fall. That was okay. She'd conducted a lot of hand-to-hand combat training with men as well as women, and some were not only muscular but big-bellied, too, unlike Jock. She'd always managed to defeat even them.

She knew her best moves.

She turned and rose at once, putting herself out of Jock's arms' reach temporarily. Or so she thought.

One of his hands was suddenly on her middle, the other grasping for her neck. Was he going to strangle her? Maybe the military was trained to do their worst, act harshly as if prepared to kill even its own, presuming that the other guy was as well trained and could get out of it.

Well, she could, too.

"No!" she yelled, another kind of distraction as she twisted away from him, then quickly turned and attempted to swing her arm and aim at his face while her leg again moved around his.

This time, he apparently let her. No resistance. At first. But before she could trip him, he moved once more and had one of his arms about her chest while the other moved farther below.

Interesting, to have him touching her there. All over. Apparently, he thought so, too, since she heard a whoosh from him that sounded like what she had heard sometimes in her training sessions with men—surprise, maybe. And interest.

His hand on her breasts moved. Squeezing just a little. Damn, but it felt good. She couldn't allow it to distract her, though—even if it distracted him.

She pretended to start going limp, then straightened, leaped back and turned, facing him again.

And noticing the thick bulge in his jeans as he, too, faced her once more, bent slightly forward, his arms at his sides, clenching and unclenching his fists.

This was definitely more heated, in many ways, than the hug they had previously shared.

Why did that position look so sexy? Or was it just her touching him—and seeing how his body appeared to be reacting?

"Enough?" he asked. He was breathing hard, even though what they'd done so far wasn't especially active.

"Not unless you give in and agree I'm part of your team."

She anticipated his rush forward. She turned sideways to make it harder for him to grab her in crucially vulnerable spots to bring her down.

That ended with her hip pressed right against that bulge she had noticed before. She drew in her breath.

Lord, how she wanted him just then. Which was crazy. She didn't know him. And she needed him to do a job here that could protect her friends, her fellow Clifford County residents and maybe even more citizens of the United States.

Would her seducing Jock cause him to do a better job? Hardly.

Even if it did, that didn't mean he would let her help.

And she was going to help, no matter what he thought.

"Okay, then, yes," he said. "You're part of the team."

Was it over that quickly? "The part of it that I say you are. And that means staying out of danger." As if he believed he had distracted her, he rushed forward, upper part of his body bent, and attempted to tackle her.

She quickly moved away, grabbing at his head and smelling his musky scent as she let herself fall, pulling him down with her.

Amazingly, he fell, too. Onto the floor. Beside where she now knelt. She flipped over, heaving her entire being on top of him. Using every ounce of her weight to press him down.

Feeling his thick muscles everywhere tense beneath her. His chest. His legs.

And the protrusion at his core that thrust up at her as she refused to move.

"You're busted!" she exclaimed triumphantly. "I win. I'm a part of your team—the way *I* say I am."

He didn't move. Didn't say anything. Not for several heartbeats—and she believed hers was somehow synced with his.

His hips moved, and his erection was thrust up against her gut, making her own insides heat and churn and ache with a desire that would not, could not, be fulfilled. Not now or ever. Not with this man.

She continued to watch his face, which, as handsome as it was, somehow remained blank, as if all thoughts, all emotions, all desires, had been erased from within him by her victory.

Even if he rocked her off him now, she still had won, so his pretending to ignore her wouldn't work. Or at least it wouldn't gain him a win over her.

And then a horrible thought struck her. "Did you let me win, Larabey?" she demanded. Well, even if he had, she was still on top—in more ways than one.

She couldn't quite read the expression that passed quickly over his face before disappearing. Smugness? Anger?

"You think I want you to join us in danger? Forget it." The movement of his chest as he spoke bumped against her, causing her breasts to tense along his muscular body. Oh, that heat within her. She'd better get off. Quickly.

"You don't need to worry about me," she said. "I can take care of myself."

"So I've just learned." She appreciated the irony in his tone. "In this kind of situation. But even so, Kathlene, you have to realize that what we're likely to be up against, if you're right about those guys being anarchists, is—"

She had to shut him up. She bent her head forward—and covered those still-moving lips of his with her own.

He responded. Oh, did he ever. His voice stopped immediately, but the movement of his lips didn't. He fastened them on her as he thrust his tongue into her mouth, hot and moving as enticingly as his body below suggested by its pressure against her, imitating the dance of sensuality that she had already imagined going on between them.

"Kathlene," he murmured against her. She responded by drawing his tongue even farther into her mouth, teasing it with hers as suggestively as he played with her.

She couldn't think. Couldn't react with the sanity of a deputy sheriff in danger. For this was danger, maybe even a kind Jock had been warning her about.

Danger that would be magnified by her joining his team. Working with him. Seeing him often while he was here, till they had accomplished—

"Hell." A familiar male voice from the doorway interrupted her thoughts that were already disjointed, thanks to Jock's continuing to drive her nuts with the movement of his body. She turned her head to see Ralf standing there.

He'd come back. "Didn't mean to interrupt anything like...
I'll go take another walk."

Jock's body heaved slightly from beneath her. He
grabbed her with his hands and lowered her gently to the
floor as he stood. "Not what it looks like," he told his fellow Alpha Force member. "We were just demonstrating
some fighting moves we'd each learned."

"Right," Ralf said. His deep complexion had grown
ruddy with embarrassment.

"It's true." Jock was standing now. He bent to offer his
hand to help her to her feet.

She accepted, still looking at the floor. Kathlene didn't
dare glance toward Ralf. Not just yet.

"Kathlene and I have reached an agreement of sorts,"
Jock said. "She wants to work with us. Be part of our team
as we investigate those potential anarchists. She'd wanted
to show me some of her fighting skills to prove that she
could hold her own, and I now agree with her. Kathlene
is now definitely a part of our team."

Had he let her win? Jock didn't think so, but he had allowed her to distract him enough with her so-sexy body
in motion that the result had been inevitable.

Besides, he'd felt reluctant to fight a female at all. Could
that have been his wolf side reacting? Unlikely. That part
of him illustrated his wildness, not holding back when it
was in his best interests. Even so...well, it was over now.

She had stayed for just a short while as they planned
their next meet-up—lunch the next day. Meantime, Ralf
and he would do a little recon on their own before getting
together with her, studying the layout of Cliffordsville and
its environs even more, maybe even doing an initial check
of the area containing the anarchists' habitat tonight.

Little did she know how he would check it.

And that was one of the biggest problems of her working with them as a team. That, and the potential danger.

He could protect her. Would protect her.

But what would she think if she knew what he was, and why he, rather than a member of any other military unit, had been sent here?

Now, after their brief discussion inside the cabin, he walked her to her car. She said goodbye to them—for now. It was getting late, darkness was falling and she said she was heading home.

She used her key to unlock the driver's door of her SUV, and he opened it for her.

"Sorry I embarrassed you in front of your partner," she said as she faced him before getting inside. Her lovely face was flushed a bit, too. Her smile seemed ironic, drawing her full lips up just a bit at the corners.

He couldn't help it. He bent and gave her another kiss.

Oh, not as sensual as last time. It was, in comparison, just a peck. But it still managed to evoke the feelings he had captured before—feelings of her firm but curvaceous body against him.

She pulled away first. "Bye, Jock. I'll be thinking about you tonight." Before he could react, she said, "About our team. And how best to investigate the anarchists together." She ducked into the car and pulled the door shut. She turned the key in the ignition and waved to him as she drove off.

"You've got an interesting way of sealing the deal, making her part of the team." Ralf and Click had come up to Jock as Kathlene's car vanished around a curve. "And I thought the last thing you wanted was for her to *help* us— and potentially learn what Alpha Force is all about."

Jock turned and motioned for Ralf to follow him back toward the cabin. "I don't know yet what kind of help she might be, but she does know people around here as well as locations. Plus, she was the one who revealed that there was a potential issue here and was credible enough for those in charge to follow up. Maybe she can help, and maybe not. But as far as her learning about Alpha Force—and me—we'll just have to make sure she doesn't. At least not unless we decide it's to our advantage for her to know—which I doubt. Speaking of which, now that she's gone, I think it'll be time soon for some very special reconnaissance."

The drive back to her home was a short distance along narrow streets now illuminated by artificial light, but Kathlene considered it a huge way from where she had left Jock. What had she been thinking?

Apparently, she *hadn't* been thinking. A hand-to-hand combat battle to convince him to let her help in finding out what was up with those anarchists?

Well, he was military, she was in law enforcement, and engaging in that kind of confrontation may have made sense...*may* being the operative word.

At least it had worked out. He had acknowledged that she would be part of his team.

Kathlene reached the cottage-style redbrick house on the residential street that she called home. She pulled into the driveway and pushed the button for the garage door to open.

She knew she wouldn't sleep much that night. She would be thinking too much about Jock Larabey, their workout together...and the feel of his body, and lips, against hers.

She made herself rehash their final conversation—and realized it felt too easy. They were going to look around. Preliminarily check out the town and the anarchists' site that she had pointed out to them. Tomorrow morning?

Maybe. But she had a feeling that these men would not wait. She turned the key in the ignition, closed her garage door and backed out of her driveway again.

They might be checking out the anarchists' location that night. If not, she'd just return here, no harm, no foul.

But if they were checking it out—well, she'd be checking *them* out.

"This should do it." Jock had allowed Ralf to drive him back along the route they had taken when Kathlene pointed out the turnoff toward where she'd indicated the possible anarchists were living. Then they had cruised a bit longer until they had found what appeared to be a nearby solitary and abandoned home, at least from what they could tell in the near absolute darkness of this forested area. The place had been built of wood in a style that looked like some bygone era's, and that wood was rotting.

Its emptiness made it a good place to conduct what they now needed to do.

Ralf had pulled behind the structure, just in case. They didn't want their car to be seen from the road if any of the people they wanted to surveil happened to drive by.

Plus, what they now needed to do could not be done with any normal, non–Alpha Force human around.

It was a secret from all other eyes. It was the heart of their supercovert military unit.

They both were out of the car. Click had remained locked in the rented cabin next door to theirs. He was vital to this part of their assignment—but only because he closely resembled the wolf into which Jock was about to change. If anyone happened to see Jock, Ralf and he would laugh it off. Show off the dog later and say it had always been Click.

"You ready, sir?" Ralf asked. He had pulled his large backpack out of the rear seat of the car and was holding out a vial of the very special Alpha Force shifting elixir.

That elixir alone was enough to entice shapeshifters to join Alpha Force. It had been developed by some of the unit's members, starting with its commanding officer, Major Drew Connell, and enhanced by formulas that other members had created independently that provided additional qualities.

"'Sir'? You're too military, bro." Ralf was a staff sergeant. Jock, as a lieutenant, was, in fact, his superior officer. But Alpha Forcers worked together too closely to stand much on military protocol. "But yeah, I'm ready."

They had decided, to save time, to have Jock shift outside the house, at least for this change. Then, when he was off performing his recon, Ralf would find a way to get inside and check the place out.

Now the only illumination was from the penlight that Ralf had taken from his sack and turned on, plus a bit of natural light from the starlit sky, visible now and then through the canopy of trees and over the road where they had been cleared. No full moon, not for another couple of weeks. Jock took the bottle of elixir and downed it slowly. It tasted somewhat minty and a bit like citrus fruit. Drinkable, but that didn't matter.

When he had finished it, he handed back the empty vial, took a deep breath and said, "Now."

Ralf aimed the other light he had taken from the backpack toward Jock, the one that, turned on, resembled the illumination of a full moon.

Jock immediately felt the stretching and pulling sensations begin. He smiled, then growled, as his body began morphing into the form of a wolf.

* * *

He prowled through the forest, in the direction of the distant sounds and scents of a large human habitat.

The one that was his target. The target of Alpha Force.

Tonight would be an overview by a wolf seeking information—one with the perception of a human, thanks to the elixir—to see what was there, to help plan what would come next.

He smelled the aromas of the woodlands—the trees. Small creatures whose sounds he heard in the underbrush, fleeing from him. Larger animals—a bobcat. A bear. Perhaps a wolverine. He scented them all, but none was near him.

A good thing. He wanted neither to flee nor to fight.

Not this night.

He soon arrived at his destination. He smelled a legion of humans. Saw the compound surrounded by a tall chain-link fence.

He slowly began circling it, careful to stay far enough away in the trees not to be spotted by curious human eyes.

He smelled fire and approached the wooded area closest to where it seemed to originate. Yes. Beyond the fence, a group of humans sat around a large campfire, apparently talking and drinking. He could smell beer and some harder stuff. Despite his keen hearing, he could only make out a hum of conversation, not specifically what they were saying.

Was it true? Were these men bent on evading—or toppling—authority and harming other humans? Or were they just a group of hunters banding together in a bond of yearning to kill wildlife?

As much as he despised that, it would not be something that merited Alpha Force intervention.

Killing or even threatening other humans did.

He needed to learn more. But he had done most of what he had intended for this night.

Observing, using his other senses that were much keener than those of a human, he nevertheless waited for another twenty minutes, but that yielded little further useful information except for the scent of gunpowder, which fit with who these people were. Explosives? Maybe, but if so they had been set off a while back.

But what he sought could still be on the property, hidden, perhaps being stored without being utilized, for now. This was not the time to check—but he would in the near future.

He had determined where the gates to this property were, including the one staffed by a guard. Other areas where the fencing was not rooted as well. Ways he could enter if he had to.

Still others where the trees and bushes and undergrowth did not end at the fence line but extended onto the property—and could hide a wolf who happened to stalk into them and hide.

He would return here.

Soon.

And then, as he began to leave, he inhaled a scent. A familiar human scent, one that trumped all he had smelled previously.

He had to be wrong. And yet his special senses were never wrong about things like that.

A woman with the anarchists?

No. Near them.

Kathlene.

What was going on?

Kathlene had headed back to the area of the cabins and arrived just in time to see the car driven by Ralf exit through the motel's gates and head in the direction of the anarchists' area. She'd had to stay far back, even drive without using her headlights, to ensure that she wouldn't be seen.

She'd watched as their car pulled into the driveway of what appeared to be an abandoned house along the road. She had decided she'd better park along a nearby turnout and walk, rather than drive, to keep an eye on them.

And, potentially, protect them. She had taken her weapon from where she had locked it in her glove compartment and now wore it at her hip.

The night was dark, especially with the canopy of trees looming overhead, obliterating the light from the half moon and the stars that, in as remote and unlighted an area as this, usually lit up the sky in identifiable constellations. And she had been right. It *was* unpleasant to come to this area at night, especially alone. But she had little choice.

She had carefully stayed on the road, walking slower than she would have liked but trying to make as little noise as possible, staying off the cover of dry leaves on the ground yet trying to remain invisible at the edge of the road. Making her way in the darkness. Staying careful, and as aware of her surroundings, and her solitude, as she possibly could.

That way, it took her a long time to catch up.

She had finally reached the house, looked inside a window, saw Ralf there in the faint illumination of a flashlight—but not Jock.

Had he tried to get inside the compound alone?

Bad move, she'd thought. What if he were seen?

Maybe he'd only intended to walk the perimeter outside the fence, just to take an initial look in the dark when he was less likely to be noticed. That made sense to her.

She'd decided to go check, just in case.

Still careful to walk as silently as possible, she had left the house with Ralf inside and hurried toward the road to the compound.

She'd wished she could use a flashlight, but at least her eyes had acclimated to the darkness. She had soon seen the light from the guardhouse and slipped behind the nearest trees, still carefully drawing closer to the area.

Then she'd started to slowly walk the perimeter. But then she had stopped. What was that?

Some kind of canine. It looked, from where she'd stood, like a German shepherd mix of some kind—but tawnier. Furrier. Like a wolf. A wild dog, maybe, that was part wolf.

As she'd watched, it seemed to smell the air in her direction. And then it moved on.

Moving cautiously, she tried to watch it but got only occasional glimpses of it. It appeared to stalk the compound outside the fence, like her—staying in the cover of the trees. It walked slowly, staring inside the enclosed area as if consciously observing what was there.

And then it disappeared. Even so, she continued to watch the area of the old ranch from her cover.

Now she had returned to an area not far from the driveway, hoping to see Jock, assuming he had come on foot to check the place out.

But after half an hour, she didn't see him. She was tired. Disappointed. Maybe she had been wrong about what the Alpha Force members intended to do this night besides exclude her.

She still didn't know what Ralf had been doing at that house. Where was Jock? Did it matter?

That wolf had most likely been hunting for food and had nothing to do with what else was going on around here.

Right?

But why was it she couldn't quite accept that?

Still careful, she headed back to where she had parked her car.

Maybe she would get some answers tomorrow.

Chapter 4

"She was there."

While still a wolf, Jock had loped through the woods back to the house near which he'd previously shifted. As planned, Ralf had gotten inside and had opened the door for him when he'd returned.

Jock had just morphed back to his human form. He'd grabbed the clothes that Ralf had folded neatly and left on a cleaned spot on the floor, then threw them on.

Now, inside the dismal and filthy hovel, he was dressed and angry and wanted to slam something. Except for spotting a few flaws in their security and some possible entry points, his initial observation had been totally inconclusive. He still had no sense of the extent of the likelihood for peril looming around the former ranch, but he definitely hadn't ruled out the conceivability of those now staying there being at least skilled and dedicated terrorists and possible anarchists, as well.

He needed to get inside, though, to check for the extent of their weaponry.

Now he knew all his frustration was evident as he spoke to Ralf.

"Who? Kathlene? Where was she?" Ralf had placed his equipment on the floor and was now stowing it in his backpack again. He stopped, though, facing Jock in the dim glow of the flashlight he had left on for illumination.

"Near the old ranch, outside the fence like I was, also hiding in the woods. But I scented and heard her, then saw her. Damn the woman. She must have been following us. Does she like throwing herself into potential danger?"

"I think you know the answer to that," Ralf said drily. Which only made Jock want to slam something all the more, like the wall. Not Ralf, and certainly not Kathlene—although, had she been nearby, it wouldn't have been outside the realm of possibility for him to grab and shake her.

And he knew what a bad idea that would be...touching her again at all. He'd want to kiss those defiant lips, and more.

Well, he would have time to cool down before seeing her at lunch again tomorrow.

By then he would have thought of a brilliant way to convince her to back off and let Ralf and him do their jobs.

At least he hoped so.

"Did she know it was you?" Ralf asked, interrupting his thoughts.

"Of course not." But Jock wondered nevertheless. Had she just shown up there because that was what she did—keeping an eye on the place where she thought a lot of dangerous people were gathering? That was a viable theory, of course. But unlikely for this evening.

Had she instead followed them—him?

That was something else he would have to check into tomorrow.

Kathlene was tired when she reported to work the next morning.

That wasn't surprising. She hadn't slept much.

Her mind kept buzzing around thoughts of her new Alpha Force best friends. Especially the so very sexy Jock Larabey, her supposed old buddy.

And their attempts to exclude her from the investigation.

Plus that strange visit of hers to the anarchists' enclave last night, thinking she would see Jock hanging around outside, near where she was, after leaving Ralf at that old house…but instead seeing only a wolf.

A particularly strange-acting wolf…

Now, inside the sheriff's station, in the assembly room waiting for the day's instructions, she kept herself from yawning by sheer willpower.

The dozens of other deputies taking their seats on folding chairs around her would only rib her about it if they saw.

The noise around her was growing—loud male voices hailing each other, chairs being dragged around the wooden floor, shrill feedback from a microphone that Sheriff Melton Frawley's top assistant, Undersheriff George Kerringston, was testing from the row of chairs up front that faced the rest.

Hardly any sound of female voices. Oh, yes, there were a couple of other deputies toughing it out like Kathlene. Or, actually, not like Kathlene. Deputy Betsy Alvers and Deputy Alberta Sheyne were perfectly happy being obedient underlings who did as Melton said, filling out paperwork at the station and bringing coffee to the big, brave men in the department.

The other couple of female deputies had resigned and moved away. There wasn't even a local police department for them to join, since the county sheriff's department was the only law enforcement in this area other than the state highway patrol on the major nearby roads. Only Kathlene attempted to keep up the job as they had once all known it.

That had become a daily fight. But she was no quitter.

And now, with her concerns about the apparent anarchists, she felt she owed it to the town, to the many people who remained her friends, to see this through.

"Hey, good lookin'."

A thin man dressed just like her sat down on the empty chair beside her, sliding over so their hips met.

"Hey, ugly guy," she said back, turning to smile up into the face of Senior Deputy Tommy Xavier Jones, the man who appeared to be her only supporter in the higher ranks of the department.

Tommy X had been a deputy for nearly twenty years. He had short gray hair, a long, almost equine face, and a lot of wrinkles. He was the tallest member of the department, was great friends with the town's ranking politicians and dated a county commissioner, who also happened to be Kathlene's friend.

He could get away with bucking the current regime within the Sheriff's Department—and did.

And fortunately, he remained Kathlene's champion, too.

"So—do you anticipate anything exciting today?" he asked, nodding toward the front of the room where Sheriff Frawley was about to take the microphone.

"Here? Nope. But I'm having lunch with my old college friend Jock, the one I told you about. I saw him briefly yesterday. He's here with a friend on the way to Yellowstone and I'll spend as much time as I can with them before they leave."

Even with someone as close to her as Tommy X, Kathlene had decided to maintain the cover story—partly because she'd been instructed to if she wanted continuing help from the elite and covert Alpha Force, whatever it was, and partly because she didn't dare allow her personal investigation of the anarchists become the knowledge of anyone here, not even Tommy X. Tommy X was a nice guy, trustworthy—but if he let even a hint of what was going on drop in front of anyone here who wanted to curry favor with Sheriff Frawley, she'd be toast.

"Attention, please." That was Kerringston, shouting into the microphone although he didn't have to. He knew that. He'd been told nearly daily since his promotion to undersheriff six months earlier, when the former sheriff had retired and Melton Frawley was promoted into his position.

Before the good old days had ended, Kathlene thought. Unlike today.

Kerringston gave his greeting and handed the mike to his boss. Melton did his usual song and dance of thanking his people, telling them to do a good job, going over the stuff that had been investigated yesterday—which amounted to nearly nothing unless one was impressed with local traffic stops.

And then the sheriff finished. He didn't look toward Kathlene. He didn't have to.

But she knew exactly whom he spoke to next, since he did so often.

"Now, we've had a few more local applications for hunting licenses. Like always. Nice for the economy since the licenses aren't cheap, plus some of the sportsmen—that's what they consider themselves, you know—are joining the others already here who're practicing their shooting skills and all. I've talked to them. They talk to me. No one's been hurt as they do their target practice—still. And no one will be hurt."

He stopped, looking over the heads of nearly all the deputies quietly facing him, some jabbing each other in the sides with their elbows as they nodded toward Kathlene and laughed.

"So…today's a new day. Anyone want to ruin our meeting by objecting to our visitors?" This time, he shot a look right at Kathlene, challenging her, even as he guffawed aloud.

She said nothing. Just looked down as if there was something loose on her utility belt that she had to check.

Same as every day. Even as she felt her face flush, her insides churn.

His discussions with the *sportsmen* suggested they didn't mind authority, so they couldn't be anarchists, could they? Or was he being wooed by them so he'd leave them alone?

Melton obviously wanted her to quit and run. She knew it. And she was tempted daily. Like now. After he had humiliated her—again.

"You okay?" Tommy X whispered without looking at her. He'd already told her that his standing up and arguing in her favor would only garner more reaction from the sheriff and nearly all his minions.

"Fine," she said. As always.

This time, though, she had something to add. For once.

"But I'm really looking forward to having lunch today with my dear old college friend," she told Tommy X.

In the late morning gloom, Kathlene had walked briskly down the busy Cliffordsville sidewalk from the sheriff's station toward the Clifford Café, the place she had chosen to meet Jock and Ralf. She'd called to let them know the address.

She had gotten there first and grabbed a table in a corner. Now she looked around. She knew maybe a half dozen patrons there, some waiting for their meals and others eating already. As she caught the eyes of a few, she smiled and lifted her hand in a wave of greeting. She remained in uniform since she would return to duty in a little less than an hour, so they clearly knew who, or at least what, she was.

This wasn't usually where she spent her lunchtime, but it seemed an appropriate place for today.

The place smelled delicious, with the aroma of grilled meats and baking bread in the air. The sound of voices was mostly a low hum. She couldn't make out what was said in any conversations, but that was fine with her.

Even so, none of the tables in this busy joint was completely immune from eavesdropping by the nosy locals who frequented it. In a way, that was a good thing. Word would get out that Kathlene had publicly dined with those friends she'd been talking about. Nothing sneaky about that. Not worth anyone spending any time puzzling over or talking about.

Unless, of course, those *friends* of hers were successful in outing, and taking federal custody of, some or all of the *sportsmen*. If word got out, that might be something worth more than some lunchtime gossip.

In any event, this wasn't Kathlene's usual midday meal. Her favorite lunch on days she was on duty was to grab a sandwich to go at one of the chains where she could choose everything from the bread to the meat and all other ingredients. That way, she could stuff it with all the salad makings she could want.

It was too hard to eat salads in patrol cars. And fortunately, the guy who was usually her partner, chosen especially for that role by her buddy Sheriff Frawley, could also get all the unhealthy menu items he wanted, too.

That way, Deputy Jimmy Korling didn't gripe at her. At least no more than usual.

Today he had griped, though, since she was actually

taking an hour to have lunch by herself. Well, not exactly
by herself. With her old college buddy Jock and his traveling companion, Ralf.

"Can I bring you a drink to start with, Deputy Baylor?" The server had obviously read Kathlene's name tag.
She wore a dress with a short skirt covered by a dainty
apron—the kind of woman, Kathlene was sure, that Sheriff Frawley expected all his female deputies to be. Not that
she had anything but complete respect for this server, who
also wore a name tag. Hers said she was Addie. But Addie
had chosen to take on this kind of job.

Kathlene hadn't.

"Just a cup of coffee," Kathlene said, smiling. "And a
recommendation for what I should order after my friends
arrive."

As she said that, she glanced past the server's shoulder
toward the front entrance. There they were—Jock and Ralf
were just entering the restaurant. As they looked around,
Kathlene half stood and waved.

"Are your friends here now?" Addie asked.

"Yes. I'm sure we'll be ready to order soon. Your sug-
gestions?"

Addie described the specials—a turkey club sandwich,
a meat-loaf platter, the soups of the day. By the time she
was through, she went over them again as Jock and Ralf
pulled their chairs from beneath the table and took their
seats. "I'll give you a few minutes to decide," she said after
taking their drink orders.

Kathlene noticed how the pretty brunette server's eyes
skimmed approvingly over Jock, who smiled back. Oh,
yeah, the server had noticed how sexy he was. How could
she help it? But that didn't matter to Kathlene. Couldn't
matter.

So why did she want to shake the waitress and tell her to go get their drinks? Fast.

"Do you have any other recommendations?" Ralf asked. This time his T-shirt was blue with a circular logo representing the Montana flag in the middle, along with the state motto *"Oro Y Plata"*—gold and silver. He'd definitely done his homework before coming here, probably ordered his shirt online. His toothy grin was friendly, not suggesting at all that he was anything but what he pretended to be: a visitor who'd come here along with a friend on a road trip.

Jock, on the other hand, was also in jeans but with a snug black T-shirt on top. It hugged his ample muscles and emphasized the tightness of his hot body. He wasn't smiling at Kathlene, though. Instead, his hazel eyes regarded her with an expression she couldn't quite read. Curiosity? Irritation? Challenge? Maybe all of the above—but she was entitled to feel each of those emotions even more than he did.

Although she had no doubt that he believed otherwise.

She turned back to Ralf. "I don't eat here often, but when I do I usually order one of the specials. I've never had a bad meal at this place, though, so just pick whatever sounds best to you."

At least here, sitting at a table, she could order a salad. The Cobb salad at this café was one of the best she had ever tasted, so she knew that would be her selection.

The server returned. Ralf ordered the meat-loaf special, Jock the sandwich and Kathlene her salad.

Then it was time for them to put on their act, pretend for those surrounding them to be longtime friends.

But Kathlene needed to give these men a reminder. They'd apparently tried to do something without her last night. Today, to maintain cordiality in their relationship, she could understand and agree with it, but only on a limited basis. And she would first make it clear that they hadn't gotten rid of her for this evening.

"So did you sleep well last night?" she began, aiming an enormous, friendly smile toward Jock.

His return grin was wry—an utterly sexy look on his craggy face. "Sure did. How about you?"

"Eventually, sure. But you know, I remembered something I wanted to tell you after I left and decided to go back rather than to just call you. Imagine my surprise when I saw you driving away down the road." She kept her smile large but her voice was very low. "I knew you didn't intend to check on that…place I'd told you about, since you'd have let me know and invited me to come along, as we agreed. Sure enough, I noticed that you'd stopped not there but farther down the road, only…" She wasn't quite sure how to continue. Things had become murky after that, and she hadn't really been able to observe either of these men or what they'd been up to. She'd essentially lost them in darkness, and neither had shown up in the area she expected they would.

Addie returned to their table and placed their food in front of them. "Enjoy," she said, "and let me know if there's anything else you need."

Oh, there was something else Kathlene needed, all right, but the server wasn't the one who could help her. Addie lingered a bit more than necessary, refilling their water glasses and making a point of joking a little with Jock, who responded as if he enjoyed it. As if flirting with their waitress was the best thing that had happened to him that day.

Which only annoyed Kathlene all the more.

Ignoring Jock, she turned to Ralf after Addie had left. "I admire the way you discovered that old, abandoned house down the road, but I wasn't sure what you were up to." Once again, she kept her voice muted even as she all but batted her eyelashes at him so anyone observing them would think she was having a grand old time flirting with her buddy's friend. "Just looking for a closer venue to use as headquarters for the investigation we'll be conducting at the ranch?"

Ralf's features seemed to grow even darker. He glanced at the man who was evidently his commanding officer.

"You could say that." Jock's smile was rigid now, his voice low but sharp. "And we will include you when it makes sense. But it didn't last night during our preliminary recon." He paused, and his hazel eyes grew icy. "You have no business following us. For all you know, there could have been some major danger there and we might not have known you were around to help protect you."

That again. He seemed determined to keep her out of danger, out of trouble. The idea should have warmed her, but instead it made her chill. Had they made no progress at all after her demonstration that she could protect herself, at least in hand-to-hand combat?

But this wasn't the place to encourage a major argument with Jock Larabey. Not with so many people around who might overhear them, especially if they raised their voices.

"I get it," she said as neutrally as she could. "But look, I really need to be able to trust you both. At least tell me what you're going to do, where you're going to go." She hesitated. "And it frustrated me last night when I lost track of you. I didn't see you anywhere near the ranch when I got there. I only saw a…well, it looked like a wolf. It seemed to be stalking the outside of the compound. Were you around? Did you see it—and me—too?"

There was no immediate response from either man. They glanced at each other, though, as if their silence spoke volumes between them.

What was going on?

"Those guys purport to be hunters," she went on when they still said nothing. "I had the sense that the wolf had some purpose to be there. Isn't that silly? But I'd have hated to see one of them shoot the animal. There is no license for killing wolves this early in the year, but I wouldn't have been surprised if they used the poor thing for target practice, anyway."

She'd been watching their expressions as she talked. Once again Jock's look appeared to say lots that she couldn't read. But he finally spoke. "You're right, Kathlene," he said, amazing her—only she wasn't sure what she was right about. "There's something we'll show you and explain after lunch. Will you have a few minutes?"

Not really, but she wasn't about to tell him that. She'd just have to face the wrath of her partner, Jimmy, after calling him to tell him she'd be late.

And dealing with his anger wouldn't be pleasant.

But she had a feeling it would be worth it...to learn whatever Jock Larabey was now willing to tell her.

Chapter 5

She had seen him. Just as he had suspected.

And she might wind up seeing him again as their investigation progressed.

Therefore, Jock figured it was already time to nip any suspicions she might have in the bud.

Not that she was likely to assume that the canine she saw was anything but a genuine wolf or dog or whatever.

He took a sip of water from the glass in front of him. He'd already told Ralf his opinion by his glance.

Jock hadn't been a member of the military and Alpha Force for very long so far, but Ralf had enlisted in the army years ago. He was an astute soldier and a smart aide to a shifting Alpha Force member—him.

Ralf knew by Jock's glance what he was saying. Jock felt certain of it.

It was time, after lunch, to go introduce Kathlene to Click.

She had insisted on driving her own vehicle since she had to return to duty soon.

Jock sent Ralf back with the car they had driven here as

Loyal Wolf

part of their cover—a nice but slightly beat-up black sedan that was owned by Uncle Sam, but with plates registered to Mr. Jock Larabey of Seattle, Washington.

He rode in the passenger's seat of Kathlene's SUV. She'd indicated that her partner was in current possession of her sheriff's department cruiser.

They had been relatively silent on the drive from town, with Ralf staying right behind them. Jock had insisted on paying for their lunch, and she'd thanked him. He didn't need to tell her it was part of his government expense account.

He wondered what she was thinking as they drove along the lane that would take them to the driveway to the Clifford Cabins—that also, eventually, would pass by the area that was the object of their investigation.

But they weren't going that far. Not this afternoon.

"So tell me what made you decide to move to Cliffordsville for your law-enforcement career," he finally said. It was similar to what they'd talked about yesterday, non-controversial—although she had grown quiet when he had asked about her early background.

"I'd just heard that Clifford County was looking for new deputies here," she said, glancing toward him.

Lord, was she gorgeous, even decked out in that uniform with her hair pulled back. Or maybe having her face barely adorned like that added to how beautiful she was, with nothing artificial making her look like anything but herself. Oh, she did wear some lip gloss. Maybe she had a little makeup on, too.

But mostly, she looked like one lovely lady. One lovely, hot, enticing lady.

"Did they hire you right away?"

She nodded. "But that was Sheriff Chrissoula. Before

our current sheriff, Melton Frawley, took over after Chrissoula retired six months ago."

"And was that around when the anarchist group started to move in?"

She again shot him a glance. "How did you know? Or did you just guess? Yes, it's my belief that Sheriff Frawley may have rolled out the welcome mat. Or even if he didn't, he also didn't tell the group to get lost."

"Do you think he's one of them?"

She shrugged her shoulders that still somehow managed to look slim and sexy despite her uniform. "I hope not, but I can't say for sure. Now—" she turned her car onto the driveway toward the cabins "—what is it you want to show me here?"

"You'll see. I think it'll explain a lot to you, at least about last night."

She parked, and Ralf pulled in beside her. The parking lot had a few more cars in it now, but no other people were visible around the row of rustic cabins surrounding the parking area.

Kathlene didn't wait for Jock to open the door for her, but he hadn't really expected her to. She clearly didn't want to rely on anyone behaving in a gentlemanly manner.

And somehow her independence only added to her attractiveness to him. To a point. Ignoring politeness was fine.

Ignoring danger was not.

She began walking along the paved path toward the cabin where Ralf and he were staying. "No," Jock called. "This way." He gestured toward the cabin next door. "Got the key, Ralf?"

"Sure do."

His aide moved to the front of the group, holding the key card in his hand.

"You've rented this cabin, too?" Kathlene looked confused.

Why did he want to kiss that puzzled frown away...?

"I'd like you to meet Click," Jock said, and nodded to Ralf.

Ralf pushed the door open and was nearly bowled over as Click leaped out, eagerly wagging his tail and greeting one of the humans who was his closest friend.

"You brought a dog?" Kathlene asked. She shook her head, then smiled. "The dog I saw last night? He's not a wolf, then? He's a pet?"

Instead of waiting for his answers, she dashed off toward where Click and Ralf were now roughhousing.

She obviously liked canines.

Couldn't he find anything to dislike about this woman—except for her carelessness in the face of danger?

He wasn't sure he wanted to find out.

At first all Kathlene wanted to do was hug the obviously excited dog. He looked familiar—moderate sized, with shining, light brown eyes, pert ears and lots of tawny fur that looked almost silvery in the light. He clearly loved people, since he bounded from Ralf to her and back again in this cabin that looked nearly identical inside to the one where the men were staying. Click basked in the attention they both gave him and snugged his head against her for multiple pats.

"He's so sweet!" she exclaimed, kneeling with one hand on the floor to keep her balance as the dog pushed at her for attention and made snuffling noises. She loved dogs. Meant to adopt a rescue someday when her work schedule was less crazy and more predictable. If it ever was. "Is Click yours, Ralf? Or Jock's?"

Why did the men exchange glances about that? It was an easy question.

Wasn't it? And if not...

"He's mine," Jock said, and he joined the excited doggy love fest, too.

But the hesitation before he knelt and roughhoused with Click had reminded Kathlene of all the mystery surrounding this dog. Why hadn't they mentioned they had brought a pet along?

She asked them. "I can understand your wanting to have a dog with you. Is Click a trained search dog?" Or was there some other reason he'd been brought here—then hidden?

And why hide him from *her*?

"That's right." Jock stepped back. "He's trained to do other things, too, like sniff out particular subjects we need to find and follow."

"Is that why he was wandering around the ranch compound last night?"

Of course it had been Click. And yet there was something about the shape of his head, the length of his legs, the fullness of his coat, that didn't look exactly the way Kathlene remembered. But she'd been stressed then. Her recollections might not be entirely accurate. Plus, she hadn't been that close to the dog.

"Yes, that's right," Jock said. "He's got some other skills we're working on, too. He's not fully trained, so we weren't sure at first about bringing him, and when we decided to we just figured we'd keep him hidden, at least initially, until we decided how best to use him."

Kathlene supposed that made sense—but she wasn't fully convinced.

And yet why would they lie to her about that?

She stood, leaned down and stroked the soft fur around Click's shoulders as she looked straight into Jock's eyes.

The guy looked the picture of innocence, as if all he had told her was the absolute truth, even if it sounded somewhat contrived.

He clearly wasn't going to give her any explanation of why he might be prevaricating.

"You look like a good friend of Click's, too," Kathlene said to Ralf. "Are either of you skilled trainers, or does someone else do that?"

"A little of both," Ralf said. "I like to work with canines, tell them what to do, that kind of thing." He gave a big grin that he aimed at Jock, whose return smile looked almost nasty.

What was the gist of their unspoken conversation?

They obviously weren't going to tell her, any more than they'd explained Alpha Force or included her in their planning.

"Can we take him for a walk now?" she asked the men.

Another hesitation before Jock said, "Sure. There aren't likely to be a lot of people around now, in the middle of the day when they're off doing whatever they're here to do."

Which again didn't make sense to Kathlene. They apparently didn't want Click to be seen by many people. When did they walk him, then?

After dark, at least. That was the one obvious time. Early morning, before many people were up and about? That still wouldn't allow Click to relieve himself in the middle of the day as well as other times, which might be hard on the poor dog.

She knew she wasn't going to get answers now, so she didn't bother asking.

"Great," she said. "I'll bet you're glad to go for a walk now, aren't you, Click?"

Hearing his name, the dog looked up at her expectantly. Did he understand the word *walk?* Probably. She had the sense that, as playful as he was, he was also a smart pooch.

"So are we all going?" Kathlene said after Ralf brought over Click's leash.

"Just you, me and Click," Jock said. Ralf just nodded, not appearing particularly unhappy about being left out.

It bothered Kathlene, though. She'd be more or less alone with the man who was driving her a bit nuts. His sexiness didn't let her state of mind settle down in his presence. His secretiveness drove her nuts in other ways.

Well, she couldn't—wouldn't—do anything about the former. The latter she could get around. She could be sweet or professional or just darned pushy.

But one way or another she would find out what these men had planned to do to start their investigation.

"Here we go, boy." Jock spoke to Click as he attached his leash inside the cabin. "You ready to join us?" he asked Kathlene.

"Definitely." She smiled, although it faded quickly. "I can only stay here for another few minutes, though. I need to get back on duty."

"We'll make it short, then." Jock gave a gentle tug on the leash and let Click lead them out of the cabin.

Jock was glad to have an opportunity to walk Click. Mostly, it was Ralf who figured out the best times to go out with the dog, when they were least likely to be seen.

On the other hand, he and his aide had talked often about potential timing for Jock to be the one to walk his cover dog. People seeing them together was generally a good thing. They would know there were two entities, Jock and the dog. They wouldn't think Jock even slightly resembled the pet he had brought here. Or that he was, sometimes, a canine himself.

Not that most regular humans would even imagine the possibility.

And of those that might…well, there weren't any people they needed to demonstrate anything to here, in this motel area.

Maybe not anywhere in this town. At least not yet.

Except for Kathlene.

He was both glad and sorry for the opportunity to take a walk with her. The best thing for his cover would be for them to stay as alone as possible here.

But that would be worst for his sense of self-control. He wanted this woman. He knew it, and being in her presence only kept his desires at the forefront of his thoughts.

As well as his physical reactions—which were uncomfortable at times, but definitely stimulating.

She was a bundle of contradictions, and that attracted him. A lot.

Maybe because he, too, wasn't all that he appeared to be.

"Let's take Click into the woods," he told Kathlene once they were outside. He held Click's leash. "He loves the scents there."

"I noticed," she said, then shrugged. "Fine with me."

He chose to say nothing about the woods in this motel area being any different from what surrounded the compound that was the target of their observation. In many ways, it was the same.

Although he himself had detected a lot of differences in the smells around there from what was here.

Gunpowder and explosives, for example. If Click had really been there, Jock had no doubt he'd have scented them, too, despite how they seemed to be muted by distance or age. He'd also have some sense of urgency about them, since he was a trained military K9. But he'd have waited for orders to determine what to do about them.

Jock would need to figure that out for himself, although he would discuss it, if necessary, with his commanding officers, as well as Ralf.

The closest part of the woods began only a few feet away, behind the row of cabins. Jock pulled Click's leash slightly to aim him between the rustic structures toward that direction.

"So tell me," said Kathlene once they had gone beyond the narrow lawn area and beneath the trees. "What is our next plan of action? Did you learn anything by sending Click to the encampment of those supposed sportsmen last night?"

"Click's presence there did give us some ideas," Jock said. Rather, it was his own presence. And it certainly had triggered what he intended to be their next course of action.

In wolf form, he had looked for—and found—some portions of the surrounding chain-link fence that were less secure and more penetrable by a canine observer than the rest of it.

He intended to return tonight under cover of darkness, and in his wolfen form.

He'd not seen or heard enough to understand what was really going on there, let alone how best to deal with it.

"What do you smell, boy?" Kathlene was talking to Click, whose nose was all but buried in a stack of dead leaves.

Jock scented it, too, of course. His sense of smell was much more acute than any person's besides other shifters, even when in human form. But he was hardly going to tell Kathlene that the dog was fascinated by the odor of a pile of pheasant droppings.

"Must be something interesting," Jock said mildly. "But we'd better keep on the move."

He nevertheless waited until Click lifted his leg to imbue the area with his own canine smell. And then they continued on.

"So what are those ideas you came up with?" Kathlene asked, walking directly behind him as they made their way through the towering trees that had a sweet, piney aroma.

Unfortunately, she hadn't been fully distracted by Click and his reaction to the odors of the woods.

"We need more information about what's going on inside the compound," Jock said. "For one thing, we'll want to know where the *sportsmen* hang out when they're in town. If possible, we'll act like we're of the same hunting mind-set and also want to engage in target practice and have the fun of killing whatever game is in season."

Even though that was contrary to his way of thinking. There were plenty of farm animals raised to be meat. He might feel sorry for them, but he was definitely carnivorous. He was a wolf in human form.

But in his opinion creatures that were wild, like wolves, should be permitted to stay that way. Survival of the fittest would allow them to feed on their own kinds of prey.

Humans did not need to kill or eat them.

"I can give you some information about that," Kathlene said. "There are a couple of bars in town where the sheriff's department has been called in because of some altercations between our townsfolk and some nonresidents. One's a sports bar near our headquarters—Arnie's. At least some of those who've gotten out of control came to town from that ranch."

"Good. We'll work that out soon, then."

"But not tonight?" She sounded curious. Too curious. He knew what was coming next.

"No, not tonight."

"Then what are we doing tonight?" she asked.

We. Of course she would assume it would be *we.*

Which it was. But that *we* included only Ralf and him. Not her. Not for what he had planned tonight.

Click stopped to circle slightly before defecating. Good. That gave Jock an opportunity to stop, too, and turn and face Kathlene.

He drew himself up as much as possible and looked down on her slim, yet official-looking form in her deputy sheriff's uniform.

But for this purpose, he was in charge, her job notwithstanding.

"Ralf and Click and I are going to do pretty much as we did last night," he told her. "Observation and reconnaissance at the perimeter of the target facility. Just us." He raised his hand to stop her as she opened her mouth to protest. "I know you're part of our team. You won that right. But we can't spend our time worrying about where you are and if you're okay, especially when we're just doing our preliminary examinations. You can work with us, participate in other aspects of what we're doing—but only if you listen to what I'm telling you now." *And obey me,* but he knew better than to say that.

She glared up at him. Damn, but that firm chin, that angry scowl on such a beautiful face…it turned him on. Even more than her presence already generated reactions inside—and outside—him that he'd never have imagined would occur with a woman in uniform, especially when that uniform was not one associated with Alpha Force.

"Then you promise that this will be the only time you'll not include me in your plans from now on." It wasn't a question but a statement. Her voice was chilly, but not even that forced his body to lose interest.

"Yes," he lied as he stooped to clean up after Click. "I promise—as long as you promise not to interfere with what we're doing tonight."

Chapter 6

Sure, Kathlene had given her promise.

She needed to make sure Jock considered her a member of their team, so what else could she do? She didn't want to fight him again, at least not yet. Besides, he claimed it would only be this one time they would exclude her.

Ha!

On her drive back to department headquarters that afternoon, along the winding road outside town, and even when she reached the main streets, she stewed.

Damn the man and his overprotective, exclusionary attitude!

Was it going to be like this all the time? Would Jock tell her each day that she'd be included in their plans…tomorrow. But not today?

Well, she might not be officially included in their recon plans that night.

But unofficially?

She'd been there last night observing.

She would do the same tonight.

They'd followed Kathlene back into town. No, not followed her. Not exactly. But Jock had made sure that Click was settled back in his cabin. Then he drove their car, with Ralf in the passenger's seat, in the direction that Kathlene had headed.

When they reached Cliffordsville, their first plan of attack was to drive by the sheriff's department.

Kathlene's car had been parked in the large outside lot. Was she inside the building?

She could be out on patrol already. And each sheriff's department vehicle, parked in rows nearest the building, looked like the rest, with their white color, gold logo and lights on top. Jock could definitely distinguish them from the unofficial ones also parked in that lot where Kathlene had left her car among a bunch of others—ones probably also belonging to the deputies and other department employees.

It didn't matter where she was, not now. Or it shouldn't matter.

But now that Jock had met her, he worried about her safety—her training and the way she had demonstrated her prowess in hand-to-hand notwithstanding.

Would she listen to him and stay away that night?

He doubted it.

But he had to trust her...didn't he?

"So where are we going?" Ralf asked from beside him. "Any games on TV now? I saw a sports bar not far from the restaurant where we had lunch, and it might be the one Kathlene mentioned. I think this would be a good time for beer and conversation if the place is likely to have any kind of crowd."

Ralf pulled his smartphone out of his pocket and slid his fingers over it. "Baseball, of course. But I'm not sure what teams they follow in Montana. There aren't any major league teams here. Maybe college teams. There's a baseball game between the Minnesota Twins and New York

Yankees being played in the East tonight, starting about now. Maybe they watch stuff like that in the bars, even though it's not local."

"We'll go see," Jock said.

Sure enough, Arnie's Bar, along Main Street, had a big-screen TV on the wall, and it was tuned to that baseball game. The crowd seemed rather sparse, but of course Jock was used to seeing lots of people gather in bars in the Baltimore area when he and other Alpha Force members decided to join regular humans in their celebration of the teams nearest to their headquarters at Ft. Lukman on Maryland's Eastern Shore.

Jock motioned for Ralf to join him on a couple of empty stools at the tall wooden bar where most of those present had congregated.

"Hi," he said, the epitome of friendly visitor when the bartender, a short, middle-aged guy who looked as if he enjoyed both the drinks and food he served, came over to take their orders. Both chose a locally brewed bottled beer. Jock liked beer, and drinking one that originated from around here should provide an additional topic of conversation, if they needed one besides sports. Oh, and who besides them were visitors here?

Jock glanced around at the others surrounding the bar. All eyes were focused on the large screen occupying the wall behind where the bartender bustled around filling orders. Jock looked at the score at the bottom of the picture. Close game. Just one run separated the two teams, but it was only the second inning. Plenty of time for them to jostle for position before one or the other won.

The bartender plopped bottles and glasses down in front of both Ralf and him without offering to pour. That was fine with Jock. In fact, drinking directly from the bottle seemed more appropriate to this apparent guy hangout.

He lifted his bottle in a silent toast, and Ralf did the same. Both took swigs just as some members of the small crowd around them started to cheer. Jock looked up to see the screen filled with two players dashing to the next bases. The batter for New York must have hit a double, or at least his teammates were treating it like one.

"Hey," Jock said to the guy on his left side. "Good game, huh?"

"It's okay, but it may be over already since the Yanks have scored again."

"I'm from Seattle," Jock said, "just visiting here. I wouldn't mind if the Yanks won. How about you?"

"The Twins are my team," he said shortly.

"Are you from Minnesota?" Jock asked. "Or do you live here?" He kept his tone light, as if all he was doing was making polite conversation rather than conducting his first interrogation here.

"Neither." The guy took a swig of his own beer and stared back up at the screen. Interesting, Jock thought. He might just have been lucky enough to start out finding one of the possible anarchists—or sportsmen, as Kathlene was calling them. Although the guy could, of course, just be visiting friends or relatives here, or even have business to conduct in Cliffordsville.

But his disinclination to answer suggested some degree of secrecy. Jock couldn't rule him out as being one of those hanging out at the old ranch for possibly nefarious purposes.

He felt Ralf elbow him gently and turned toward his aide. "Hey, Jock," Ralf said. "This is Hal." He gestured toward the man on his other side. "He's just visiting town for a while, like us. He's doing some target practice on a ranch not far from the motel where we're staying."

Jock leaned so he could check out Hal from behind Ralf.

He held out his hand. "Hi, Hal. Good to meet you. You a hunter?" He kept his tone light and nonjudgmental. Heck, if he were to ask, probably ninety percent of the regular humans who lived in an area like this most likely engaged in hunting, for food or sport or both and probably most complied with the laws. Just because he identified with some of the wildlife they might go after didn't mean he should give them a hard time about it.

"Sure am," Hal said. He was a moderate-sized guy and, if Jock were to guess, he probably worked out regularly with weights, judging by the way his arm muscles bulged as he, too, reached around Ralf to shake Jock's hand.

"Me, too," Jock lied. "We're only here for a short time visiting an old friend of mine, but target practice sounds like fun. Any possibility of our joining in?" Of course, they'd have to find reasons not to if it turned out this guy's target practice wasn't at the old ranch as part of whatever was going on there.

"Could be," Hal said. He stood and walked behind Ralf and Jock, approaching the guy at Jock's other side. That guy didn't look too pleased, especially when Hal said, "Hey, Nate, we got room to enlist some other hunters?" If Jock wasn't mistaken, Hal, who was even taller than Jock had first thought and had a substantially receding hairline, half winked toward the man he called Nate.

"Probably not just now," Nate said, not sounding especially inviting. "But I can check. You guys done much shooting before?"

Jock started making up a whole story of how he'd loved hunting since he was a kid. He added what he thought might help make up this Nate's mind if he was one of the leaders and the group actually was composed of anarchists. "Thing is," he ended up saying, "there are so many damned laws about who can own guns and where you can shoot them and what you can shoot where we come from—well, it's just damned frustrating."

"Yeah," Nate said. "Where I'm from, too." He held out his hand. "I'm Nate Tisal."

Jock introduced himself and Ralf, too.

Tisal appeared to be in his fifties, with a lot of gray in his dark hair and divots resembling parentheses emphasizing the narrowness of his lips. His light brown eyes seemed to study Jock, as if he were trying to dig into his mind and learn what he really thought about hunting and guns.

"Where's that?" Jock asked in a tone that was studiedly casual yet friendly.

"Another state," the guy dissembled. "How long you here for?"

Obviously turning the topic back to him, Jock thought. "Just a few days. Ralf and I are on our way to Yellowstone, but I wanted to take the opportunity to visit a friend from my college days who lives here."

"Who's that?" Nate immediately shot back.

Jock had already talked about this with Ralf. Since they were likely to be seen in town with Kathlene, who wore her deputy sheriff's uniform a lot, it would be better to be up front about that so none of the possible anarchists they met would assume they were talking to the authorities about their newest acquaintances.

Even though they would be.

"My old buddy Kathlene Baylor. Who'd a thunk back then that she would go into law enforcement? She's with the local sheriff's department, of all things." He shook his head as if he was totally befuddled by the idea.

"She is?" Despite the casualness of Tisal's tone, he sounded interested. Worried? Probably not.

"Yeah. I don't get it. But damned if she doesn't look good in a uniform." Jock looked around. "Hey," he said, and waved toward the bartender. "I'd like another beer. How about you?" He looked at Nate. "I'm buying. And you, Hal?"

Jock paid for a round of beers for the four of them, who were now good buddies. Or at least he had made some inroads, he hoped, into finding out more about these men and those with them—and whether they were, in fact, terrorists or more.

He realized he hadn't fully established, not yet, that they were among those hanging out at the old ranch. But he'd have bet another round of drinks for everyone there, including the additional dozen or so guys also still at the bar, that these two were part of that group.

And were they anti-law? Anti-government? That remained to be seen.

But with their initial attitude about hunting and guns... well, he couldn't rule it out, either.

"Hey, the sheriff's got a job for you for tomorrow afternoon."

Kathlene had just gotten back to work, logged in and contacted her partner, Jimmy Korling, who was going to come by and pick her up in their patrol car. She was heading outside to wait for him when Undersheriff George Kerringston hustled from the doorway to catch up with her.

She pivoted to face George. If Sheriff Frawley had personally chosen an assignment for her, it probably involved hanging out in their cruiser on the street where some town muckety-muck's kid was having a birthday party inside.

George Kerringston had been with the sheriff's department for twenty years and bragged about that often. He was slightly tall, slightly plump, and all dazed most of the time. Kathlene had wondered whether their old boss, Sheriff Lon Chrissoula, had kept George on out of kindness to him or to his large and needy family, and had thought their supervisor particularly sweet to have done so. Back then, George was just a deputy, like her.

But Sheriff Frawley had promoted him. Kerringston couldn't have been happier. Or more loyal. He probably had few thoughts of his own, anyway, so he'd undoubtedly been delighted to become Melton's second in command and pass along anything and everything his boss told him to.

"Thanks, George," Kathlene made herself say. "Do you know what the assignment is?" She braced herself for something minor and useless that she'd hate.

Instead, though, it was something potentially important. "Yeah. You and a few others are being sent to patrol tomorrow afternoon's meeting of the county commissioners."

"Oh? Great. I'm on my way out now but will check more about it when I go off duty later."

"Okay." He looked her square in the face, then let his gaze roll lustfully down over her body, which made her freeze and want to go take a shower. When she glared angrily back at him, she'd have sworn he was about to drool.

Before she could say anything, he turned. Lord, couldn't the man even remember to tuck in his uniform shirt? He wasn't only a sleazy, unintelligent goon, but he was also a slob who only made the sheriff's department look bad.

But Melton obviously didn't care. He had this guy's undivided allegiance.

Some other deputies were just entering the building. They looked at her curiously, and she just shot them a smug smile that was intended to tell them this was a fine day and she was doing just great, thank you. Never mind what she was thinking inside.

She wondered what overprotective Jock Larabey would

have thought about her exchange with Kerringston. Good thing he wasn't here.

At least her trading of lustful expressions with Jock was mutual—and they both understood that acting on any real sexual interest between them simply wouldn't happen.

Kathlene scanned the street in front of her. There were only a few pedestrians along the sidewalk. Not much automobile traffic, either. She wasn't sure where Jimmy was, but he was obviously taking his time getting here to pick her up.

Well, that was fine. She would use the time to her benefit. She decided to make a quick phone call—to Commission Chair Myra Enager. Myra was Tommy X's lady friend. She was also a friend of Kathlene's. Maybe even a reason why Kathlene remained with the Clifford County Sheriff's Department. Myra was both a role model for a woman's being in charge of something important around here and a sounding board for Kathlene to vent when things here didn't go well.

Not that she would abuse her authority and tell Sheriff Frawley where to go on Kathlene's behalf. And that was fine with Kathlene. She would handle this, like everything else in her life, herself.

As she would tonight, when she was supposed to pretend that she wasn't part of the team she had gotten in place here. Jock and Ralf might have heard her promise to stay away this time.

But she would use her own definition of staying away.

"Hi, Myra," she said after a secretary at the commissioners' offices had gotten her on the line. "I hear there's a meeting tomorrow afternoon."

"That's right," Myra said. "I was going to contact you about it. You might want to attend. The main topic to be discussed is my proposal for the enactment of local laws to help enforce state regulations that protect wildlife and require the arrest of poachers."

Passage of those laws locally should have been a no-brainer. They were simply following what was already enacted in the state.

But there were opponents on the commission.

And even more, the timing of the arrival of the first of the supposed sportsmen had begun just after Myra initially proposed enactment of the local law—right after Sheriff Chrissoula retired six months ago.

"Great. Not only will I be there to hear it, but I've been told I'll be on duty then, with other deputies, as well. I don't know about Tommy X, though."

Silence on the other end. Then Myra said, "Your boss is anticipating some controversy, then." It wasn't a question but a statement.

"Guess so, although I haven't talked to him directly."

"Well, don't." Myra, more than anyone, knew how much Kathlene hated conversations with her highest-up boss. "We'll be fine, especially with some of the best deputies in your department there keeping the peace. And you're definitely the best."

"Thanks, Myra. We should grab a cup of coffee one of these days." Should Kathlene tell her friend more about what she was up to? "I've got something in the works that just might help get your law passed. If nothing else, I'm checking out my theory that those guys who're showing up in town need to either get arrested or leave."

"You're not doing anything foolish, are you, Kathlene?" Now Myra sounded worried.

Kathlene glimpsed her patrol car driven by Jimmy pulling up at the curb. "Gotta run," she said. "And no, I'm not doing anything foolish. You know me better than that. See you tomorrow."

She wondered, as she hurried to the car, what Myra would really think if she knew Kathlene had not only gotten the federal government involved, but a secret military unit that wouldn't reveal, even to her, what they were really about.

Chapter 7

They were back at the cabin. After Jock and Ralf had returned, they'd taken Click for a walk around the motel area, saying hi to the few other guests and staff members they ran into.

The place seemed to be getting busier, but that was okay. They still maintained their extra cabin for Click, and his being seen with Jock now and then was a good thing.

Now they were inside, ready to report to their superior officer, Major Drew Connell of Alpha Force. He was at Ft. Lukman, and it was a couple of hours later there, nearly nine o'clock.

Drew didn't mind. The members of Alpha Force were sent all over the country and abroad for special assignments, and he'd made it clear to Jock that he expected periodic call-ins, no matter what the time.

Jock didn't have a lot to say…yet. But he knew it was time to make a call.

He motioned for Ralf to join him on the couch. Each had a bottle of water on the low table in front of them.

No more alcohol that day. Or that night. They still had something to accomplish after this call.

"Anything in particular you think we need to report?" Jock asked Ralf, then chugged some water from his bottle.

They discussed all they'd seen and heard in Clifford County so far, underscoring to one another what sounded most important. Then Jock took his phone from his pocket and keyed in the number for their commanding officer. He pressed the button that would put the call on speaker.

"Jock?" The major's voice sounded alert and interested. He was obviously using caller ID. "Ralf with you?"

"We're both here, Drew," Jock responded. "Just wanted to give you a rundown of what we've learned so far, which isn't much."

"Go ahead."

Jock proceeded to relate all that had happened in the past couple of days, from Deputy Kathlene Baylor's showing up at the cabin she had reserved for them soon after he'd called to let her know they'd arrived, to the brief interchange with the guys at the bar that afternoon.

He stressed what they had done last night. Of course. It was the crux of why Alpha Force was involved. "I shifted into wolf form and prowled outside the enclosed area," he told Drew. "Ralf stayed at the deserted house where I'd changed. I was able to find some potentially vulnerable points of entry into the encampment but I mostly stayed in the surrounding forest using all my senses just to orient myself. I'll be going back tonight, once we're done talking, to do a bit more digging."

"Anybody see you shifted?" Drew asked.

"I'm pretty sure none of the hunters or whoever they are inside the fence did, but Deputy Baylor did."

He didn't mention that he had told the stubborn woman to stay away from them, nor did he tell his commanding officer that the deputy now believed she was an integral part of their team. Jock had to deal with all of that in the best way he could. Kathlene's proclivity for involving herself was his problem, not Drew's. He could deal with it, although he might avail himself of Ralf's help now and then.

What he also hoped he could deal with—no, he *would* deal with it—was his attraction to the strong, determined and completely frustrating woman.

"We diffused any concerns she might have about seeing a wolflike dog at the site by introducing her to Click," he added. He didn't tell Drew that she appeared to be fond of canines. That was irrelevant.

"And those men at the bar—you think they're among those hanging out at that site, the possible anarchists?"

"Maybe," Jock said. "We started to foster a good relationship with them, although how good remains to be seen."

"Carry on, then." Drew paused. "Oh, and Jock?"

"Yes, sir?"

"Be damned careful—but do a good job. We need to maintain our stellar reputation."

"We will. Count on it."

His affirmative reply was seconded by Ralf.

The two men grinned at each other as they hung up. But then Ralf's expression faded. "You think there's a problem with Alpha Force's reputation?" he asked.

"Not with Drew in charge."

Every member of Alpha Force knew the covert unit's background. It was started a few years back by Drew, who was a shifter. He had begun developing the extraordinary elixir that helped shapeshifters change not only during the full moon, but at any time they chose, as well. Not only that, they could also keep their human mind, and knowledge, intact while in shifted form.

The unit consisted of shifters from wolves to lynxes to hawks. It also included aides for each of them.

Not to mention their cover animals, as close to the others' shifted forms as Click was to Jock's.

The unit's operations had occurred all over the U.S. and occasionally elsewhere, and had involved rooting out terrorists, including some who had intended to create biological weapons, and others who had aimed to destroy glaciers much faster than global warming and effect all the harm that could involve.

It was definitely a covert unit, and yet Drew and his operatives always kept their eyes peeled for other shifters they could recruit.

Like Jock himself had been about a year ago.

He hadn't regretted it. Not for a moment.

He had mostly worked with other Alpha Force operatives before. This was his first assignment in which he was the sole shifter, in charge of initial surveillance and determination if more Alpha Force members were needed to stop any harm from being inflicted on people or this country.

He definitely would perform as Drew had commanded—and do a good job.

"Let's get ready," he finally said to Ralf, who was playing with Click. "We need to put him in his cabin and then head for that deserted house again. I intend to learn a lot more about what goes on beyond that fence tonight."

Jock thought about Kathlene. He didn't feel guilty at all about leaving her out of whatever was to occur. This time he had even told her to butt out, though he would do as promised and include her as part of their team. Whenever he could. Whenever it wasn't too dangerous for her.

For tonight at least, team member or not, she was safe.

Kathlene drove a circuitous route toward the back of the fenced-in compound, lights turned off, then parked off-road so her car couldn't be seen from what passed as a partially paved lane way off in the forest.

This time she'd had plenty of time to change out of her uniform. Tonight she wore a long-sleeved knit shirt and jeans, both black. So were her athletic shoes. Unlike when she was on duty, she hadn't clipped her long hair behind her head. Its dark color might even help hide the lightness of her facial skin, in case anyone happened to glance in her direction.

She stared into the blackness of the forest and saw nothing. That was good. It meant she was unlikely to be seen, too.

She sat motionless for a few minutes, going over plans in her mind.

She had once again hung out near that old hovel of a house, observing from a distance as the two men went in, but only the dog came out. She hadn't seen Click at first, but they were clearly relying on him to observe what was going on at the nearby enclosed ranch.

And then she had carefully slipped away and driven here.

By being there, she wasn't disobeying orders. Sexy but annoying Jock Larabey might be in charge of Ralf Nunnoz and whatever he was doing here, but he wasn't in charge of her. He wasn't her superior officer, and he had no authority to tell her what to do.

And extorting her cooperation by telling her when she was, and wasn't, a member of his team, simply didn't work.

She cracked her window just a bit. A light breeze was blowing. She heard a couple of owls hooting not far away. No other wildlife, though.

And no Click barking anywhere around. Not that a dog as well trained as he seemed to be would be making noise when he shouldn't.

Jock had told her that Ralf and he—or apparently just Click again—would be conducting some kind of surveillance at the old ranch once more that night. She wasn't sure what that would accomplish, unless the group centered there had decided to conduct an exercise under cover of darkness. Did they ever do that? Maybe.

They at least practiced the use of different kinds of weapons, although the muted explosions she'd heard a few weeks ago had been late in the day, but not nighttime.

She didn't really know what they did, though, except act secretive and threatening while pretending to be nice guys off to practice hunting skills. As sportsmen.

As they planned some nasty uses in the future of the weapons they tested now...? That was her fear.

But hanging out here tonight was likely to be fruitless, just as last night had been.

Still, if Jock decided that Alpha Force would check the compound out again that night, then so would she.

She hated doing everything in near total darkness, but fortunately, in the area where she was now, the trees weren't quite as close together so there was a little illumination from the stars overhead.

Lovely to see them this way, the constellations and all. The moon was only a sliver, so it didn't provide much light, but she loved looking up in the sky toward the stars.

Not that she dared do that very much. She had more important things to watch.

For now she would just stay in this area and conduct her own little bit of surveillance.

If she didn't see anything, she would carefully move toward where she had first seen Click maneuvering around the compound last night.

Surely she could glean more information than a dog could. Or even if she couldn't compete with its superior senses, she could certainly verbally divulge a lot more than a canine could.

Unless…she hadn't asked, but maybe they had equipped the dog with some kind of camera or other recording equipment. That would make sense.

And if she was part of the team, they should not only tell her but also show her what had been filmed.

She could take some shots herself. She pulled her phone out of her pocket, held it down so any illumination wouldn't be visible outside her car and reset it so it showed no lights—but would nevertheless take pictures.

No other kinds of shots, though. Not tonight. She purposely left her Glock in the glove compartment of her car.

She wasn't here as a deputy, but as a curious and concerned citizen.

But now it was time. She cautiously opened the door of her vehicle, prepared to get out quickly, even though she'd turned off the interior lights, too. This far from the fencing no one was likely to see her, anyway, but just in case…

She slid out fast and pushed the door closed, careful not to make any slamming sounds. Then she stood still for a few minutes to orient herself.

The air smelled tangy and moist, as if humidity was hovering, determining when a rain shower should begin to pummel the earth.

She heard nothing now, not owls or anything else. It was time to draw closer to the perimeter of the compound. And watch for Click, who would probably be circling the whole thing.

She had done a bit of surveillance before trying to enlist help from the federal government, but she hadn't done this.

Nor had she been competing to convince anyone to keep her involved. She had, back then, been the only one who'd tried to do anything.

And now, if she was lucky, she would get a lot more useful stuff than the dog did. Show Jock that she was an important part of the team.

Show Jock that—

"Hands up, lady." The voice that growled at her was off to her side, and she was suddenly bathed in so much light that she was blinded and couldn't see its source. "What the hell are you doing here?"

"I was just—" she stammered.

"Don't matter. You're coming with me."

Damn!

While preparing to sneak in through a particularly vulnerable and worn area of fencing, Jock had caught the scent of Kathlene in the distance.

The woman was impossible. Never listened.

Always put herself in danger.

And once he had loped in her direction in his shifted form, careful to stay hidden in the trees, he had seen that she had been captured.

The man who had found her kept a gun trained on her back. He marched her toward a nearby gate in the fence— one that had been secured and was not a potential entry point for Jock. He watched as Kathlene was forced to go through the gate and onto the fenced-in site.

He tore back to one of the vulnerable areas he had located before, where the chain-link fencing had apparently been hit by a car or otherwise damaged. There was enough of a gap that a canine could squeeze through it.

He did.

He looked around cautiously, engaged all his senses to ensure that there were no humans nearer than those now congregating around Kathlene and the man who had captured her.

He knew how to help her—maybe. And then only if she was astute enough to follow his lead.

Too bad he hadn't come with a collar and leash to further resemble the dog who was his cover. But he would improvise, and so, he hoped, would Kathlene.

Assuming a submissive position, he all but crawled on his stomach, using all four legs.

As he maneuvered, he listened to the conversation. Rather, the way Kathlene was being chewed out and threatened.

"Why the hell are you here?" "Ain't you a deputy sheriff?" "You don't belong here. We don't like snoops." "Tell us what you want here." "Let's just shoot the nosy bitch. No one will ever know."

Jock wanted to growl. To attack. But his human mind overshadowed his wild-animal instincts. Instead, he just continued to draw himself closer.

"What's that dog doing here?" he heard one of the men say. "That's no dog. It's a wolf."

Jock maneuvered his way up to Kathlene's side, pretending to ignore the crowd of ill-smelling, menacing hunters who surrounded her in what appeared to be a stable yard of the old ranch. A floodlight had been turned on and illuminated the entire area. When he glanced up briefly, he recognized one of the men Ralf and he had seen in the bar earlier.

That man—Nate Tisal—appeared to be in charge.

Jock smelled Kathlene's fear, but the woman stood straight, chin up, scowling at her captors...until she saw him.

"Click!" she exclaimed, as if he was her savior.

In some ways he was—if she figured out how to play this.

He hurried up to her, nuzzled her side with his nose, whined a little as if in fear.

"There you are," she said. "You bad dog." Did she get it? It sounded as if she did. "He belongs to some friends of mine who're visiting. I love dogs but don't have one right now, so I was walking him for them. He apparently likes to go into the woods and usually stays near the road, but this time he ran away. I was out here looking for him." She slipped to her knees and hugged him. He wished he could hug her back but instead licked her cheek.

She tasted sweet and salty and nervous.

"You were walking a dog out here?" Tisal's tone was scornful.

"No," she said, rising again to look the tall, hefty, scowling man in his gleaming brown eyes. "Like I said, I was walking him in the area, a distance from here, near the road, but he ran away and I've been looking all over for him."

She sounded affronted and sure of herself.

"I'm sorry if I bothered you, Mr. Tisal. Although," she continued, "I don't understand why you're all so defensive. Are you doing something here that you shouldn't be?"

Damn her! If he could have, he'd have slapped a muzzle on her to shut her up.

But then he realized why she'd done it. To maintain her character, since at least some of these men apparently knew she was a deputy sheriff.

"Not at all," Tisal countered smoothly. "It's just that most of us were heading for bed and it was startling that someone spotted a prowler. We weren't sure if you were doing something here that you shouldn't be. Were you?"

"Of course not. Just looking for my friends' dog. And now I won't even have to tell them he went missing. I'll just take him and go home." She looked at him. "I left his

*collar and leash, though. Do you happen to have a rope
that I can use to lead him?"*

"Yeah." Tisal nodded toward one of his minions, who
dashed off. "Okay. You can go home with your dog. No
harm, no foul. I apologize that some of my friends might
have sounded too harsh but we were all startled by your
being here. And in case anyone asks, I hope it's clear
enough to you that we're not doing anything wrong, just
hanging out and practicing till hunting season."

"I got it," she said. "And I can certainly understand
why your friends overreacted." Jock wished she would
aim such a bright smile toward him but realized how false
it really was.

And he felt sure she didn't forgive them for their
threats—which convinced him more that she'd been correct about the nature of these guys and what they were
doing.

Smart lady, he thought again. Turning the situation
so it appeared as if it was resolved in favor of these men.

And maybe it was. Would real anarchists rehearsing
for some terrorist attack actually let her go?

Or were they simply using Kathlene as a foil?

And if the latter, she should only remain in danger as
long as these men were around.

Chapter 8

One of the men, a guy in an open shirt and jeans, stayed with Kathlene while she walked Click back through the woods to her car. She tromped in the near total darkness on uneven clumps of dead leaves, not caring about the noise she made now and not looking at the guy—but aware every moment of his presence.

The odor of impending rain filled her lungs, or maybe they just felt constricted because of the nervousness she had felt before, with vestiges still hanging on now.

Fortunately, the man who'd gone after a rope had found something that let her keep Click secured loosely at her side. She just hoped their escort didn't insist on her showing him Click's actual collar and leash. She'd have to go into an act about how she'd thought she had left it in the car but must have instead lost it in the woods when she let the dog run free.

She reached her car in about five minutes, yanked the key from her pocket and pushed the button to unlock the doors. She opened the one on the passenger's side and gently pulled the rope around Click's neck to get him to jump in first. Then she nodded to their unwelcome com-

panion without saying anything as she circled the car, slid
into the driver's seat and locked the doors.

Only then did she feel she could breathe again.

"That wasn't any fun," she said to Click as the light
inside the car faded. "Those guys are definitely nasty."

He whined, and she interpreted it as agreement with her.
But the way the wolflike dog looked at her—it seemed like
a glare, scolding her for having been there in the first place.

"I'm reading too much of your master into you, guy,"
she told the dog. And despite knowing she would be
scolded, at a minimum, by Jock, she half wished he were
there, too. No, more than half.

Whatever Alpha Force was, she would really have appreciated it if the strong, determined Jock had had her back
during this ugly incident.

Well, his dog had had her back, and the situation had
ended a whole lot better than she'd figured it would.

And Click? Well, she really liked this dog. Appreciated his help.

Still wondered why she had recalled his head as being
flatter, his legs longer, his coat a little shorter and less
wolflike.

Well, no matter. She turned the key in the ignition and
drove off slowly through the woods toward the barely
paved road.

If she hadn't had Click with her, she'd have driven
straight home. Maybe had a glass of wine to help calm
her nerves. Or two glasses.

But since Click was with her she needed to take him
back to Jock and Ralf. That meant she would have to explain to them what had happened.

Where she had been.

And how their dog had been a lifesaver.

This time she didn't turn off her exterior lights. She

soon reached the main road, which was a shred better maintained than the one she'd been on. It only took another few minutes to arrive at the hovel that the Alpha Force guys had settled into as their apparent local command center. She pulled into what passed for a driveway and parked.

"Come on, boy." She again took hold of the rope that looped around Click's neck and remained careful not to pull it too hard, not wanting to choke him.

But the dog didn't seem to want to go to the house's main door. Instead, he pulled slightly toward the back area, then led her to the rear door. Interesting. But of course Click had been here before with the two men, and maybe they had started using this as their main entrance. It was less visible from the nearby road, so that made sense, especially since they had also parked in back. Maybe she should have, too.

As she knocked on the door, Click raised one of his fur-covered legs and pawed at it. That made Kathlene smile. The dog was clearly trained to act at least somewhat human.

The door was pulled open nearly immediately. Ralf stood there, and he looked downward toward Click first, then let his gaze dart upward toward Kathlene's face. "Er... Hi, Kathlene. Come in. How did you—where did you find Click?"

"I'll tell you all about it but I'd rather just describe it one time, to both Jock and you. It wasn't pretty, but it'd have been a lot worse if Click hadn't been there to save me."

"What?" His tone sounded aghast, and his dark eyes turned huge.

Kathlene managed a laugh. "I'll explain." She glanced around. "Where is Jock?"

"Uh...he's probably out looking for Click. He...went

with Click to check out the exterior of the ranch again. And since Click is here with you, he's probably still there searching for…for the dog."

Ralf seemed to be hiding something, but Kathlene had no idea what it could be. No matter.

"I'll wait here with you, then, till he shows up."

"No!" Ralf's tone was sharp. He ran his thick hand over his short crop of graying hair. What the heck was really going on? "No, Jock and I already made plans for this kind of situation. I'm to take Click back to our cabin and wait there. If…if Jock doesn't show up within a short while, I'm to head back here to wait for him. Since you probably won't see him tonight, it'd be better if you just gave me a brief description of what happened that I can convey to him, then you can go home and get some sleep. We'll all talk about it more tomorrow."

He clearly wanted her to spill her story then leave. At the moment he hadn't really even let her go very far inside. They stood near the door, talking.

Maybe that was a good thing. The place smelled musty and unpleasant. But she didn't need to stay there long. Only long enough for Jock to arrive and listen to her story.

She didn't want to argue, though. Ralf obviously didn't want her to wait for Jock. And as exhausted and frustrated as she felt, going home sounded great.

"Okay," she said. "Let me sit down, and I'll tell you what happened."

Ralf showed her to a rickety chair that had apparently remained in this disaster of a house. She gave him the abridged version of her horror at being caught, threatened and virtually imprisoned, and how she had been able to use the very unexpected presence of Click inside the property's fence to make up a good enough story that, even if the anarchists didn't buy it, they wound up letting her and the dog leave, anyway.

Ralf, seated on another equally decrepit chair, kept exclaiming and shaking his head.

Surprisingly, Click stayed at her feet, sitting there and seeming to enjoy the sound of her voice. At least the dog kept looking up at her and even made some small whining noises in his throat.

When she finished with how it had felt to slip into the car with Click and drive away, Ralf leaped to his feet. He took her hands and squeezed them.

"I'm just glad you're okay. Jock'll be glad, too. I've got to go look for him now since he won't have his phone on. You go ahead home and get some sleep. I know he'll want to talk to you more about it, so plan on getting together with us sometime tomorrow."

She told him about the county commissioners' upcoming meeting and that she would be there on duty. "And I'm glad—since I heard that some measures that might evoke reactions from those sportsmen are being discussed. It's a public meeting, so I'd suggest that Jock and you attend, too. I'll go off duty shortly after it's over, so we can grab coffee and talk."

"Sounds like a plan." Ralf glanced down at Click, then back up into Kathlene's face. "We'll see you there."

And then he ushered her back out the door.

She rehashed a lot of things as she drove back home as quickly as she could: her horrible situation with those men. How that smart dog, who was unbelievably sweet despite resembling a combo between a wolf and German shepherd, had helped her diffuse and escape.

And then Ralf's attitude, and the absence of Jock.

She absolutely had to get those men to explain Alpha Force. Something about that covert military unit would clarify at least some of their part of what she had just undergone. She felt sure of it.

Those two men should not keep her in the dark any longer.

Jock sat on the chair that Kathlene had vacated half an hour before, his hands clasped, his head bent as he attempted to maintain his temper.

He had spent part of that time shifting back to human form and getting dressed.

Now he was ready to head back to their cabins with Ralf. To check on the real Click and make sure he was okay.

And grab a drink, not at the bar where they'd met up with Tisal but by themselves. By *him*self, preferably.

He knew that Ralf was full of questions but had been astute enough not to ask them—yet.

What he did ask, though, was, "You okay, Lieutenant? I mean, Jock."

Jock shot a glare at his aide, who again sat in the chair he had occupied when Kathlene was here. Ralf was grinning, knowing he was intentionally prodding Jock's dander by doing as he'd been ordered not to—acting even somewhat military right now.

"I'm fine," he grumbled back.

"Except for wanting to strangle Deputy Baylor, right?"

Jock closed his eyes and counted to five before opening them again. "Yeah," he said. "Except for wanting to strangle Deputy Baylor. But that would be most imprudent considering I pretty much saved her ass before, while shifted."

"Yes, she does have a pretty ass." That grin of Ralf's twitched, and Jock knew he was only trying to goad him. And succeeding.

"Maybe I should strangle you, instead, Staff Sergeant." Jock started to rise, but only got a laugh out of Ralf.

"Maybe I can just pin you to the floor like Deputy Baylor did," Ralf countered. He paused and continued more seriously, "I know you don't like her putting herself in danger like that, Jock. I don't, either. But until we figure out what's going on around here and stop it, you know she's just going to keep at it. And if she hadn't wound up calling in federal help and getting Alpha Force here she'd probably have remained in the thick of it all by herself."

"Yeah, I know," Jock conceded. "But she did wind up with us here, even if she didn't know exactly what she was getting. And like it or not, I realize we'd better plan on her inclusion and interference."

"And maybe on her finding out what Alpha Force is really about."

"Not if I—" Jock stopped himself. "Maybe you're right. Whether or not we want her to. But I suspect a woman like that, once she got over the shock, might not hate the idea."

"We may just find that out," Ralf said.

"True." He forced himself not to sigh or react in any other way—this time. "Now, let's go back and see how I—rather, my counterpart Click—is doing right now, shall we?"

"Yes, sir," Ralf said.

"On the way, let's discuss what we're likely to hear at tomorrow's county commissioners' meeting, okay?"

"I just happen to have downloaded their agenda onto my smartphone while you were out playing wonder dog and saving Deputy Kathlene's butt. I'll drive—which I should, anyway, since your body may still be morphing here and there—and you can look it over. The agenda, that is. Not our deputy's butt. Or ass. Or whatever."

Jock glared at Ralf. He shouldn't give a damn that his

aide happened to have noticed Kathlene's lovely, firm, enticing rear area. What red-blooded male wouldn't have?

And just because he found the woman much too damned sexy didn't mean he had any priority over any other man in looking at, or wanting, her.

He'd have to keep telling himself that in the next few days, especially since he had no doubt that she would insist on staying involved.

And that meant he actually had to treat her as part of their team—at least enough to keep an eye on her and attempt to keep her out of trouble.

"You ready, Kathlene?" asked Deputy Jimmy Korling, checking his duty belt without glancing at her. Jimmy was a somewhat nice-looking guy, with short, wavy black hair and a youthfully muscular body.

He was also clearly not pleased about having a woman as his very first partner after joining the department. Most of the time he was very cordial, if remote.

Most of the time…

"Just about. How about you?" She, like her partner, was confirming that her uniform, including the equipment on her belt, was complete and that she was ready to report to the county commissioners' meeting as one of the law-enforcement officers there on duty.

"I sure am," Jimmy said.

"Great. Just give me another minute." She worked to finalize her check.

Right now it was the morning after her unpleasant visit to the sportsmen's ranch. She was at the department headquarters, in the dispatch room, where all officers congregated before heading off to duty. It had chairs for them to sit, plus mirrors on the wall so they could get last-minute glimpses of themselves and assure that they appeared professional and ready for the day's assignment.

She had arrived at department headquarters right on time that morning despite the wet roads after some overnight rainfall—and after getting little sleep the night before.

That was mostly because of her nighttime rescue, thanks to a dog, from the people she deemed to be anarchists. Thinking about it—the situation, and how she had managed to exit it relatively gracefully—had occupied her mind much of the night.

But she wasn't about to tell any of her colleagues about that. Would the men from the ranch mention it to any locals?

To Sheriff Frawley?

Kathlene didn't like the idea but couldn't assume it wouldn't happen.

And where had Jock been? Had Ralf found him? Were they back at their cabin?

She believed so. She hadn't wanted to call them in case they were sleeping in, or were up early and out and about doing whatever they were doing undercover, maybe hanging out in local restaurants pretending to be visitors.

She was their team member, though, and they should have let her know.

She'd texted Jock just before reporting for duty, while still in her car. She'd received a brief response:

All fine. Glad Click helped you yesterday. See you later.

The only question he'd seemed to answer was whether he'd gotten back with Ralf and Click. Unless, of course, Ralf was responding on Jock's behalf.

She knew she was one suspicious lady. But she was an

officer of the law. Suspicion was her job, even when she wasn't involved in a potentially threatening situation—like now.

But she wasn't going to resolve anything here. Would she at the upcoming meeting?

No, but it might turn out to be quite interesting—and the discussions there could be highly enlightening.

"Okay, partner," she finally said, aiming one last look at the mirror on the wall, then facing Jimmy, who now seemed to be studiously ignoring her. "Let's go."

As she had been ordered, Kathlene, in uniform and with her weapon in its holster at her side, stood just inside the door to the large public meeting room in the 1950s-style building that housed the Clifford County government offices. Straight and alert, she maintained a position that wasn't quite at attention, but nor was it at ease.

Far from it.

She was there to be visible as well as to watch all that was going on. Her gaze scanned the room, confirming that everything looked peaceful and friendly and not in need of official sheriff's department intervention. Not yet, at least.

She scented perfumes and shaving lotions as people walked by her to enter. She heard snatches of conversations, received a few friendly hellos, which she responded to, but otherwise stayed silent and alert.

She knew most of the people walking in. So far, they hadn't included Jock or Ralf. Where were they? Today's session could be important to their ability to determine who those who'd infiltrated that old ranch were and what they wanted.

Even if it wasn't, they should be here to find out.

At least none of the men who'd accosted her when she'd been saved by Click had arrived yet, either. But she felt fairly certain that Nate Tisal, who'd appeared to be in charge of the sportsmen's outpost, would be here.

Her partner, Jimmy, was stationed at the door directly across the room from her. He appeared bored and not especially alert, but the meeting hadn't yet gotten started.

Kathlene hoped he would do his job. Same went for the other couple of deputies who'd been deployed here, both of whom stood outside in the hallway at the moment. She wasn't sure when or if they'd come inside.

A lot of people had already entered the assembly room. Most were seated in the folding metal chairs that had been lined up in ten long rows. A few stood in the aisles at each end of the rows, chatting. The noise level was high in this room that had clearly not been built for the best acoustics, but Kathlene knew the sound would level off once the meeting began.

She glanced at her watch. Five more minutes. That's when the commissioners would enter the room and begin their session.

She had attended county commissioners' meetings before, mostly as a local resident interested in what was going on in the area.

Now, though, the commission had requested a visible presence by the sheriff's department for the third time— and each of those times Kathlene had attended in uniform.

Which she had been glad to do. She had discussed the situation with her friend Commission Chair Myra Enager each time, before the session and after. Both of the prior times, there'd been at least a few of the men hanging out at the old ranch who'd come in and even tried to speak. But they hadn't followed the commission protocol so they'd not been able to present their opinions.

Not vocally. But their glares had spoken volumes.

So had the anonymous and general threats delivered by

email and otherwise afterward, although no one could definitely attribute any of them to the apparent anarchist group.

These sessions and what had occurred afterward had added to Kathlene's concerns about who the people were who were staying at the old ranch. But it didn't take a law-enforcement officer to note the cold stares leveled by the visitors who appeared at those earlier meetings and sat at the front of the room when something about hunting restrictions or gun licensing was being discussed.

Today the mayor of Cliffordsville, Larry Davonne, was also there, sitting in the front row with some of his aides. He wasn't in charge of anything here, since he was a city official and this was a county meeting. But Kathlene felt certain that the commissioners had requested his presence to ensure that he knew what was going on. Maybe to get his input.

Kathlene had been watching for the mayor, since Jimmy and she had been told to pay special attention to him and to a couple of commissioners who had expressly requested the law-enforcement presence and surveillance. The deputies were to make it clear that the crowd at the meeting was under guard, if necessary.

That included Myra, of course, and her closest ally on the commission, Wendy Ingerton. The other five members were men. All appeared to get along reasonably well, but the members besides Myra and Wendy had been fairly tight-lipped about their opinions on the matters that clearly riled the visitors: local laws to help enforce new state regulations that protected wildlife and required the arrest of poachers. A certain amount of gun control was involved in those matters, too—licensing, at least, and some background checks for the purchase of ammunition.

Despite the controversy surrounding those concepts even among members of the sheriff's department, Kathlene thought them quite reasonable to impose on strangers whose real purpose for being here remained hazy—and potentially threatening.

"Hello, Kathlene." The low voice at her ear caused a soft shiver of pleasure to ripple through her body. She tried not to smile, to stay professional, as she turned to see its source.

"Well, hi, Jock," she said. "Hi, Ralf." It was okay to smile now, since she was playing the role of longtime friend of the tall, sexy, grinning man who stood closest to her after slipping in the door near her. "So you decided to see how my town works? Good. I'm glad. Go ahead and grab a seat. I'm on duty, like I told you."

But she felt a lot more comfortable with these two men in the room—which was also perversely irritating. She knew they were military men, probably could handle a lot of stuff, but she was the official law-enforcement officer here, not them.

"I should have told you to save us some seats near you," Jock said softly. It was true; most of the chairs on her side of the room had filled up.

But there were a couple near the back, although not on the aisle. "How about there?" At the moment, it really didn't matter if they were close by. Even so, the idea of their having her back, even unofficially, allowed her to relax just a little and ignore her internal grumpiness.

"Okay."

Ralf waved at her as he followed Jock through what was left of the crowd in the aisle. Nearly everyone had found seats.

Kathlene glanced at her watch. Time for the fun to begin.

As if she had called them, the county commissioners

began filing into the room from the door near the front that led to a separate hallway to their offices.

That was when Kathlene saw Tisal and some others she recognized from her confrontation the night before begin to enter the chamber from the door nearest Jimmy.

Showtime.

Chapter 9

Jock didn't like this, but he wasn't surprised.

The possible anarchists slipping into the commissioners' meeting at the last minute could just have been because they were running late—as Ralf and he had been. They'd just spoken with Major Drew Connell again, this time about the day's proposed agenda, and had gotten a delayed start.

But with the newcomers, including that guy Tisal who'd been involved in the nastiness against Kathlene last night—well, they'd wait and see if those guys tried to disrupt anything, but Jock wasn't at all pleased to see them even if they kept quiet and just listened. Not that he was surprised by their presence.

"Let's come to order here." That was the woman in the middle of the group of seven commissioners, all seated at a long table facing their audience on a slightly raised stage. Her name was Myra Enager, Jock found out a moment later as she introduced herself and the other commissioners. She was the chairperson, an efficient and serious-looking, middle-aged woman, who didn't look like she would brook any nonsense from this group.

Jock had heard of her and wasn't surprised. The information Kathlene had provided that resulted in Alpha Force being deployed here had mentioned Myra's name and status on the commission.

It had additionally said what proposed local laws the commission had been considering, and the nonspecific threats to its members had been part of why the military presence was determined to be critical. The situation had sounded potentially way beyond the ability of locals to resolve peacefully, if at all.

Myra also introduced Mayor Laurence Davonne, who sat at one side of the audience and appeared to be surrounded by assistants dressed much like he was in dark suits. He waved but didn't seem very enthused about being mentioned.

"Now, here are the items we will be considering today," Myra continued. "We've had some changes in our agenda."

Interesting. The woman leveled a glare toward the part of the room now occupied by the group who'd stomped in at the last minute—Tisal and his gang.

"We'll once again defer consideration of the matters I have proposed to the commission, those regarding enactment of county statutes to help enforce the latest state regulations to protect wildlife and to arrest and incarcerate anyone found poaching."

"What? Why defer it again?" This was another of the commissioners, one toward the end of the table—Grabling was his name, per Myra's intro. He half stood and glared at the chairperson.

"From the start, I intended my proposal to be helpful, not controversial. However, for the past several months it has generated a lot of discussion at our open meetings—and more." Myra glared into the audience toward the corner of the room where the newcomers still stood. They glared right back. Jock figured that what she wasn't saying was that the arrival of that group had made her decide to remove the controversial matters from the agenda.

Possibly due to prior bad experience.

Tisal raised his hand as if he wanted to be called on to speak.

"We are currently not open to any further discussion, at least not here and now," Myra said.

Jock glanced toward Kathlene. She was obviously on alert, standing stiffly with her hand poised over her firearm. He doubted she would use it—unless she had no choice.

But just the gesture should make any sane person in this audience back down.

Tisal didn't. His hand was still raised, and it was waving. "Madam Chairwoman," he shouted. "I wish to be heard."

"There is nothing for you to be heard about, sir," Myra called back to him. "We have no motions on the table, and in fact, we are about to adjourn."

"But we haven't done anything," Grabling protested. "We owe it to our county residents who've come here this afternoon to at least describe what they came to learn more about—your damned…er, your proposals regarding hunting. We and they can talk about those proposals further and put them to a vote if not this afternoon, then next time for sure."

"If anyone here is unhappy about this, I do apologize," Myra said, "but in the interest of safety and security of all of us—"

"At least tell us what proposals are still on the table." That was Tisal. He was no longer with his gang at the back of the room but strode forward toward the podium. "We're curious, that's all. Then you can adjourn or do whatever you'd like, Madam Chairperson."

He spoke completely reasonable words in a completely reasonable way—and Jock didn't trust any of it. Not after his own supposedly innocent discussions with Tisal, the *sportsman*—or the way Tisal had allowed Kathlene to be badgered last night.

By now the entire crowd was stirring, mostly chattering in apparent support of Tisal. Kathlene was still alert, her expression suggesting incredulity. Were the apparent anarchists always so rational-sounding in public? Unlikely, but they were garnering a lot of support here.

Two other deputies were now inside, too. They stood near the other uniformed guy across the room, apparently listening.

Or not. They all seemed to glare at Myra as if she was being unreasonable, and maybe she was.

Or maybe she was just being smart. And protective.

"I think we can accommodate that gentleman," Grabling said. "Here's what we are considering, sir. Earlier this year, our state named some additional wild animals as endangered and requested that individual counties where hunting permits are granted add those animals to their lists. We're also requested to step up our gun laws and the penalties that can be imposed for violating them."

"We told everyone that before," said Wendy Ingerton, the other woman on the commission. "And making it public generated all sorts of…well, let's just call it discussion."

"And threats," Myra added. "Even though we assured people that we're not against hunting when done appropriately and in accordance with law. Nor are we against using guns, again if they're used safely and in accordance with law. And never used against people." She shot a glance in Kathlene's direction. "Except when enforcing the law, of course." Then Myra moved her gaze toward Tisal. "You wouldn't know anything about that, would you, sir?"

The man's smile was so sorrowful that it all but shouted its falseness to Jock. But others in the room might buy it. The buzz of conversation grew louder.

"Are you accusing me of something, Madam Chairperson?" Tisal asked in a soft tone that mirrored his expression.

"Only if the shoe fits," Myra said.

"But I'm sure you're just speculating," Tisal responded. "Can you provide proof to these nice people?"

"I think we're adjourned," Wendy Ingerton said. "All in favor?"

Myra's hand went up immediately. "Aye."

Grabling seemed to want to protest, but Myra's accusatory stare was leveled next at him. "Aye," he echoed.

So did enough of the others at the table to actually adjourn the meeting.

But as everyone poured out of the room, including the mayor and his minions, Tisal and some of his gang flowed forward while the council members filed out.

"We'll see you all next time," Tisal said as he reached some of those council members, his smile still innocent but his eyes full of malice.

Before she left, Myra gestured an invitation toward Kathlene, who hurried to join her at the front of the room on an edge of the raised meeting platform. Myra's charcoal suit looked rumpled, her face looked stressed.

"I'd like for you to come with me," Myra said. "I've called for a private session to start now. I don't think my colleagues are thrilled about it, and they may even let those…men know. If you could just stand there, looking official and guarding us, it might help."

"Of course." Kathlene would need to report in to let her superiors know what she was doing, but she doubted they'd mind an extension of the assignment they had given her earlier.

She glanced around. The rest of the room was nearly empty of people. She saw Jock and Ralf move in her direction. She wanted to talk to them, to get their take on what had happened at the meeting, but that would need to wait until they could go somewhere private.

The expression on Jock's face was icy and serious, but when she motioned for him to join them his look softened—after he gave her one sexy, assessing look.

"Come here, you guys," Kathlene said cheerfully. "I want you to meet Commission Chair Myra Enager. Myra, Jock is an old friend from college, and Ralf is one of his friends." She quickly told Myra their cover story about the men being from Washington State and stopping to see her before heading to Yellowstone.

Could she tell her friend about bringing in a covert military unit to help confront the *sportsmen?* Maybe, but she'd been sworn to secrecy. And if she told Myra, Tommy X would undoubtedly hear about it, too.

"I found your meeting very interesting," Jock said to Myra. "But I was really concerned when you mentioned threats. What kind of threats?"

He actually knew more about them, of course, Kathlene thought. The threats to the council had all been part of the reports she had submitted when she sought help. But she figured he wanted Myra's description, too.

As well as how concerned she really felt about those threats. But Kathlene knew that Myra was an intelligent, sensitive and politically savvy woman. And in their discussions about the threats, she might have laughed them off a bit in what she said, but the seriousness of her tone and expression told a different tale.

"I don't have time to talk about them now," Myra said. "My private meeting's about to begin. But Kathlene knows about them. She'll be with me at that session but I'm sure she can fill you in later. Nice meeting you." Without another glance, Myra headed out of the room.

"I do need to be with her," Kathlene said. "But I'll want to get together later. Dinner?"

"Sure," Jock said after sharing a glance with Ralf. "An early one."

"What's going on later?" she demanded. They weren't going to keep her out of it this time, no matter what it was.

"We'll talk about it at dinner," Jock said cryptically. Kathlene wanted to strangle it out of him.

Better yet, kiss it out of him...

No. She wouldn't think like that, no matter how much his amused, hot gaze turned her on. He was just trying to discombobulate her. And succeeding.

"I'll call you as soon as this meeting is over," she told him.

And as she followed Myra down the hall she made another call—one to Tommy X. He was high enough in the food chain that he could report to those who needed to know about what she was doing, and a close enough friend that he wouldn't argue about it.

Pizza. That was what they were going to have for dinner that night, Kathlene learned after the relocated and abbreviated commission meeting was finally over.

Her first phone call had been to Jock, and his deep voice, filled with amusement and charm, asked first where she was, how she was, whether she needed backup, all of which made her feel both annoyed at his lack of confidence in her and gooey that he seemed to give a damn. And then they talked about where to eat—in about half an hour.

She was walking along the relatively empty sidewalks of Cliffordsville now, back to the sheriff's department to officially sign out for the day and get on her way to meet Jock and Ralf. There wasn't much traffic on the streets, either. She simply strolled between official administration buildings, almost alone. The sun was going down, and the structures cast shadows along the pavement, keeping her comfortably cool.

Nothing much had been accomplished at the reconvened meeting. Not unexpectedly, the seven members were divided into two factions: Myra and Wendy Ingerton on one side, along with one of the men. Three men, including Grabling, were decisively on the anti-legislation side when it had to do with more restrictions on hunting or weapons. And one guy was undecided, so they might as well not have met again. That commissioner, Mertas, was likely to be accosted by lots of attempts to sway him to one side or the other, Kathlene felt sure.

She called Jimmy after her conversation with Jock ended, a courtesy since he was her partner. He seemed a bit grateful that he hadn't been enlisted to stay, too.

She finally reached the department headquarters and went inside. Asking around, she learned that the sheriff and his head deputies were in a meeting of their own. They might not even have known—yet—that Kathlene had remained at the county commissioners building after the main meeting broke up.

Tommy X, ducking out of that meeting for a restroom break, took her aside briefly in the department's main admin room as she signed out for the day. "What actually happened?" he asked. "I've heard all sorts of versions. Is Myra okay? Was there any trouble?"

"She's fine and, no, there wasn't any trouble—not at the private, post-meeting meeting," Kathlene told her tall, middle-aged ally, who leaned on the nearby wall for extra support. Of course he would be most concerned about the woman he was dating.

Now that she wasn't in the middle of things, Kathlene could relax—and she felt exhausted. Good thing they were alone in this vast room, at least for the moment. She just wished she was out of her uniform and into something a lot more comfortable. "I suspect there was a lot that churned in the background and remained unsaid at the adjourned public meeting. The an…er, the sportsmen now living at the old ranch had a presence, and they seemed very well behaved, but that doesn't mean they weren't the source of the threats."

It wasn't appropriate to call those men *anarchists* in Tommy X's presence. She'd run that by him before, and, despite his awareness that there was some animosity toward Myra, he wasn't buying Kathlene's accusation, not without more proof. Continuing to call them sportsmen was a good compromise.

"It doesn't mean they were, either." Tommy X's gray eyebrows knitted in a chastising frown. "I know you don't like or trust them. But don't let your opinions cloud your thinking."

Good thing he didn't know about her trespassing the night before, Kathlene thought. Or how it had turned out.

"I won't," she said. "See you tomorrow."

Jock and Ralf were already seated at a table at the pizza joint when Kathlene walked in, still in her uniform as usual on a day she was on duty.

She made the outfit look almost beautiful—because she was beautiful.

She also looked tired, Jock thought. Being on duty in the middle of an overtly peaceful yet underlyingly antagonistic crowd must have been wearing on her.

The restaurant was only moderately crowded and smelled of a lot of tangy spices. Even regular humans would probably sense the sharp cheese, oregano, peppers and more.

Kathlene spotted them in the middle of the room nearly immediately, and Ralf waved toward her. As soon as she was near them, Jock rose to pull her chair out for her.

"Hi," she said softly, looking up at him. He could imagine her sleepy blue eyes trained on him similarly in the dark after an exhausting, fulfilling bout of lovemaking.

His body reacted to the image, and he moved quickly to get her seated and resume his own chair.

Surprisingly, she ordered a beer. He'd have assumed that would put her right to sleep. But she seemed to perk up a bit as they started talking.

"What did you think of Tisal and the way he acted at the meeting?" she asked them. "I mean, he mostly just seemed so nice and low-key, like any other attendee. And yet—"

"And yet it didn't take anyone with psychic ability, if there is such a thing, to know what he was thinking," Ralf said. He'd been dressed in a nice shirt and slacks at the meeting but they'd had time to return to their cabin and change. And check on Click. Now Ralf wore a Cliffordsville T-shirt that he had just bought.

Jock had stuck with a solid color navy knit shirt. "Or implying," he added. "Threats? Who, him? He acted so innocent that it should have been obvious to anyone who knew there'd been some threats that they'd come from him or his gang."

"Amen," Kathlene said.

Their server brought their beers and they ordered a large

pizza with a variety of toppings that they would all split. Kathlene also ordered a small salad.

For the rest of their time together, they discussed what should come next—in lowered voices and language couched in tourist kinds of planning.

Kathlene pushed for details, reminding him that he'd said they'd discuss plans over dinner. He kept things general, though, mostly talking about how Ralf and he were still determining their best approach to learn more about the men at that compound. For one thing, he told her, they'd already started acting interested in joining the group as hunters and would follow up on that.

Jock didn't mention how far along their intended process really was, or that their plans didn't really start the next day, but sooner. He had a feeling that there'd be some interesting discussions that night at the anarchists' hangout.

He wanted to listen to them. And the best way to do that would be to shift first.

That wasn't something Kathlene needed to know.

When they were all done eating, they squabbled a bit over the check but Jock remained adamant, hinting about their expense account. It wasn't really that generous, but, although he didn't want to admit it to himself, he did feel just a touch guilty about not letting Kathlene know more of the truth. Not that he wanted her to know he was a shapeshifter, of course, but he also wasn't telling her that the Alpha Force members at this table were again excluding her from their team for what they intended to do that night.

"No need to follow me home," Kathlene told them when they were outside after eating. "I need to grab my car at the department lot. I'll just be heading back to my place. I almost got my second wind while eating with you, but I'll sleep well tonight."

The look she aimed at him was almost challenging, as if she was hinting that she wouldn't mind company.

That was just wishful thinking, but he didn't hide his own lust from his eyes as he said, "Okay, then. Good night. We'll meet again for lunch tomorrow and let you know if our sightseeing in the morning in the areas of gun shops and all yields us anything useful."

"Great," she said. "Good night."

He wished that he could turn that last smile of hers into a very different activity with those gorgeous, full lips.

She had gotten her second wind, fortunately.

Kathlene had also learned something about the Alpha Force guys who were supposed to treat her as a member of their team.

They did what they pleased when it came to making plans to surveil the presumed anarchists. She knew they weren't telling her everything. And after the events of today, when Tisal and others had shown up so unbelievably innocently at the meeting, she had no doubt something was about to happen.

And that her best buddy Jock and his friend Ralf thought the same thing. And intended to go check it out... without her.

That was why she broke speed limits getting back to her home and quickly changed clothes into a dark-colored, long-sleeved shirt and snug pants, along with black athletic shoes.

She was going into surreptitious mode.

Once more she hurried, driving her car toward the hovel where Jock and Ralf had hung out for the past couple of nights, sending Click to the anarchists' outpost to do whatever recon they had planned.

Best she could figure, as she'd considered before, the

dog must somehow have a video camera that recorded what he came up against. Only, when she had been with Click that previous night, there'd been no indication of even a collar, let alone any electronic wonder toy attached to it or to the dog.

Well, she intended to hide in that house and see and listen to whatever transpired before the men took Click to the old ranch area to do his unexplained assignment there.

She again drove faster than she should. Once more, she parked some distance from her goal, hiding her car behind some trees near the crumbling roadway.

She walked quickly but quietly to the house—and was delighted to find that she was, in fact, there before the men had arrived.

Assuming they did show up there that night. And she had a feeling, a very strong feeling, that they would.

She'd have to play it all by ear…but she relished the thought of, tomorrow, telling all to an astonished Jock— that she had figured out what they were up to and showed up there to learn more. She would once again outmaneuver the hot and commanding man who had gotten her body to react in ways she hadn't felt in years. If ever.

And wouldn't she have fun laughing at him? Oh, yeah.

Her only fear was that Click would scent or hear her and give her away before he was taken out and about for his task for the night.

As a result, she maneuvered her way into the dilapidated house and, using a flashlight, looked around the foul-smelling place, knowing she had to be careful about where she ended up. And *up* was the operative word. She found an area above what had once been the living room where she could climb the wall thanks to some holes in the deteriorating plaster that revealed wooden framing strong enough to act as a ladder and also opened into her target

area. It was up above the ceiling but below the roof. Even
if Click smelled or heard her and started barking about
something above them, they surely wouldn't suspect there
was a person up there—let alone her.

She hoped.

She was glad her arms were strong from her training,
as she had to mostly pull herself up since the footholds in
the wall weren't plentiful, but eventually she was exactly
where she had hoped.

She settled in as best she could into the uncomfortable
and uneven area that consisted of broken slats above a partially plastered ceiling. And waited.

And hoped she had been right that the men would show
up here for a third night in a row.

After maybe half an hour, she heard something outside—a car engine that was quickly cut off.

Good. Only…was it definitely the men she hoped it
was?

Well, she would see.

And she wasn't stupid. She had brought her service
weapon, just in case she ran into trouble.

Sure enough, though, she soon saw, through the hole in
the ceiling that she had adopted as her viewing point, the
faces of Jock and Ralf illuminated slightly by the flash-
lights they carried.

She held her breath, watching for Click, waiting for the
dog to sense her and react.

But she didn't see him. Didn't hear him.

Had they left him back at the cabins that night? Had
they dropped him off at the ranch by himself? Or were
their plans to conduct some other kind of surveillance?

They didn't hide what they said, so she listened.

"You ready?" Ralf asked. He had put what she assumed,

in the faint light, was a backpack on the floor and was digging in it. She couldn't tell what it was that he extracted.

"Sure am," responded Jock.

Ralf handed him something that looked like a large bottle, and Jock drank from it. Kathlene wondered what it was. Did he need to fortify himself with alcohol to do whatever it was they had planned?

When he had apparently finished it, he sat down on the floor. "Okay," he told Ralf. "It's time."

"Yes, sir," Ralf said, and laughed as he turned on some kind of bright light and shone it on Jock. He was nude! But why? Did it matter? Maybe not, but she wanted to learn more.

Lord, was his nude body gorgeous. As masculine and sexy as she'd imagined when he was fully clothed. She loved the view...at first.

But in a minute, Kathlene had to chomp on her hand to prevent herself from calling out. She couldn't believe what she thought she saw as Jock began to roll around on the floor. And moan. And change.

Oh, how he changed. His limbs seemed to tighten. His face grew longer. He grew fur all over his body.

And when it was all over, Kathlene could finally understand why she had seen Click around here but not Jock. Not at the same time. Not after Ralf and he had been at this house before.

Understand? No, not really.

But Jock Larabey had become the wolflike dog who had rescued her yesterday in the anarchists' compound.

Jock Larabey was a werewolf.

Chapter 10

A werewolf? A shapeshifter? She didn't believe in such things. She was a peace officer. A realist. A… An incredulous fool.

For she had seen what she had seen. She couldn't deny that, even though everything inside her screamed that she was hallucinating.

But she knew she wasn't.

Kathlene attempted not to move. She knew she hadn't cried out; she'd stuck her fist in her mouth to prevent it, not an easy feat considering the cramped position she was in here, above the room.

Even so, once he had stabilized and stopped changing, the wolf—Jock—froze in place, then moved his head to stare straight up in her direction. He growled, but only for a second. And then he barked.

Ralf followed the canine's gaze, moving his head to look up toward her. Could he see her?

"What is it, Jock?" Ralf asked. "Something up there?"

The dog nodded, growled again, pawed the floor with one paw, then stopped right beneath her.

"You want me to check it out." It wasn't a question but

a statement. And why not? Kathlene figured that, if what she'd seen was true, Ralf had done something to help Jock change. He might be able to help him in other ways.

"I didn't see a ladder, but it looks like I can scale that messed-up wall. Maybe. I'll try to go up and..."

"No need," Kathlene called down in a small, defeated tone. "He—whatever he is—knows I'm here."

"Kathlene!" Ralf's voice was sharp and angry. Kathlene could only imagine what Jock would say, and how he would say it, if he could actually talk now. "What are you doing up there?"

"Right now, I don't know. I'm coming down."

She hadn't really thought through how she would retreat from the area above the ceiling but figured she would just do as she'd done to climb here, only in reverse. It wasn't quite that easy, not with using flimsy handholds and places to stick her feet into the partly destroyed wall areas, but, with Ralf's help, she managed.

And when she was back down on the main level, she just stood there, staring. At the wolf, who stared right back at her.

She was anthropomorphizing, sure, but with good cause, when she read in the canine's gaze anger and frustration and a need to chew her out.

"Is this what your Alpha Force is about?" she finally demanded, looking first at the wolf, then at Ralf. "Why didn't you just tell me?"

"As if you'd have believed it," Ralf countered. His dark eyes looked even darker now as he frowned at her, his thick arms crossed over his chest. "And now what are we going to do with you?"

The wolf gave a quick bark. He dashed toward the large bag that Ralf had carried into the house and pawed at it.

In moments, he dipped his muzzle in and extracted a leash.

"You want me to take you for another walk…Click?" Her hand raised to her mouth. "Not Click. It wasn't Click yesterday, either, at the ranch, was it?"

"Nope," Ralf answered.

Jock brought the leash to Kathlene. But instead of holding it for her to take and try to attach it to him—without a collar—he took an end, dropped it on the floor, then held the other end in his mouth and, slowly circling her, wrapped it around her legs.

"You want to leash me?" she asked incredulously.

The canine looked at her, then at Ralf, and nodded his head.

"We've worked out some ways of communicating without talking," Ralf said. "I'm interpreting this to mean that he wants you to stay here while he conducts the recon we already planned. He'll change back on his return, then we'll talk. Right, Jock?"

The wolf-dog gave one bark and nodded once more.

"And if I don't want to stay? If I want to just get out of here and digest what I just saw, and—"

Jock growled again, then sat down on her leashed feet.

Kathlene thought about how funny this situation could be if it were played out in a movie or TV show. But the reality?

It felt anything but funny to her.

Was she nuts? Were they all nuts? Had they somehow drugged her or… Well, she wasn't going to find out now.

She wouldn't find out until they had that conversation that Ralf had mentioned.

"Okay," she finally said with a sigh. "I'll wait here with Ralf. But I expect you both to fill me in later. On everything."

And if she could, she'd push for Ralf to tell all in Jock's absence.

But she had a feeling that lower-ranking members of this supersecret Alpha Force military unit wouldn't do anything without their superior officer's verbal, human-type, okay.

She had seen him shift.

Jock loped through the woods now, toward the encampment that was his target. Again.

He had to concentrate on his mission, what he needed to accomplish this night.

How he needed to accomplish it.

But his mind was filled with human thoughts other than those he had to focus on.

She had seen him shift.

She had seen him naked, and that somehow made him glad. He wanted her to return the favor. Soon.

But she had also seen his fleeting but intense discomfort as he had changed from human form into wolfen.

And then they had communicated somewhat. She had agreed to stay. To obey his command.

But he knew better. If he had been in human form and gave her orders, she would never have agreed to do as he'd said.

She was confused. Unsure what to do, so she was heeding him. For now.

But later…

Why hadn't he scented her before he shifted? He had caught her fragrant scent before when she had been where she wasn't supposed to be. The old house was filled with ugly smells, so why not pick out one good one from the rest?

His only excuse was that he had been focused on shift-

ing. If he had smelled her, he might have sloughed it off, anyway, as a residual scent from yesterday.

There. He had arrived at the area just outside the fence.

Time to concentrate. Time to meander around and eavesdrop and see if those inside were discussing the meeting that had occurred today—and how their presence, even acting like interested bystanders, had changed the outcome.

And if he were lucky, he would overhear how they intended next to levy their threats on the county commissioners who wanted to put further restrictions on their abilities to hunt and arm themselves...and hurt people.

That was why he was here: to learn what they were actually up to.

And to stop them.

A good time for it, too. For the first time since he had started recon on this old ranch, he heard an explosion. Small and muffled, yes. But he needed to find out more about it—and the very slight scent of plastic, perhaps C-4 explosives, that accompanied it.

Kathlene had gotten Ralf talking. Not a lot, and not comfortably.

But at least she knew a little more now than when Jock had stalked away toward the ranch site.

Rather than on the dilapidated chairs, they sat on the warped wood of the house's floor with the flashlight pointing toward the base of the wall to give off a minimum amount of illumination that could let them see around them. She leaned against the wall, her legs bent with her knees pointing toward the ceiling where she had been hiding before. Ralf had his legs crossed and looked highly uneasy.

But he had answered a few of her questions—*few* being

the operative word. Some responses were interesting and hinted at even more fascinating data behind them. But none were in depth.

"So Alpha Force somehow recruits different kinds of shapeshifters—mostly wolves, but also lynxes and cougars and even hawks," she repeated back to Ralf, trying to buy into the concept. But she'd seen a shift with her own eyes. If a man could change into a wolf, why not all the other kinds of animals, too?

"That's right," Ralf said. "But I can't tell you anything about the recruitment process or how they're utilized on missions or anything else, really."

"Are you a shifter, too?"

"No, but I was a member of Special Forces before I was recruited into Alpha Force. I'd gained the trust of my commanding officers so they must have figured I could handle this…different…kind of assignment."

"Do you like it?"

"Oh, yeah. I always liked trying something new and outrageous, and you can't get much more outrageous than this."

Kathlene pondered what else to ask that wouldn't trigger a refusal to answer. "What do you do as an aide?"

"Whatever's necessary—but some of it's classified so I can't answer any more of your questions about it."

"Right." She tried to sound perky and understanding and accepting of all he said. What else could she do? He could be lying about everything, but after what she had seen she might believe stuff that was even crazier than reality—like, was Ralf himself going to shapeshift in a few minutes into King Kong?

How could she be certain that he couldn't?

A noise sounded at the front door, like something scratching on it. A dog's paw?

Ralf must have heard it, too, since he stood quickly and dashed over then opened the door.

Sure enough, a silver-furred figure leaped inside, panting. A dog. A wolf.

Jock.

"All okay, sir?" Ralf asked, obviously trying to be funny. For her, or for his commanding officer, or both?

Kathlene had already figured out that, whatever happened to Jock when he shifted, he obviously maintained his ability to understand what people said, even if he couldn't respond in kind. Otherwise, how could he have helped her so much at the ranch compound last night?

And how could Ralf joke with him?

The sound Jock made in response was like a muted growl. Maybe he didn't find Ralf so funny after all. He barked again and loped over to Ralf's backpack that still lay on the floor. He pawed at it.

And then he stared at Kathlene.

"He wants to shift back right now," Ralf said. "He could do it on his own in time, but I can help him do it faster with the light. But the thing is, when he shifts back he'll be…er…"

"Naked. I got a glimpse when he shifted into being a wolf before," Kathlene reminded him. "No problem. I can just leave now."

Jock barked again, giving a decisively negative shake of his head.

"He wants you to stay," Ralf interpreted unnecessarily. "Maybe he saw or heard something that means danger if you go outside now. Tell you what. Why don't you just turn your back?"

"Sure," she said, pivoting to face the wall that had been nearest her back in the house's main, and most decrepit, room.

But she couldn't help it. She turned just slightly, enough to see that Ralf had his back to her as he pulled the light from his backpack and aimed it at Jock.

Jock wasn't looking at her, either. Especially not when he growled, then moaned as his body started lengthening, the fur pelt receding into him, his muzzle and pointed ears retracting.

The process was fascinating. Kathlene couldn't have forced herself to turn away even if she'd wanted to.

Which she didn't.

The most intriguing part of the process was to see Jock's taut, all-masculine, human muscles forming and tightening once more.

Not to mention the nether part of his body. His sexual organs, before the evident but not so interesting form of a canine's, morphing into all human, large and erect and utterly enticing.

Why did he have an erection? Did he know she was staring at him or was this what always happened to him?

The process was nearly over now. Both men would be more aware of her presence very soon.

At least now Kathlene was able to force herself to turn back toward the wall.

And go over, in her mind, the miraculous change she had just witnessed.

How often did he do this? How much did it hurt?

Why did it seem so sexy to her?

She suddenly heard whispering behind her. It was so soft that she couldn't make out what the men were saying.

Too bad *she* didn't have any canine abilities. Dogs had excellent hearing. Did a werewolf?

She prepared to call out, ask if it was okay to turn around, if Jock was decent.

But before she could, someone touched her elbow, startling her. Why hadn't she heard movement on this irregular wood floor?

"Kathlene," said Jock's voice. She turned to see him standing right behind her, tall, fully dressed and with an ominous look on his handsome, chiseled—and now all human—face.

"Oh, hi," she said, making an attempt to act nonchalant and unaffected by the night's offbeat occurrences. "I'd really like for you to tell me more about what's going on."

"Yeah, I will. I hope you're not tired tonight, because we have to talk—right now."

Could they trust her?

They had to. Jock knew that. But he wanted to make sure she understood there would be consequences if she even unintentionally alluded to what she'd seen in front of any of her sheriff's department people, or anyone else, for that matter.

"Okay," she said. "But could we go someplace more comfortable to have this conversation? Your cabin would be a whole lot better than this."

"Fine," Jock said. "I'll ride with you."

He didn't really believe she'd try to drive off and ignore them, or, worse, shout what she had seen to the world, but just in case...

"Okay."

Was it that easy? He'd anticipated some argument from her.

But on the other hand, she'd made it clear that she had a lot of questions. Maybe she thought he'd answer them more freely if they were one-on-one.

And maybe he would, depending on her reactions.

"We'll see you back at the cabins," Jock told Ralf, meeting his aide's eyes in an attempt at reassurance that this was the best way. "If you could take care of Click first, that would be great. We'll wait for you in the other cabin before we have any major discussion." That part was for Kathlene. Maybe he'd talk with her in the car and maybe he wouldn't, but the main part of their conversation would have to wait. "Although you both should know that I heard one small explosion this time—like the ones you described, Kathlene, that helped in the decision to send Alpha Force here."

Both Kathlene and Ralf reacted to that. "Interesting timing," Ralf said.

"Sure was," Jock agreed. What neither said was that the information would need to be passed along to their Alpha Force superiors.

At least waiting to talk more about his shifting would also give him time to consider the best way to present the facts—and which ones he actually would tell her.

"I want to hear more about what you heard," Kathlene said. But she was clearly distracted by his shifting, which was okay. He'd rather talk about that now. Give her an explanation that she—and he—could live with. "Although... well, was the dog you introduced me to in your cabin next door actually Click?" Kathlene had started walking with him toward the house's back door.

"Yes. He's my cover dog," Jock explained.

"Yeah. That gives me two canines to take care of." Ralf, always willing to joke to lighten a difficult situation, followed them. He'd picked up his backpack, and as they all exited the house he was the one to make sure the door was shut behind them.

"Interesting," Kathlene said. She paused and looked up into Jock's face in the near total darkness outside. "That's why I was so confused—one reason, at least. I'd seen you, and I'd seen Click, and I thought there were even some differences in appearance between that dog and the one who saved me yesterday, but that didn't make sense to me...before. And I never even considered the possibility of your—do you call it shapeshifting?"

"That's right," he said, then asked, "Where did you park your car?"

"Just down the road a little ways, in a small clearing in the woods."

"Okay. We'll see you in a few, Ralf." Jock picked up his pace a bit, taking Kathlene's hand. "So neither of us falls in the dark," he explained to her. It was partially true. It was also true that he didn't want her to dash off and leave him here—although at this moment he doubted she would do that. And if she did, he had his phone along and could call Ralf to pick him up—and to chase her with him.

What he hadn't counted on, though, was what it did to him to have her firm, warm hand in his. It somehow seemed to irradiate a path of heat from their fingertips all the way inside him to his groin, where an unbidden erection started to grow once more.

Last time, as his shift ended, it had also been because of Kathlene, because he knew she was peeking, saw him naked.

This woman was going to drive him nuts in more ways than one.

They reached her car quickly and he did his usual thing of opening her door for her, then getting into the passenger's seat. She drove slowly at first, which gave him an opportunity to sense their surroundings by sight and scent as they reached the road.

Nothing out of the ordinary. That was a good thing.

Her next question wasn't such a good thing, though.

"Why, Jock? I mean, what causes you to shapeshift? Have you always done it? I thought werewolves changed under full moons, although that's not even true anymore sometimes in movies. But what's the reality? Do you like it? And—I think I'd better shut up." Her gaze was straight out the windshield. She didn't even glance toward him, but he could smell a slight tangy scent that suggested she was afraid.

Of him?

Damn.

"I'm not going to hurt you, Kathlene," he said softly, reaching over to stroke her warm, smooth cheek with the back of his hand. She tensed up, but only for a moment as he continued to touch her.

"I know," she responded, but he heard the slight tremor in her voice.

Touching her like this, even just to be friendly, wasn't a good idea. It gave his body thoughts of touching her all over—and not just with his hand.

"Tell you what," he said. "This isn't the kind of conversation to have in the car, and what I need to talk to you about with Ralf along isn't going to touch on what you asked, either. Once we've had that conversation, I intend to see you back to your home, anyway, since, even though I didn't hear anything threatening at the ranch compound before, after that county commission meeting today I don't trust anyone in this town. Especially around you, since you and your fellow officers were there representing local authority, and you've already made noises against the group in question. I'll answer your questions then, okay?"

She hesitated, but only for a moment. Was she still afraid of him?

Or of herself? For when she finally aimed a brief glance at him before turning from the small road onto the main highway, he saw something on her face and scented something other than fear and her underlying perfume.

Something that suggested that she might feel as turned on, and interested in touching and more, as he did.

But her ultimate response made him smile.

"Okay," she agreed.

Chapter 11

They were back in the motel cabin she had reserved for the two men from Alpha Force, once more sitting on one of the two chairs. Ralf was already inside with Click when they'd arrived. He had walked the dog briefly and had fed him a late dinner.

Kathlene studied Click as he now sat near the cabin's kitchenette. Yes, he looked similar to the wolf-dog she had seen earlier after Jock had shifted, but they were not identical. As she had noted but not understood before, his head was flatter, his legs longer, and the color and fullness of his coat, although similar, was less of a tawny-silver than Jock's.

Jock's. Jock, the shapeshifter, the human-wolf combo.

She liked dogs. A lot.

But she liked Jock in human form even better. He was gorgeous. Even more, he was hot. Maybe the sexiest guy she had ever met.

Shouldn't the fact that he was so…different…turn her off?

Maybe so, but it didn't. How weird was that?

He'd sat beside her briefly but had stood to confer with

Ralf and pat the dog that looked so much like him—sometimes. Were they discussing the sounds he had heard? She hoped so.

She finally felt more vindicated. She'd want to talk more about them, too, later.

But for this moment, she wanted to know more about Alpha Force—and Jock.

He returned and handed Kathlene a glass of soda with ice in it. "Now," he said, "let's talk."

That sounded ominous. But she knew what he was going to say.

"Okay," she said, and waited for his orders.

As she'd anticipated, they were, in fact, directives. Jock leaned toward her, his hands clasped near her knees as if he would grab and shake her if she dared to argue with what he said. Kathlene glanced toward Ralf, not expecting any support from the other military man. Ralf sat beside Click, who had lain down on the cabin's polished wooden floor. Everyone's eyes seemed to be on her, waiting for her reaction.

Even Click's.

"I know you have questions," Jock began, "and we'll go over them later, the way we discussed. But right now I need to be sure that you understand the circumstances. Alpha Force is a highly covert military unit, and I'm a member."

When he paused, she nodded to signify she understood and didn't disagree. At least not yet.

"You saw me shapeshift. That's fine, since we've already established that we're on the same team. But you can't mention, can't even hint about it, to anyone. Do you understand?"

She nodded. "Yes."

"And do you agree?"

"Of course. But—well, I know you said we could talk

later about what shapeshifting is and all that, but I'd love to understand why Alpha Force was sent here to help in this situation."

Jock looked a little irritated that she had dared to interrupt what he intended to say, but his expression softened immediately. "Because things here, if they're as you represented, could get pretty dangerous if the only undercover personnel deployed here happened to be all human."

Kathlene laughed and was a little surprised that both men did, too.

"We have a general idea how you asked for help," Jock continued, "but why don't you describe that to us now and maybe it'll help us explain."

She ran through the facts. She had seen—and heard—what appeared to be going on at the old ranch, and more men with guns appeared to arrive daily. When no one here, especially not Sheriff Melton Frawley or even town mayor Laurence Davonne, had paid attention to her, she knew she needed help.

She told them now how she'd stayed in touch with her friend from college, Bill Grantham, whose father had been an army colonel then but was now a general working at the Pentagon. Bill had listened to her, and so had the general.

Despite asking, Kathlene had never been told why he'd decided to call in Alpha Force. All she knew was that he'd contacted her and discussed the cover that the military men to be deployed to Cliffordsville would undertake. She'd been glad that they'd taken her seriously, at least.

"Got it," Jock said. "I know of General Grantham. He's a friend of the general who oversees Alpha Force, General Greg Yarrow. Guess that's why we were called in to help. General Yarrow knows all about us, who we are and what we can do."

"Yeah," Ralf said. "If they'd brought in the usual kind

of military or other guys to go undercover, they might have been able to infiltrate that group as fellow sportsmen to see what's going on, and Jock and I still might resort to doing that, depending. But we have the choice of what'll work best, unlike anyone else."

"You sound proud of Alpha Force," Kathlene noted.

"Damn straight!" Ralf responded.

"Then it sounds like I did the right thing." Kathlene sure hoped so.

But the ultimate success of the team consisting of Jock, Ralf, Click and her still remained to be seen.

They talked a little longer about Alpha Force without going into detail about how many there were in the unit or what kinds of missions they'd undertaken before.

But the upshot was that Kathlene was definitely a temporary member of their team now—since she knew what she knew.

And if she blew their trust, she would be sorry.

Eventually, she found herself stifling a yawn.

"Guess it's time to get you back safely to your place," Jock said. He told Ralf that he would follow Kathlene to assure her safety.

She wanted to tell Jock that she'd be fine. She could head home alone.

And yet she could hardly wait for the private conversation Jock had promised her.

She wanted to know more about shapeshifting and shapeshifters and what they thought and how they felt.

"Sounds good," she said. "Good night, Ralf." She headed toward Click, then bent and hugged the wolflike dog, whose tail was wagging fiercely. "Good night, Click. See you tomorrow—although Jock and I need to discuss tomorrow's plan of action."

She looked at the man who waited near the door for

her. His mouth had thinned as if he didn't like what he'd heard, but then his stance relaxed.

"I guess we do," he said.

Once again, Jock followed Kathlene as she drove. This time, at least, he would get to see where she lived.

He had the address, of course. He'd contacted the military computer geeks who unearthed all private information when necessary for Alpha Force. So far, he hadn't felt a need to go there.

Tonight would have been different even if she hadn't agreed for him to follow her.

Before he had left, he told Ralf to call Drew Connell. He was sure that the major would be very interested in the report of his hearing that explosion, though not particularly strong—this time—at the old ranch, as well as getting the small, yet distinct, scent of explosives.

He wasn't surprised to see Kathlene pull off the main Cliffordsville streets into a nice residential neighborhood. After a few turns, she pulled into the driveway of a small but pretty redbrick home on a block of other similar, well-maintained houses.

Jock parked on the street and followed her to the front door.

For her safety and security, he reminded himself. That was all.

"Nice place," he said.

"Thanks." She opened the front door with a key she had taken from the large bag she carried—which he felt sure hid her weapon. And then she walked inside, with him close behind her.

They entered into a living room with textured beige walls, floral-patterned and fluffy sofa and chairs and a huge wide-screen TV along one wall. It smelled of tangy cleaning fluids and unlit jasmine-scented candles on the end tables.

The woman was a bundle of contrasts. A peace officer with feminine furniture and aromas in her home.

But the ability to watch the news in high definition.

He told himself yet again that he wasn't here because he found her attractive—and so sexy that he wanted to take her into his arms and undress her, seduce her and make love till she screamed.

He'd never considered getting close to anyone outside of his old home neighborhood or Alpha Force.

He'd certainly never thought about getting close to a deputy sheriff.

But that was before he had met Kathlene Baylor.

Still, making love with her, a supposed team member with whom he would have to continue to work until this assignment was complete? Bad idea.

He would just have to keep his thoughts, and body, in check.

"It's a little late for coffee," Kathlene said. "Would you like a glass of wine? A bottle of beer?"

"Just water will be fine," Jock told her. He was looking closely at her TV.

"I can turn that on for you, if you'd like." She figured, though, that he could do it easily by himself.

"No. I don't think it would make good background noise for our talk."

"Right." She went through the doorway in the far wall and entered her kitchen, glad to be out of Jock's presence for even just a minute.

What had she been thinking, inviting him to her house?

Even though what they'd said they would talk about fascinated her.

Good thing he hadn't taken her up on her offer of alcohol. She didn't want any, either. She needed her wits about her.

Otherwise—well, she might just jump Jock Larabey's bones here, knowing they were alone.

Knowing he was the sexiest man she had ever laid eyes—and lips—on.

As long as he was in the form of a man.

She quickly brought him a glass of water and carried one for herself as she joined him on the sofa.

"Now," she said, "tell me all about what it's like to be a—do you call yourself a shapeshifter? A werewolf? What?"

"Either is fine. And I love who and what I am."

He described growing up in the less-populated areas of Wisconsin with his family and other shifters around. "I don't know whether the regular humans around had any idea of who we really were, but if they did they were still friendly and pretty much left us alone."

"Amazing," she said. What would she have done as a kid if she'd known there were actually such things as shapeshifters, and some lived near her? She'd have been fascinated.

She'd always loved to watch sci-fi shows on TV and in movies.

But that's what they were. Science *fiction*.

Or so she had always believed…until now.

"And Alpha Force?" she asked. "How did you learn about it?"

"They found me," he said. "The unit is always on the lookout for shifters who would fit a specialized career in the military. And Alpha Force—well, I can't really talk much about it, but one of the perks is the special elixir we use that gives us a lot of benefits that regular shifters don't have."

"Like not having to wait until a full moon?" she asked. "I always thought the original legends said that werewolves only changed then."

"And it's true," he said. "Except for Alpha Force members and others who've found a way to get around it. Plus, we can keep a lot more of our human awareness and intelligence with Alpha Force's elixir. But like the other information you now have about Alpha Force, that's something you can't talk about." His hazel eyes bored into hers as if attempting to see inside her brain for her thoughts about whether to blab all to the world.

"I get it," she said. "And, yes, I'll keep it to myself."

Those eyes stayed on her, but their expression changed from icy inquisitiveness to something warmer. A whole lot warmer.

Which made her smile even as her insides turned molten.

Oh, yes, it was a bad idea to have Jock here alone with her in her home.

"Would you like some more water?" she asked quickly, needing a reason to stand up and run away, even by just a few feet.

But his glass wasn't empty.

"No, thanks. So, your turn now. Tell me, Kathlene. Why did you decide to go into law enforcement?"

She didn't have to tell him. It wasn't something she talked about much, if at all.

But he had been honest with her. She supposed it was her turn.

"I wanted to fight for justice," she said with an ironic grin. "As if there really was any out there."

"Because…?" he prompted, his gaze still not leaving hers.

For this moment, at least, her body stiffened and had no interest in doing anything but leaving the room, leaving the topic.

Instead, she said as nonchalantly as she could, "My parents owned a convenience store in Missoula. One day, a couple of thugs came in to steal their cash and wound up murdering them. My folks' killers were caught and prosecuted and went to prison—for all of a year. But they appealed their conviction and got off on a technicality. Now they're free. Maybe even robbing and killing other people, but maybe not. I keep track of them as best I can. Justice? Maybe I can't create it, but I sure as hell can seek it and try to make sure it sticks."

"I'm so sorry, Kathlene." His expression had turned full of compassion. And suddenly, she found herself in his embrace.

She closed her eyes. She couldn't allow herself to give in to her desire because this man—no, man-wolf—was also a really nice and caring guy.

Only…as his mouth sought, then captured, hers, she realized for a fleeting moment that this was what she had been hoping for all day long.

No, from the moment she had first met Jock Larabey.

They were going to make love. She knew it. She also knew how foolish it was.

But for this moment, foolishness be damned. She opened her own lips, allowed her tongue to seek out his, even as her body pressed up against him.

Her breasts became the epitome of sensitivity…especially when, as they stood, she felt his hard erection pushing against her. She sighed, even as she maneuvered herself closer.

"Jock," she whispered against his hot, searching mouth.

"Yes," he responded without missing a moment of their increasingly sensual kiss.

"My bedroom is just down the hall."

Jock had promised himself before to keep his libido in check. His wayward body parts, too.

But his erection had a mind of its own. Oh, yeah.

And the erotic dance with this woman on their way to her bedroom was filled with deep, deep kisses, not to mention hugs and caresses and touches outside his clothes to his most sensitive and responsive areas. Which he reciprocated, and then some.

He couldn't wait to strip. And to strip Kathlene, too.

The thought aroused him even more, if that was possible.

Her scent was spicy and salty and altogether sexually incredible. The atmosphere was enhanced by the sound of her deep, irregular breathing, her soft, sexy moans.

"In here," Kathlene gasped momentarily against his mouth, and he responded by kissing her even more deeply, even as she guided him through a doorway and flicked on the lights.

To her bedroom.

Like the furniture he had already seen, this room, when he managed to pry open his eyes and look at it, had a floral motif, from the carvings on the mirror over the dresser to the rose-and-lilac design on the comforter on the bed.

The bed. That was the way they were heading. Good idea.

Better idea was how he at last started removing Kathlene's clothes on the way over to it. First her knit shirt over her head. Then his hands on the buttons on her slacks, and they soon slid to the floor.

"Now me," she said, and it was his turn to lose his shirt, his pants, his briefs. He was naked first.

Fine by him. He quickly got the rest of Kathlene's stuff off, too.

And then they tumbled right onto that pretty, flowery bed.

Yes, oh yes, Kathlene thought. She refused to even consider how unwise this was.

Not with Jock's gorgeous, hot, muscular body on top of hers, writhing gently, obviously trying to feel all of her against him without squashing her with his substantial, tense weight.

He was still kissing her mouth. At this angle, she couldn't do much more than kiss him back, squeeze his delightful, firm buttocks in her hands.

Feel his thick arousal pressing against her.

But she wanted more. A lot more.

She wriggled, whispered, "My turn," and maneuvered so she could get loose from beneath his body.

He let her, without removing his hands. Which was a good thing. Otherwise, she would have felt bereft if she no longer had his touch upon her.

As it was, he gently grasped her breasts, rubbing his thumbs against her nipples so erotically that it made her feel like crying.

Instead, she moved, curling up a bit so he could no longer reach her chest…but she could reach his hard shaft, which she took into her mouth.

And reveled in the sound of his gasp even as she tasted its heat and hardness and enticement.

"Now," she heard him say, and it sounded as if he spoke through gritted teeth.

But she couldn't quite comply with what he said.

If she remembered correctly…she pulled away from him entirely and left the bed, giving only a quick glance to his narrowed eyes that stared at her so sexily.

She opened the top drawer of the nightstand nearest her and reached past the makeup and other inappropriate contents toward the back.

And found exactly what she sought: a box of condoms. Unopened. There for years, a box of unfulfilled hope that she'd never been tempted to use with any man she'd met recently.

Until now.

She pulled it open, took out a foil packet, and tore it, holding it out toward Jock.

"You do it," he said. "I'm busy." That was when he reached toward her, claimed her hot and wet and aroused area with his hand and stroked it, inserted a finger, then two…

She cried out even as she got the condom in place over him. He pulled her onto the bed, rolled her back into the position she had been in before, beneath him, and entered her.

She reached a climax nearly immediately and was happy to hear Jock's own cry of fulfillment.

In moments, his body became a loose weight on top of her. He panted as he laughed, moved off her and said, "Too fast. We've got to get in more practice."

More?

Did she want to do this again with this man?

Oh, yeah.

Chapter 12

Lying there beside Jock, Kathlene was still breathing heavily from what they had just done together when he asked to stay the night.

She graciously said yes. Heck, she wasn't just being gracious. He was fulfilling her dream. Her desire.

For even though they both talked about how tired they were, she knew that they would make love again. And, maybe, again.

First, though, he left her bedroom, ostensibly to use the bathroom. She saw him grab his phone from his trousers before he left. Her head on her pillow, her body beneath the sheet, she soon heard his voice as he talked to someone else. Ralf?

She couldn't distinguish much of what Jock said, but she did hear the word *protection*. Was that what he called what they had done?

More likely, he was just giving an excuse to Ralf for staying here.

But if protection was really on his mind…

No. He surely wasn't using his body to try to control

her, to make her more amenable to his staying around her. Protecting her.

She didn't need that.

He returned to the room. She sat up, ready to confront him, to make sure he continued to remember, despite their amazing lovemaking, that she wasn't just some needy woman, a female who wanted a man around who would take care of her.

She could do it all by herself.

But as she sat up, the sheet dropped from her…and her upper body showed. Her breasts.

They began tingling as he looked at them.

And when he slid back onto the bed with her and reached out for them, touched them, slid his fingers back and forth over their sensitive nubs, she forgot all of what she intended to say.

He actually got some sleep that night. In between delicious interludes of lovemaking with this all-human, all-female woman who knew his secrets. Was she somehow turned on by what he was? Or did it simply make no difference to her?

He counted at least three more times when he rolled over in her erotically smelling bed to find her awake, too. Or maybe they were simply in sync.

They made love over and over, and then he slept.

Not that he felt well rested when he awoke in the morning, listening.

He heard sounds outside—Kathlene's neighbors walking their dogs and chatting with their kids, cars driving by, noises that were not familiar to him in this area while staying in the remote cabins.

"Good morning," whispered a soft voice from beside him.

He rolled over to find Kathlene's half-open blue eyes looking at him, her still-sleepy face smiling.

Why did that look sexy? He didn't know, except that there they were, still in bed, still nude. He reached for her, and they made love yet again.

"Are you interested in breakfast?" Kathlene asked once she had returned to her bedroom after showering.

Jock and she had finally arisen after their most recent round of luscious sex that took enough out of her that she could have stayed in bed all day. Except that she had to report for duty in about an hour.

And except that spending any more bed time with Jock nearby was not a good idea. She had questions. He probably had answers. They had discussed only the generalities of Alpha Force last night at his cabin, and more specifics about his shapeshifting when they had arrived here at her home. But she had other questions about what he did. And if they didn't get up, she wouldn't even be able to try to draw responses out of him. They'd be too busy engaging in other, more enjoyable things. Assuming they could find any more energy after last night.

So she had tossed him out of the bedroom first to shower. Then she'd dashed to her wonderfully appointed kitchen—her favorite room in the house—in his absence, still in the robe she had thrown on, to see what she had in the way of breakfast fixings.

Fortunately, she had a few eggs, some bread, cereal and plenty of milk. Coffee, too.

"Sure," he said now. "Where would you like to go?" He undoubtedly meant for her to pick a restaurant.

Instead, she said, "Down the hall, to my kitchen. I'll take care of it." She gave him her available choices. Seemingly glad about her offer to cook their breakfast, he chose toast and coffee, with a couple of scrambled eggs thrown in when she said she was making some for herself.

But she liked the fact that he apparently didn't want to create extra work for her, even when she offered it.

A short while later, they both sat at her oval wooden kitchen table, their plates of eggs and toast, and large white mugs of coffee, on red woven place mats in front of them.

Jock once again wore the outfit he had had on last night, of course—T-shirt and jeans, his and Ralf's usual undercover uniform.

She, on the other hand, wore her deputy sheriff's uniform.

"Now let's backtrack a bit," Kathlene said, smiling as Jock took one bite after another of the eggs that she had seasoned with thyme and oregano to add a slightly Italian flair to them.

"Okay," he said. "This is really good, by the way."

"Glad you like it." Kathlene took a sip of her hot coffee. "Now, last night. When you were wandering around the old ranch area."

"When I was shifted," he said with a nod, gazing at her as if waiting for her reaction this morning, after she'd had time to sleep on her initial thoughts.

Well, heck, neither one of them had actually slept much….

"That's right," she said. "Tell me more about what you saw and heard. And whatever else you did while you were—while you were a wolf."

His grin at her was obviously meant to be a sexy leer. "I'm always a wolf, but which kind depends on what form I'm in."

"Right," she said drily. "While you looked like a wolf."

"Sure." Their limited repartee had been enough for him, she figured, for he spent the next few minutes describing what he had seen and heard as he walked, in wolf form, around the outside of the old ranch's fence. "I heard a couple of guys I couldn't see talk about the county commissioners' meeting and how they needed to teach the town a few lessons about backing off when it came to adding any possible limits on hunting."

"Did you see who they were?"

"No, but I might be able to identify them through their voices and scents, although I was too far away to be sure."

"Oh. Of course." His other senses besides sight were undoubtedly sharper when he was actually a wolf, she figured.

Which gave more credence to why the feds would send this kind of secret unit here to deal with the situation she had described.

"Then there was the noise I heard—probably like the explosions you had mentioned hearing a while back. I wasn't close enough to really get a good scent, but I thought I smelled a hint of plastic, like C-4. The sound was muffled, though, so could be they were just experimenting and keeping it under wraps—troublesome, anyway. Something we need more information about, as well as the ability to disarm anything that has the potential of injuring anyone, including the county commissioners this group clearly has no love for."

Kathlene shivered. She felt vindicated, but that didn't really make her feel good. The danger still existed.

"I'm glad you heard it, too," she said. "And smelled it. And are checking into it, even though no one else around here seems concerned."

"Nothing but peaceful target practice," Jock acknowledged. "And if I believed that's all that was going on there, Ralf and I would be on our way to Yellowstone—or that's

what we'd tell anyone here who asked. Which is probably no one."

"Do we need to get you more involved in the commu-
nity?" She had wondered about that. Maybe they needed
to be more than just her buddies. But how?

His smile looked both amazed and…tender? A teasing
warmth crept up her back. She was beginning to care too
much for this man, and she had to get it under control. He
was only here for a short time, till he accomplished his
very important mission.

Then there was the fact that he was so different from
her…

"I knew we were on the same wavelength," he said, "but
I didn't think you'd anticipate this. And maybe you haven't.
But here's what I wanted to tell you. Let me preface it by
explaining there was another thing I heard. Something else
you might be particularly interested in."

Her curiosity was suddenly almost overwhelming.
"What's that?"

"I want you to bring me to your sheriff's department
this morning, introduce me to all your coworkers as your
longtime buddy, even though I've already met some of
them, okay?"

"Sure," she said, but he hadn't answered her question.
She needed to know more. "But tell me why."

"Because one of the things I heard and sensed last night
was a presence I didn't expect. Or maybe I did, but you
might not."

"Who's that?" she asked.

"Sheriff Melton Frawley."

Jock took another bite of the delicious eggs that Kathlene had cooked while waiting for her response.

Her beautiful blue eyes had widened, and she was staring at him. "Sheriff Frawley." It wasn't a question, but a statement. "Did you hear anything he said?"

Clearly, she had suspected his involvement.

But then again, why wouldn't she? From what she had told her friend that had led to Alpha Force's being deployed here, she'd tried to get her boss's support in investigating the people she had become concerned were anarchists and had gotten nowhere.

"Sure," Jock responded. "That's how I knew he was there. I recognized his voice from when I'd heard him before, yesterday at the commissioners' meeting. But if you're asking if he said anything that would implicate him as being part of whatever those guys are doing, the answer's no."

"What did he say, then?"

"All the most circumspect stuff, thanking Tisal—I heard his voice, too—for inviting him there and showing him around…again. That wasn't his first time there, apparently. And also apologizing for the way the county appeared to be criticizing a group of licensed hunters like the people camping out there."

"Really? He…he sounded as if he assumed someone was eavesdropping on him."

Jock nodded. "I wouldn't be surprised if that's what he thought. Not that he would assume it would be a shapeshifter, but there are a lot of tiny, hard-to-find electronic bugs these days. He certainly did sound like he was covering his butt."

"He also seemed to be protecting the guys who are hanging out there." Kathlene looked so affronted and woeful that Jock had to fight the urge to kiss away her bad mood—or at least try. "What are we going to do?"

"Okay, team member," he said. "Here's what I want. Like I said, you'll need to introduce Ralf and me to your colleagues, including the higher-ups. And pretty soon, you and I, old buddy, are going to have a very public difference of opinion—when Ralf and I make it clear that we're sportsmen, too. We like hunting and are all for those who don't want to add any more protections to the animals that should be fair game for us all. Period."

"And then?" The worry on Kathlene's face only got more obvious.

"Ralf and I are going to join the anarchists."

"But how will you do your shapeshifting then?"

Kathlene knew she was acting almost confrontational with Jock, but she now realized that there was a good reason for Alpha Force to have sent members here to deal with the possible anarchist situation.

Yes, she liked the idea of the two men going undercover with the people she suspected were anarchists to find out what they really were up to.

But if Jock was there with them, she might not be able to communicate with him anymore except in apparent anger.

And his very special abilities, which might help lead to more answers than just some ordinary—even well-conducted—undercover work might wind up being extraneous and unusable.

"Don't worry about that," Jock said. "You can be sure I'll work it out." He stood up from the table, his now-empty plate in his hand. He took it over to the sink, rinsed it, and placed it in her dishwasher.

Which she liked. He was a guy who didn't assume that women were the ones who had to do all the cleanup chores, unlike so many of the men she now worked with.

He returned to the table and picked up his coffee mug. He didn't ask her to refill it for him but instead went to the tile counter and picked the half-filled pot off the coffeemaker and poured more into it. And then he brought the pot over and refreshed her coffee, too.

That made her smile. She looked up at him, right into his intense hazel eyes that were so much like the eyes of the wolf he was while shifted—and like Click's eyes, too.

As much as she wanted to stand up, place herself close to him, into his arms, she pulled her gaze away, took her phone from her pocket and checked the time on it.

It was getting late. She had to go.

"Time for me to head to work," she said. "You go ahead and pick up Ralf. Maybe give me an extra half hour to see who's around and figure out the best way to handle your further introductions at the department—and get you in a position to speak with Sheriff Frawley. We'll have to figure out later how best to keep our *friendship* going on, in secret if necessary. Okay?"

"Okay," he said, and he was the one to take her coffee mug and place it back on the table, then pull her into his arms. "One for the road," he said, then engaged her in another deep, sexy kiss.

Chapter 13

Kathlene's uniform felt fresh, slightly stiff and generally comfortable, as it always did—but she was entirely conscious of being dressed as she drove to the department headquarters building along the pleasant town streets of Cliffordsville.

Dressed wasn't how she had been for the entire night—in Jock's arms.

But she commanded herself not to think only about him and sex as she headed to work.

She could think about him some, yes. In fact, she could think of little else—especially in light of the secret she now knew about him.

Yet instead of constantly recalling who and what he was, and—somehow, amazingly, even more mind-boggling—how incredible their bouts of lovemaking had been, she had to consider Jock in the scheming she needed to do.

She had to figure out the best plan for bringing Jock and Ralf in to meet up with Sheriff Frawley in a manner that wouldn't appear odd or suspicious.

The two secret Alpha Force members needed to interrogate Melton about his relationship with the group of sportsmen in a way that couldn't possibly be interpreted to indicate that one of them had actually discovered the sheriff at the old ranch and overheard at least some of his conversation there.

Not that Sheriff Frawley, or anyone else who was reasonably sane, for that matter, would have the slightest glimmer of what Jock Larabey actually was or how he might have seen the sheriff, and even eavesdropped on him, during his visit to the possible anarchists' camp.

And once the scheming Kathlene was involved in bore fruit, she reminded herself, and the sportsmen's true nature was determined and dealt with, Jock would be gone. Out of here.

Leaving her to maintain the position she loved, as a deputy sheriff in Clifford County.

Which was the perfect reason to enjoy him while he was here, but not get emotionally involved.

Hear that, heart? she made her mind assert to herself.

Her heart's only reply was to continue to beat. A good thing.

She would survive this interlude with Jock. And then she would survive without him.

Better that way, of course. She didn't know how she had somehow accepted that he was a shapeshifter, but that was all the more reason not to form any relationship with him. At least no more than she already had—an amazing one, yes, but definitely short-term.

At least now, with what she knew, Jock and Ralf couldn't treat her as someone outside their team. She could always blackmail them into including her. They didn't know that wasn't her way. And she wasn't going to tell them…yet.

Kathlene soon pulled her SUV into one of the spaces behind the sheriff's department headquarters and got out. She wasn't the only one arriving then, which wasn't surprising.

The daily meeting in the assembly room for those on duty during this regular shift would begin in—she checked her cell phone—ten minutes.

She still hadn't decided how to achieve what she needed to do. But she knew she would figure it out.

She glanced around at the others who were also heading toward the rear entrance to the building. Her partner, Jimmy Korling, was among them, but she didn't hurry to catch up with him. They'd have enough time together that day when they headed out on patrol.

She spied Deputy Betsy Alvers, one of the other few remaining female deputies. Kathlene usually went out of her way to avoid her overweight and irritatingly accommodating counterpart because Betsy's way of dealing with the strife at the department was to simper and smile and act as if that was the way things should be.

Consequently, Sheriff Frawley and Undersheriff George Kerringston seemed utterly pleased that Betsy was one of their deputies—especially since she seemed thrilled to bring them coffee and agree with everything they said.

Unlike Kathlene.

But maybe Betsy was the ideal person for her to talk to now. Whatever she told the young and obnoxious deputy would undoubtedly be passed along to the brass.

She had to finesse this well, though. More often than not, Kathlene avoided talking to Betsy since it was so difficult not to show her scorn—and that would be highly inappropriate behavior for someone who wanted to keep her job around here.

So she would need to find a way to get Betsy to address her first. Then it would be impolite of her *not* to respond. All would look good then…she hoped.

She sped up a bit as she headed toward the door. She figured that spacey, controversy-avoiding Betsy might be best approached as if Kathlene was in the throes of sadness. She put her head down and turned her mouth into a sorrowful pout.

She met up with Betsy as they neared the door. "Hi," Kathlene said, glancing up with a tiny smile that she intended to appear more mournful than false.

"Hi, Kathlene," Betsy gushed in her usually enthusiastic tone. "How are you?" But before Kathlene could respond, Betsy got the gist of what she was faking. "Oh, is something wrong?"

"No," Kathlene said hurriedly, reaching for the door handle. "Well…maybe."

She held the door open so Betsy could enter first. Fortunately, there was a gap between them and the next group of deputies heading in their direction, and the lobby area into which they entered was already empty. Everyone must have headed to the assembly room right away.

"You want to talk about it?" Betsy's dark brows were raised sympathetically over her small brown eyes. She wore too much makeup and her puffy rouged cheeks looked as if she had been in the sun too long. Her white-blond hair was pulled into a clip at the back of her head, as all female law-enforcement personnel were directed to do. The result almost made her look like a large, overdone doll. An overdone deputy doll, since she, too, wore a uniform—hers larger and more rounded out than Kathlene's.

Kathlene felt a snap of conscience. The young woman was actually acting nice. And in fact, she usually did. The problem was with how she caved under the orders of the most chauvinistic men around here.

She might really make a good deputy, given a chance to prove herself besides exercising her waitress and secretarial skills.

The room they'd gone into was more of an entry that

led to a variety of hallways within the building, including a stairway at one end. They'd need to scale it to reach the assembly room. But for the moment Kathlene moseyed in a way she hoped looked sorrowful toward a far corner.

"It's really not much," Kathlene said. "And I probably shouldn't be talking about it at all." Especially to you, she thought—except now, when she hoped to use the deputy who had good connections thanks to her submissive nature.

"Sometimes it helps to talk about things," Betsy encouraged. Kathlene wondered how often others had caved in to the young woman's sympathetic demeanor and revealed stuff they shouldn't—and had it used against them.

She, at least, would only say things she wanted to get to the ears of their bosses.

"I guess. And really—well, it's not so bad. I'm just feeling a little disappointed. One of my old-time friends is in town, a guy I've known since college. He brought another friend along with them, and the two of them told me that they plan to leave here sooner than they originally said."

She looked up at Betsy's face, hoping her expression showed both frustration and sadness.

"Did they tell you why?" Betsy asked. Good. Kathlene didn't have to prompt her to ask that question.

"Well…yes. They live in Washington State and came to visit me before going on to visit Yellowstone. I didn't know they'd had the idea of doing some hunting in Montana. Or maybe they hadn't thought about it before. But they're looking into the possibility. The thing is, they attended the county commissioners' meeting yesterday out of curiosity and were…well, concerned about the issues being discussed that might outlaw hunting completely in this area. I told them that wasn't the case, and even further limits were somewhat iffy, but they decided they'd only stay another couple of days, anyway."

"But didn't they understand that there's a nice, solid faction here that is discouraging the commissioners from passing any more laws that would make it hard for people to hunt in this county?" Betsy peered at Kathlene. "Or are they mostly upset with you, since I gather that you're in favor of that kind of law."

Kathlene shrugged. "It could be partly that, I guess, even though I try not to get into my opinions with them too much. But no, they just think this area's government may be too dictatorial. Or at least that's what I assume."

"What if someone talked to them, tried to convince them otherwise?"

Kathlene forbore from rolling her eyes, instead attempting to look happy and pleadingly into Betsy's face. "Oh, would you?"

Betsy shrugged. "I'm probably not the best person. Maybe someone who's a hunter, or who at least is in favor of allowing hunting, would be better."

"Do you know someone who'd talk to them?" Kathlene hoped she appeared the picture of clueless innocence.

"I've got a couple of ideas," Betsy said. "Let me ask around."

"That would be wonderful," Kathlene gushed. "My friends will be here in about half an hour. I told them to come so I could give them a quick tour after our assembly but before Jimmy and I go out on patrol. They were interested in seeing where I work and what the local sheriff's station looks like."

"Fine," Betsy said. She glanced at a watch on her puffy wrist. "We'd better go upstairs. And I'm not sure I can get anyone to talk to them this soon, but I'll see what I can do."

"Thanks so much," Kathlene said, and followed Betsy to the flight of stairs across the room.

Jock and Ralf entered the reception area at the front of the sheriff's department building. They approached the desk and told a uniformed guy behind it who they were—at least who their undercover identities were—and that Deputy Kathlene Baylor was expecting them.

"I'll let her know as soon as the meeting she's in is over," the smooth-faced deputy, who looked as if he still belonged in high school, told them.

"Thanks."

Ralf and he sat down on chairs at the room's perimeter. Jock picked up a couple of magazines and leafed through them—some on law enforcement and on the wonders and delights of Montana.

Two women sat across the room from them. A man and woman entered behind them and also approached the reception desk. "We want to file a complaint," the man said. "One of our neighbors has a dog that he lets do his business in our front yard."

"I'll give you the paperwork to file a complaint," the deputy told them.

Jock glanced at Ralf. "Sounds like this town has some nondog people," he said with a rueful shrug.

"Yeah. Maybe we should get their address so you can leave a deposit in their yard sometime." Ralf had kept his voice very low. His smile looked as if he was trying to appear diabolical but he failed.

Jock couldn't help laughing back.

He looked up as other people in uniforms started entering the area both from the stairs and from the couple of doors into the room. "Guess the meeting's over," Jock said.

"Guess so," Ralf agreed.

In a minute Kathlene hurried down the stairway toward them. How could she look so beautiful and sexy with her dark hair pulled starkly away from her face, and in a unisex gray uniform?

Maybe it was the beauty of her face. The way she filled out the uniform.

The way he could visualize, from experience, what was beneath it.

"Hi," she said. "Are you ready for your tour?"

"We sure are. You ready to show us around?"

"Absolutely," she said, loud enough for others to hear her. "I definitely want to show you where I work." And then, more softly, she added, "I tried to initiate something that'll get you an audience with one of the guys in charge—preferably Tisal. But we'll just have to see whether it works."

Jock played his role well, or at least he intended to.

Ralf and he had both dressed in button-down shirts and nice trousers as an ostensible show of respect while getting a tour of the sheriff's department headquarters, Kathlene's base of operations as a deputy. Dressing well wouldn't guarantee them the meeting that they hoped for, but it probably wouldn't hurt.

The three of them had discussed their approach before—definitely treating Kathlene as a member of their team.

She, in turn, was following through quite well. She was in uniform and acted utterly professional.

Now, leading them down hallways and into various rooms, Kathlene spoke loudly enough for anyone around them to hear what she was up to. She repeated often that she really couldn't spend much time doing this since she and her partner were scheduled to go on patrol in less than half an hour.

In turn, Jock acted, in reaction to Kathlene's cheerful prattle about what he was seeing, as if he appreciated what she said but wasn't overly impressed. Ralf undoubtedly appeared to be the nicer of the two of them. Maybe that was actually the case.

After all, the man Jock was supposed to be at the moment was a potentially frustrated hunter who wasn't particularly happy with this town that considered enacting further hunting restrictions.

A hunter who in fact wasn't wild about towns or any other kind of government authority that attempted to tell its citizens what to do.

In other words, a budding anarchist.

Ralf? Well, his assumed character had similar values but perhaps wasn't as vocal about them.

They'd reached the end of the second-floor hallway and Kathlene had just pointed out the assembly room where she and her fellow officers met daily for a general assessment of what was going on and what to look out for before being sent off on their assignments.

"Now let's go up another couple of floors to the offices of the sheriff and his primary officers and staff," Kathlene said with a wide, too-bright smile. "That will have to be the end of the tour, at least for now. I've got to go on patrol in just a few minutes."

"Sounds good," Ralf said. "I'm really enjoying this. How about you, Jock?" The guy certainly knew how to play his role well. All his Alpha Force roles.

There wasn't any better aide to shifters than his was, and Jock knew it.

Especially since they'd also had a talk about Kathlene.

Ralf wasn't stupid. He knew what was going on. Was non-judgmental. Only told Jock to be careful, which he was.

"Definitely," Jock replied to Ralf. "But let's hurry. I don't want to hold you up any more, Kathlene."

A couple of other people in uniform were standing nearby, conversing. If any of them eavesdropped, they'd most likely believe exactly as Jock wanted them to. All was well. His old buddy Kathlene was merely showing him and his friend around where she worked. Everything was aboveboard. No underlying issues or goals.

False.

They'd started out on the lower levels, where Kathlene had pointed out the rooms of emergency staff and others who responded to phone calls, as well as locker rooms, storage areas and places that were of great use but wouldn't yield them the information they were after.

But that was part of the act. They really had to behave as if this was a genuine tour of the building—even though they were only just now about to dig into what was important here.

Rather than waiting for an elevator, Kathlene showed them up the couple of flights of steps to the upper echelons of this building.

They emerged into a hallway much wider and more brightly lit than those downstairs. The floor was gleaming wood. The walls between the numerous doors were covered with photos of faces of smiling men in uniforms, probably former sheriffs and their seconds in command.

"I don't get up here very often," Kathlene said. "The officers stationed up here mostly come downstairs if they want to interact with us. But—"

A door at the far end of the hall opened, and Sheriff Melton Frawley emerged. With him was a young uniformed deputy, a woman. Jock assumed she was the person

Kathlene had said she would talk to about Ralf and him and their opinions about the town.

The woman who had Frawley's ear because she did as he said and waited on him hand and foot, if what Kathlene had said was true. And Jock had no doubt that it was.

Frawley strode toward them. Kathlene smiled again in a way that struck Jock as nervous yet determined. Instinctively, he moved to her side and was glad to see Ralf do the same.

"Deputy Baylor," the sheriff said, "what're you doing on this floor?" To his credit, the guy wasn't scowling at her, and his tone sounded more curious than angry or dictatorial.

Sheriff Melton Frawley struck Jock as being a tall stick of a man who'd fought his way into a job with power and would do anything to maintain it. When Jock had seen him the previous night at the old ranch, the guy had been in his uniform as he was now, maybe to assert himself as in charge, or maybe just because he hadn't had time to change. In either event, he'd swaggered a bit while talking to Tisal and the others in charge of the supposed sportsmen.

"I was just giving my friends Jock and Ralf a tour of our headquarters, sir, but we're done. I'm off to find Deputy Korling so we can go out on patrol."

"You do that," said Frawley. And then the man turned to Jock and Ralf. "Meantime, I'll continue with your friends' tour." The man grinned, and Jock figured that the other lady deputy had done as Kathlene had hoped: told their story to this man.

And with luck, Ralf and he would get an invitation to meet the sportsmen in person. Tonight.

While Jock was still in human form.

Chapter 14

As the sheriff spoke, Betsy Alvers had remained just behind him, peeking around to aim a sympathetic smile toward Kathlene that said she'd done as Kathlene had anticipated and revealed to the boss the earlier conversation they'd had—whether or not Kathlene had expected some discretion from her.

But fortunately, Kathlene had expected exactly what had happened.

And the results? Well, now Sheriff Frawley must know how concerned Kathlene was that her dear long-term friend Jock and his buddy Ralf weren't on the same page as Kathlene about hunting and hunting laws and maybe even about people who tried to restrict other people's rights.

So as Kathlene hurried downstairs to meet up with her partner, she kept telling herself those results were perfect, just what she'd wanted: a probable conversation between the undercover Alpha Force guys and the sheriff, one that could lead to her team members learning a whole lot more about what was going on with the sportsmen and what they were up to.

So why did Kathlene feel so bummed out now?

As if she didn't know.

What they were doing wouldn't, couldn't, include her.

At least not right now…

She reached the downstairs area where Jimmy waited for her, nearly alone since others in their shift had already hit the road.

"You ready to go, partner?" Jimmy asked, frowning in what she interpreted to be barely concealed irritation.

"I sure am. Let's sign out and get on our way."

They'd both officially gone on duty before the morning's assembly, but now they followed the standard process to confirm that they were about to enter the patrol car assigned to them and get out there to protect the town and county.

"Let's go," Kathlene said a minute later when she had completed her entry on the department computer system, tossing a grim smile toward Jimmy. She strode determinedly through the doorway and down the concrete steps to the parking area, hearing him keeping up with her.

Today she had the keys. She would drive them around.

And would get nowhere near the old ranch unless there was a call out for assistance from law enforcement.

That wouldn't happen.

Nor would she get back here, or anywhere else where Jock and Ralf were likely to be hanging out.

No, she would get an update from them later about how their ad hoc meeting with Sheriff Frawley went, and whether they would get a visit to the sportsmen's camp out of it.

Kathlene would have to wait.

And Kathlene was not a patient person.

All had gone perfectly, as if Jock had whispered into the sheriff's ear exactly what he wanted, and the guy had been nothing but an obedient servant—even while Frawley undoubtedly assumed he held all the cards in anyone's pockets around this department and the county where he was in charge.

At the moment, Jock and Ralf were just ending their meeting in Frawley's surprisingly small but neat, and expensively appointed, office.

"We really appreciate all you've said," Jock said, leaning forward in the smooth wooden office chair he'd taken that faced the sheriff's desk.

Ralf was right beside him. "We sure do," he said. "I'd been telling Jock that maybe it was a mistake to come here, at least for any length of time. It's okay for him to say hi to an old friend, but we're on vacation, and the idea of not being able to do any hunting before visiting Yellowstone and then heading home… Well, I, for one, didn't like it."

"And like we said, before we talked to you we really had the impression that things around here were about to get even worse. I mean, your county commissioners' ideas about passing even more restrictions?" Jock shook his head, hoping he was as good an actor as he was trying to be. Those restrictions could save lives, including lives of wolves.

And his kind had an affinity for the true, wild, nonshifting canines as well as for their own.

"Well, when you come tonight to the barbecue, you'll get to meet other people who think like you do."

"We're looking forward to it." Jock knew his smile was genuine. They'd gotten an invitation to visit the ranch. They would be able to talk to the men staying there, listen in on what they were saying to one another, get a better feel—he hoped—for what those explosions were about and whether the residents there genuinely were true sportsmen.

It still was possible that they were innocent of any wrongdoing despite all Jock's doubts, including those raised by the snippets of conversations he had been able to make out while patrolling the area in wolf form. And that one small explosion he'd heard and smelled.

"I'll let them know you're coming, and I'll be there, too, at least for a while." The sheriff stood, still grinning at them. Even if Jock didn't have other reasons to doubt the man's sincerity, that too-bright smile on the narrow, aging, yet falsely friendly face would have given him the same sense of crawly insects along his back as he had now. "And don't you worry about your friendship with Deputy Baylor," Frawley drawled. "I'm a bit older than you gentlemen, and sometimes youthful relationships don't last forever, especially since people often go in different directions that you can't imagine when you're kids in college."

Very philosophical for an old, curmudgeonly—and most likely deceitful—sheriff, Jock thought. But this one had an ax to grind, apparently against anyone who didn't think the same way he did.

"Thanks," Jock said.

"See you later," Ralf added as they both rose and left the room.

It was late afternoon, and Kathlene was off duty. She was glad that she'd gotten a few minutes to join up with Jock and Ralf at their cabin before they left to go to the barbecue at the fenced-off ranch.

"We need some kind of signal or code," she said. "You can always call me and say it, and then I'll come to help."

Jock had been standing by the cabin's unused fireplace, but now he strode over to her. He was wearing a white T-shirt and jeans with a light hunting jacket over it. Ralf, just coming in with Click on a leash, was dressed similarly.

"Thanks," Jock said, "but we'll be fine." He drew close enough to look down at her, and the heat in his brilliant hazel eyes looked both fond and damnably sexy. Too bad she couldn't just seduce him to keep him from going into what could be a lion's den of trouble.

"Well, will you be able to shapeshift if things get too rocky?"

"No. I don't want to have the equipment and elixir along just in case things do get out of hand, and I doubt we'd be able to slip away long enough to do anything, anyway. But don't worry. We'll be fine. We're well trained by the military, even though we also have some secret kinds of missions that the rest of the troops aren't sent on. I doubt things will get so out of hand that we'll need to engage in any kind of self-defense or combat, but if so, we'll deal with it."

"Yeah, but Kathlene already bested you in hand-to-hand," Ralf called from behind them. "No wonder she's worried."

She couldn't help smiling, but only for a moment. "That's not the point. I should find a way to go with you, to help if—"

"No need," Jock interrupted.

"But—" Kathlene didn't get to finish. She was suddenly in Jock's arms, held tightly against his muscular body, his mouth silencing her with a hot kiss.

When he finally let go of her—just a little—Jock pulled his head back and looked down at her again.

"We'll be fine," he repeated. "And I'll call you just as soon as we're far enough away from there to have no repercussions. I'll tell you what we learn, I promise."

Kathlene wanted to contradict him yet again. Sure, he could distract her with an unexpected kiss, but only for a moment, and not from her deepest concerns.

None of them spoke much more before the two men left shortly thereafter—although Kathlene had to glare at

Ralf to fend off his amused glances. When they were gone, Kathlene stayed in their cabin just a little longer, glad to have at least Click's company this time.

She sat on one of the two rustic chairs, and the dog seemed to sense her malaise. He came over and sat on the wooden floor beside her, putting his head onto her lap.

"Thanks, Click," she whispered, bending over to hug the dog. She patted him for a while, then reached for the TV remote. Maybe she'd find some brainless sitcom to take her mind off those men—that man—and his attitude, and the potential danger to both of them.

But that was impossible. She was damned worried.

She was part of their team. They'd confirmed it before, and her knowledge about the nature of Alpha Force now made it even more critical that they accept her.

They had, therefore, told her all that they'd said in their discussion with her boss, or so she believed. Sheriff Frawley had undoubtedly invited them that night because of her. His sportsmen should supposedly be able to convince these visitors that there were others in and around Clifford County who weren't like her and who didn't like the kind of authority that she espoused.

She was concerned, of course, that the sportsmen just wanted to get to know Jock and Ralf better, to learn if they truly were of a similar mind-set to them—or potential enemies, as she was.

They were aware that she and Jock were supposedly old friends, so that could give them cause to mistrust him, no matter what he told them.

Her showing up with them for this barbecue, as part of their team, wouldn't work. She knew that.

But she could at least wait here, on their turf, for their return.

Unless…

* * *

This felt novel. Instead of Jock's creeping around while in wolf form, Ralf drove their car right up the narrow, pitted driveway through the woods to the locked metal gate in the fence surrounding the old ranch.

It was late now. Evening was falling. A good time for a party, Jock supposed.

A guard came out of the small shed that was right next door, a guy in a camo uniform, of all things. If this group was composed of anarchists, why did any of them want to look like official military members?

Or was this just for show, to make any visitors realize that not just anyone could enter here?

Jock got out of the car and approached. He was careful not to raise his chin or do anything else that might look unusual, but he did use his stronger senses to check out the area a bit. There was nothing unusual, though, except the hint of a fire in the distance, probably the barbecue.

That didn't mean the entire facility was pristine.

"Hello," the guard called through the gate. He looked like he must have been around for a while, a senior citizen with a wrinkled face and suspicious frown. A long-time anarchist?

Jock motioned for Ralf to join him. Ralf turned off the engine and they both walked toward the gate. "Hi," Jock called. "Sheriff Frawley invited us to the barbecue here tonight."

When the guard didn't move for a moment except to study them with dark, distrustful eyes, Jock thought of Kathlene and what she had said and her concern for them.

Maybe she'd been right—not that he doubted they could be putting themselves in a dangerous position just by coming here. But maybe they should have called in backup first.

Their orders, though, were that backup would be readily available, but no Alpha Force members would be flown in until their surveillance yielded more than suspicions that these guys were ready to blow up civilians and others to support their hatred of authority.

Jock had put his superior officer, Drew Connell, on alert after hearing, and scenting, that one explosion, but more was needed.

And Kathlene as backup? No way! He needed to ensure her safety, but not vice versa.

"Your names?" the guy finally called.

Beside Jock, Ralf moved a little. He apparently felt uncomfortable with this situation, too. "I'm Ralf Nunnoz," he called, "and this is my friend Jock Larabey. We visited with Sheriff Frawley at his office this morning, so if there's any question about our being here, you can call him."

His aide at work. Jock suppressed his grim smile. He knew he could always count on Ralf to have his back.

"No need. He's been in touch. You can come in." The senior guy moved away and pulled something out of his pocket. It must have been a control of some kind since the gate started to roll sideways as it opened.

"Thanks," Ralf called. Both returned to the car and Ralf slowly drove them inside.

The guard approached the driver's window, which Ralf opened. He told them to continue down the narrow road until they saw a parking lot. They were to leave their car there and someone would meet them.

Once again, Ralf thanked the man, and they followed his instructions. Jock was surprised to see that the parking lot was fairly substantial in size and nearly full. Perhaps twenty cars were there beneath the canopy of overhanging trees. It was still light enough that Jock could see that, straight ahead, there was a clearing beyond a narrow row of vegetation, and in it was a structure he'd noticed before, while prowling the area, that looked like a ranch house.

Sure enough, as the guard had said, they were met by a man walking from that direction. He looked familiar—one of those they'd met at the bar and at the county commissioners' meeting.

Ralf had parked in one of the few empty spaces and the guy joined them. He was tall and appeared as muscular in his bright green knit shirt and jeans as Jock remembered him. "Hi," he said. "Welcome. We met before. I'm Hal."

"Hi, Hal." Jock reintroduced himself and Ralf. "This is really nice, our being invited here. I understand from the sheriff that there are a bunch of you and that you're into hunting."

"That's right. Come on and I'll introduce you to some of the others." Hal motioned with his long arm, and both Jock and Ralf followed him along the unpaved path through the trees. "I hear you're not from Montana," he continued as they walked.

"That's right," Jock said. "I went to school in Missoula but I live in Washington State now."

"I gather that you wanted to do some hunting here, but this isn't a good time, and we've got some strict laws against poaching. People generally have to apply for permits before now, and there's a lot of game that's not yet in season. But we'll fill you in."

"Don't you have a way to get around that?" Ralf inquired. He was staying closer to Hal's side than Jock, which was fine. It gave Jock more of an opportunity to view what they were passing—and use his more powerful senses to also scout the area.

"Like I said," Hal responded, "we'll fill you in."

They reached the clearing. At its far side was the large wooden ranch house that was painted a deep red. There was a white door in its center, and equal-sized wings on each side.

He couldn't tell the depth, but Jock had the sense that quite a few *sportsmen* could be housed right here, for as long as they were needed to train…or whatever.

Jock smelled the aromas of barbecuing meats and the fire cooking them more strongly here. He also scented a number of different people, although there were enough that he couldn't distinguish one from another—not the way he'd have been able to in wolf form. He did think, though, that he smelled the other person, Tisal, whom he'd met at the bar and who had gone to the commissioners' meeting.

Sure enough, when Hal led them around the back to a large stone-paved patio filled with chattering men, most with beer cans in their hands, Tisal was the first in the crowd to approach them. Jock didn't see the sheriff there, but he might come later.

"Welcome, gentlemen," the man said. "As you know, I'm Nate Tisal, and I guess I'm the guy in charge here. As Sheriff Frawley probably told you, we're a little selective in who we invite since there are a lot of people these days who're tree huggers and don't like what we do—hunting."

"That's not us," Jock said immediately. "In fact, we told the sheriff that our inability to hunt around here was making us leave sooner than we'd originally anticipated."

"Well, we might be able to help with that. Come on, let's grab you some beers and I'll introduce you around."

The next hour or so would have been enjoyable under other circumstances. Tisal introduced them to everyone there—all men, and all dressed casually in clothing that ranged from snug, sleeveless T-shirts and jeans to full hunting apparel.

Food was served buffet-style on a table near the barbecue pit, and all the guys grabbed seats at the three rows of picnic tables on the large patio.

"Good stuff," Jock said after tasting the meat. "What is it?" He knew, of course. Venison. But as far as he knew deer wasn't yet in season here.

"What do you think?" Tisal asked. He'd sat down at the same table, as had Hal and four other guys.

"Venison?" Ralf said.

"Well, if anyone outside these gates asks, you had some damned good steak," said one of the other men.

"That's right," Tisal said. "There aren't any poachers around here." They all started to laugh.

"Definitely not." Jock made himself grin as he took another bite. Of course they were poachers. But the sheriff probably knew that and had no intention of arresting them.

Nor would Alpha Force have any interest in hauling these guys in if that was the only kind of law they were breaking...although if the poaching included wolves, wild cats or birds there'd be a bunch of controversy within their very special military ranks.

For now Jock just ate and stayed as quiet as possible. Ralf knew the deal. He was the friendly one who answered questions and asked some of his own about how this group had moved into the ranch area and started growing. The men described how they all were sportsmen who practiced at a shooting range on the property that their latest visitors would be shown after dinner. How they nearly all had their hunting licenses already and would brag about using them in town when the time was right—but not talk about anything else they might be using their guns for before that.

And Jock? Well, he listened to the conversation and chimed in now and then. He looked around them, believing he could, through some breaks in the trees around this part of the property, get a glimpse of the chain-link fence surrounding the ranch thanks to the lights that had been lit on the property, since it was already nightfall.

But mostly he used his acute hearing to eavesdrop on what those at other tables were saying.

And, yes, some were complaining about the laws that wouldn't let them legally hunt much now, and the talk that those laws might even be made stronger.

There were also complaints about government in general, and how other people, who claimed they had rights under stupid laws that should never have been passed, should be shot for telling these guys what they could and couldn't do.

These guys, as they continued to swig down beer after beer, complained even more. And said they would do something about those laws and the people proposing and enacting and enforcing them.

General stuff, though. Not enough to call in reinforcements to bring this group to justice. Were they planning to do something to back up their complaints?

Jock didn't hear anything like that—but Ralf and he cheered what they did hear and made it sound like they agreed with everything said at their table.

A while later, four new guys who hadn't been there previously joined the party. Jock had heard a car enter the parking lot at the other side of the house, so they'd apparently just arrived. They all wore black and seemed highly muscular beneath their tight shirts, but otherwise they didn't resemble one another at all. Two were bald, though one of them, a short guy, had a dark mustache and the other was probably six foot five. One newcomer with short dark hair had a skinny, lined face and the final guy, with fuzzy light hair, looked about sixteen. Their scents varied, too, from popular aftershaves to sweat and garlic.

Jock was curious about them, especially when Tisal

rose quickly from the table to join them. With all the other conversation going on, increasingly loud and rowdy as the men drank a lot of beer, all Jock could make out were a few words—ones that concerned him. Words like *follow-up* and *warning*.

But when he rose to ostensibly go after another helping of food, all four guys seemed to melt into the crowd.

Even so, despite how interesting this was, it didn't dispel the suspicions they had about this group; neither did it scream out that they were all dedicated anarchists who planned to do something about it...like kill people.

At least this evening was a foot in the door. Hopefully, Ralf and he were making friends and contacts, and would be invited back to interact and listen some more.

Maybe get the lowdown on the men who'd arrived late.

And...

Jock froze suddenly, then lowered his fork to his plate. He wanted to raise his head, to aim his nose into the air so he could verify that what he'd thought he had smelled was real.

But that would look damned odd to this group, so instead he sat quietly, allowing himself to inhale as unnoticeably as possible.

Yes. There it was, the scent he'd thought he smelled.

Two scents.

Somewhere beyond the patio, beyond the fencing that he could only glimpse here and there...

Were Kathlene and Click.

Chapter 15

Good thing Click was well trained, Kathlene thought. Otherwise, he'd surely be barking at what was going on beyond the trees and fence, maybe even tugging at his leash.

She had stopped at an area where the trees were thick but she still, after angling herself, could see inside the well-lighted compound. Click undoubtedly could sense a lot more, but the wolflike dog sat down, panting slightly as if expressing frustration and glancing up at her often.

"Good boy," she whispered and patted his furry head while she stood there looking. And worrying.

The night was warm, the air still and dry. She heard rustling in the trees around her, possibly from creatures of the night, but fortunately Click didn't react to them. Nor did he react to the pulsing sounds of noises beyond the fence, as if people were partying. They sometimes raised their voices to cheer.

Was that where the night's dinner was being served? Probably.

As far as she knew, this was Click's first time here. The other visits to the exterior area of the ranch had not been by the actual dog, but by Jock, while shapeshifted.

Shapeshifted. Amazing, but she had accepted the idea. She had no choice, after what she had seen. But that didn't keep her from worrying.

Maybe Jock could take excellent care of himself when he was in wolf form. But tonight he was pretty much all human.

In case he needed to shift, though, she had brought the backpack that was usually in Ralf's possession. It contained the stuff she'd seen the two men use to get Jock shifted.

She had also brought her Glock.

She had come here because she was worried. She still didn't know if that worry was justified.

She hadn't stayed long at the cabin after the Alpha Force members had left for the evening to do their undercover work—without her, their team member. This time, she understood and agreed with it. If a deputy sheriff turned up at the supposed sportsmen's complex for dinner, she'd no idea what their reaction would be, but it certainly would be as bad as she'd experienced when they'd caught her in the area before. Maybe worse, since she was supposed to have learned her lesson.

So tonight she'd intended to simply head home and wait for Jock to call and tell all that had occurred, as he'd promised.

But things hadn't turned out that easy. When she started to leave the cabin area, she'd parked at the opening to the main road to check her bag because she'd wanted to make sure she hadn't left her phone at the cabin. She wasn't sure why she'd turned off the engine, but it was a good thing she had.

Despite her car lights being off, thanks to the minimal illumination outside the registration cabin she'd seen a reflection on the side of a vehicle driving down the road without its lights on, either. It appeared large and dark.

It headed in the direction of the old ranch.

Her law-enforcement instincts had immediately shrieked silently at her that something was wrong. After all, she, too, kept her lights turned off at times she didn't want to be seen while driving at night. But she knew her own motives, and they were essentially law-abiding.

What were the motives of whoever was in this vehicle?

She didn't know for sure, of course, that the sportsmen's compound was the car's destination. Nor did she have any reason to believe that her teammates would be in trouble.

She didn't know that they wouldn't be, either. And the idea of something happening to either of them, particularly Jock, especially when she might be able to help… Well, she had hurried back to the cabin and gotten Click, just in case she again needed an excuse to be out and about if she were caught. It hadn't worked well last time but at least it had worked.

And this time, with a real dog instead of Jock in wolf form…

It didn't matter. She had to be there in case she was needed.

So here she was.

Filled with frustration. She couldn't be certain that this compound was where that car had been heading, but she hadn't seen it again when she'd driven in this direction a few minutes after spotting it.

She didn't know who had been inside the vehicle, had no real idea why she'd worried so much about Jock and Ralf…except that she had learned to trust her instincts.

Plus, she admitted to herself, she had come to care much more than she should for her teammates. Especially for one of them.

Jock.

Was he okay? Were things within the compound—

Wait. There.

In the bright lights beyond the fence, she saw more movement than she had before. The area she observed appeared to be an outer wall of a house, and she'd caught sight of cars parked to one side and heard noises like a party beyond it.

She hadn't seen any people…before. But now several men appeared to be walking from the noisy area toward where the cars were parked.

Four or five men.

They included Jock and Ralf.

Those two appeared to be engaged in a rollicking conversation with their companions. Having fun.

Maybe Kathlene's instincts had been all wrong. That could be a good thing.

She and Click would leave soon. Carefully. At least, having seen Jock, she could assume that he was okay.

She stifled a gasp and a laugh. Oh, yes, he was okay. As she watched, he lifted his hands as if aiming a rifle. He was evidently getting into his role there as a hunter. But while he was pretending, one of his hands went over his head. His hand moved in a strange gesture. As if he knew she was there and he firmly motioned her away.

He turned, and the group headed back toward the party area. She'd no idea why—other than he was protecting her, keeping anyone from driving away while Click and she headed from the area toward where she had parked her car.

Instead of her protecting him, he had wound up protecting her.

She didn't like that…and yet she appreciated it.

And she would have to tell him so.

* * *

Fortunately, no one had blinked when Jock, in a completely friendly manner, asked for a short tour of the property. He'd acted as if he'd drunk too much beer and was in the mood to see the shooting range, maybe fire a few rounds, which gave him the ability to perform his gesture to Kathlene without anyone suspecting that he was doing anything but being an idiot who'd OD'd on alcohol.

He'd asked Hal to show him around and invited lots of others. Only a few had come along.

When they'd reached the area pointed out to them as the firing range, a cleared area surrounded by trees that he believed to be near the back of the property, no one had given in to his requests to practice firing any guns, even at targets, with him in such a soused condition. No matter what these men were, they at least didn't agree to put themselves in danger. Not here. Not now.

But the other goal of his performance, trying to get closer to the men who'd slipped in late, hadn't been successful. They had dropped a few more words that captured his attention, hints about other, bigger, more powerful guns that they may have brought that were perhaps still stashed in their vehicle.

But then they had shut up and begun just partying, too.

Ralf had gone along with him. His aide knew him well enough to realize he had a reason for acting so loony. But not even his looniness got him close enough to the large black SUV the latecomers had driven here except to see it at a distance. Were there guns hidden inside? Were there other guns more powerful than regular hunting weapons already hidden somewhere on the ranch?

He needed to look, to find out somehow. But that wouldn't happen tonight.

It would happen soon, though. He had to make sure of it.

Now Ralf and he were back on the patio. He started to wind down, then approached Hal again.

"Sorry," he muttered. "I'm not...I'd better go back to our cabin now. Thanks so much for inviting us. I'd love to come again."

"Me, too," Ralf said. He put a hand under Jock's elbow, as if trying to steady him. Good. That added another element of believability to the act he was putting on.

"Of course, of course." That was Tisal, who had joined them. "Glad you came."

He got a little closer, making Jock more uncomfortable although he didn't show it. What was the guy up to?

"We're always interested in having men of similar interests...and ideas...join us. I know you don't plan to be here long, but consider that."

Jock suddenly wanted to do a fist pump but of course stayed still. They were being accepted. Right?

Or was this just an act so these *sportsmen* could keep an eye on them?

No matter. Ralf and he had achieved most of what they'd hoped to do on this visit—including some level of being accepted here. Now they were leaving, but they would return. By invitation.

First thing he wanted to do after leaving this compound?

Go find Kathlene, give her a big kiss...then chew her out for showing up here and potentially endangering all of them.

A noise at the door woke Kathlene, followed by the excited scratching of doggy nails on the wooden floor as Click jumped around near the cabin's entry.

She hadn't intended to fall asleep, but after seeing Jock's motions that told her to leave, she had headed back to the cabins to return Click. Then she'd decided to stay for just a short while to see if Jock and Ralf came back quickly.

She'd sat down on the bed and picked up a brochure on the Clifford County area that the motel had left in the cabin for its visitors…and that was all she remembered until now.

She wasn't sure what time it was, but she knew she'd been here a while.

Click's excitement told her who was about to enter the cabin. Even so, her law-enforcement instincts kicked in and she reached toward the weapon she had placed in her bag and left on the floor near the bed.

When Jock and Ralf entered and were jumped on in greeting by Click, she put her bag back down, relaxed and smiled at them. But only for a moment.

Jock was scowling at her.

"Hi." She attempted to sound friendly and ignore what she assumed was his irritation.

"Hi, Kathlene," Ralf said as he knelt to hug the ecstatic dog. "What are you doing here?"

"More important, what were you doing around the ranch? Didn't you learn your lesson last time?" Jock stood with his arms folded across his buff chest that was now covered by a white T-shirt and open hunting jacket. If it weren't for his attitude, she might have felt turned on by his stance, his obviously toned body.

Instead, she made herself ignore what he looked like as she responded, "Yes, I keep learning lessons around here. But I also know that there are times my primary focus is to protect people. I hadn't intended to go to the ranch, but I saw something that worried me."

"What's that?" Jock's response was immediate.

"Possible invaders. They might have been hiding from whatever they left behind, or whatever was in front of them, but I needed to make sure you two remained unharmed." Standing to face them, her own arms folded across her chest, Kathlene described the darkened car she had followed and why it had worried her. "Once I got there, I didn't see them anymore so I figured they'd driven into the compound. I walked around it with Click to try to make sure that, whoever they were, they weren't doing anything to harm either of you."

"Even if they were slaughtering us, why on earth did you think you and Click would be able to do anything about it?" Clearly Jock wasn't going to back down.

She wasn't going to allow him to get away with his attitude. Not now. "You mean you're the only one who can act protective? Hell, I'm the one in law enforcement around here. You're—"

"I'm one of the people you called in for help. Don't forget that."

She wilted, but just a little. "You're right," she acknowledged. "And tonight? If I'd seen you in trouble, I'd have called for help...but it couldn't have been a standard call-out of my department. Not when the sheriff himself is apparently allied with that group. I'm just..."

"Just?" Jock prompted when she stopped talking and looked over at Click, who sat between the legs of the two men facing her.

"Just glad you're both okay." She lifted her eyes, looking first at Ralf, whose gaze was clearly sympathetic, and then at Jock, who at least wasn't scowling at her now. In fact, his expression had softened quite a bit. Enough to make her want to throw herself into his arms, so she could feel, as well as see, that he was all right.

But she wouldn't do that now, even if they'd been alone. Maybe he was right. Was she worrying too much about him? He was a big boy, a soldier...and more. He surely could take care of himself as well as she did for herself.

"It's getting late," she finally said. "I'd better head for home."

"Yes," Jock said, "but not yet. We need to make sure none of my newest best friends followed us here. If they see a nonallied deputy sheriff leaving here, that could blow everything."

"Oh." Kathlene realized she should have considered that. She had been so wound up in her concerns about the men's treatment at the ranch that she hadn't thought about what might happen next around here. "I'm parked back in the lot outside. Umm…maybe I could sneak out behind this cabin and you could…" But she couldn't figure out how to move her car in a way that she wouldn't be spotted if they were under surveillance.

"No, best thing is for us to go out and check." Jock turned to look at Ralf, and they exchanged glances that seemed to communicate volumes.

Volumes Kathlene could read, too.

"You're going to shift and go out as if you're Click," she stated.

"Exactly."

That would mean… Hell, she was a professional. The fact that Jock would have to get nude again was just part of the process, and she didn't have to react to it, even if she observed it. "I'll help," she said.

"What do you mean?"

She pointed toward the backpack that now lay on the floor near the cabin's couple of chairs, near where Ralf had left it before. "I'd brought that along on my venture, just in case you'd need to shift to get out of there. I wasn't sure how, but I figured it didn't hurt to be prepared. I saw you shift before, and even if I have to stay in here while Ralf walks the canine who looks like Click, I can assist Ralf in doing his part to help you change—pour your elixir, maybe, or get the light ready, or—"

"You've really bought into the reality that I'm a shifter." Jock's grin was huge now.

"I don't actually need assistance," Ralf added, "but I'd be glad to show you what I'm up to, step by step, so you'll be ready if you ever have to do it on your own someday."

"Great! How soon should we get started?"

"How about now?" Jock answered, and his flashing hazel eyes caught hers.

He knew what she was thinking…and he started to remove his clothes.

He made it look good.

Jock didn't bother to glance toward his aide. Ralf would know exactly what he was doing.

Teasing, tempting the hot woman who was staring at him. Not that they could do anything about sexual urges now, and he knew better than to give in to them later.

But he might as well have fun for the few minutes it took for him to shift.

True to her word, Kathlene stood beside Ralf. She held the vial that had stored the elixir, which Jock had already drunk. She knelt beside Ralf as he aimed the light toward Jock.

And watched closely, very closely, with eyes that shouted appreciation and more, as Jock finally removed the rest of his clothes.

He didn't have much time, though, to continue the silent seduction of the woman who watched him strip. The pulling began inside him, outside him along his skin, and the discomfort turned into more.

He was changing. Fast.

* * *

Kathlene watched…everything. As much as she appreciated seeing Jock's hard, bared body—and how his erection grew and pulsed as if aware of how intensely she watched it and the rest of him—she also found herself amazed and intrigued as that wonderful male body changed and contorted, shrinking in many places, growing in others, sprouting the same kind of fur that covered Click.

Click. The dog had been banished to the other room for this process. Had he seen it before? Interacted with the man who looked, when all was through, so much like the dog?

No matter. The process seemed to take forever, yet no time at all.

And in just a few minutes, it was complete.

After another short time frame, Ralf glanced at Kathlene. "It's time for our walk. Click will stay here with you. Everything okay?"

Kathlene admired how the man who had undoubtedly watched this process countless times could act so nonchalant. She looked into Ralf's dark, inquisitive eyes and said, "I'm fine. I'll be here. Go ahead."

Ralf slipped a collar around Jock's neck and attached a leash. "Okay, my friend," he said. "Let's go."

Chapter 16

*T*he area around the cabins was busier this night than
Jock had seen before. He did not know the identity of any
of those who darted between cars and into other buildings.

That did not matter.

As Ralf and he walked around the area, Jock continued to use his enhanced wolfen senses, his sense of smell,
his hearing, to determine if anyone here had also been at
the old ranch this day.

He detected no one from there.

He continued to stay at Ralf's side, sniffing the ground,
occasionally lifting his leg, doing as he would if he truly
were Click or another domesticated canine.

Ralf, above him, whispered now and then, asking if
there was anywhere Jock wanted to go, to examine more
closely.

Each time, Jock shook himself as a dog would do, sig-
nifying that the answer was no.

They remained this way for quite a while, although
Jock, in this form, was not certain how much time had
passed even with his enhanced human abilities thanks to
the elixir.

Eventually, Ralf said, "We've been around the whole place twice. Is there anything else we need to do?"

Once more, Jock shook himself. Then he pulled forward a bit on the leash that he forced himself not to resent.

He much preferred freedom while in shifted form. Freedom to roam. To be as wolfen as he desired.

But in this situation, he had to conform.

In a few more minutes, they had returned to the cabin. The cabin that still contained Kathlene...for now.

Since he had sensed no others around who could harm them, it was time for her to go home.

She would be glad.

And so would he.

They were back, on the wooden platform outside the door.

The real Click's skittering around on the bathroom floor where he'd been temporarily confined confirmed that, and so did his soft woofs.

It had taken all the self-control Kathlene possessed not to follow the man and apparent dog, not even to pull back the curtains and peek out to watch what she could, knowing they might not be in her line of sight at all.

They walked into the cabin, Ralf still holding the leash attached to the collar around Jock's neck.

"Did you see anyone?" she asked Ralf as he bent to remove the collar from around the gorgeous, wild-looking wolf.

"No, and Jock didn't sense anyone, either."

"Is that what he told you?" She couldn't help the smart-alecky question. Or was it? Despite earlier conversations in his presence, for all she knew this werewolf did actually know how to talk to his aide in English.

"He communicated it, yes." The smile on Ralf's dark-toned face appeared smug, as if he was proud of his ability to understand his shifted charge.

That charge, sitting on the floor beside Ralf, cocked his head and gave a muted bark—one that Kathlene interpreted to mean that he might choose to honor her with direct communication, too, if she earned it.

Okay, this was weird. Definitely. And yet knowing someone who shifted—and not only knowing him, but being part of his team, at least for now—was a whole lot more fun, a whole lot more intriguing, than she could ever have imagined while reading books or seeing movies or TV shows that featured shapeshifters. Fictional shapeshifters, at least in those media.

But never, ever, had she considered the fact any part of that could be real.

Till now.

"Are you going to shift back now? I mean—" She'd started aiming the question at Jock as if he would be responding directly, but she gave a short laugh and looked back at Ralf. "Will he be shifting back now?"

But Jock did in fact provide the first response. His pointed ears moved farther forward and his head nodded. He gave a short "woof" in emphasis.

"That means yes," Ralf said unnecessarily. "When Alpha Force shifters take that elixir so they don't have to rely on a full moon, they'll shift back on their own in a few hours. But like I've said, we can help them by aiming that same light on them, which quickens the process. I don't know how it works. I only know it does." He had been looking at Kathlene but now turned and looked down at Jock. "You ready to change back?"

Again his ears moved, along with a nod and muted bark.

"Good." Ralf looked around. He apparently spied his backpack in a corner along the wall, where Kathlene had seen him put it after returning the elixir container and light once Jock had shifted. Ralf approached it and pulled out the light.

"Let's go," Ralf said.

Kathlene braced herself. The amazing immediate transformation she had seen before was about to happen again.

And this time, when it was complete, Jock the man would be there.

Once again in the nude.

And also this time, neither of them, Ralf nor Jock, had told her to leave or even to look away.

She watched, feeling sorry for the tawny-silver wolf as he began writhing and moving and changing in the light, his fur receding, his body elongating…and then, very soon, it was Jock lying there on the floor, unclothed and buff and enticingly gorgeous.

You're a professional, she reminded herself—even if it was law enforcement and nothing related to what she was watching. She pasted a vaguely interested expression on her face and stood near the wall, behind Jock's head so he wouldn't see her.

Not that he'd be surprised she was still there.

"You okay, bro?" Ralf soon asked his charge.

"Yeah," Jock said somewhat breathily. Kathlene had anticipated his panting like that. That shift looked terribly uncomfortable, probably painful. "Yeah," he repeated and sat up—shielding the most intriguing parts of his body from Kathlene, but not before she had gotten a really good glimpse of them again. Now her best view was of his back, including his butt resting on the floor. His firm, amazingly great-looking butt…

Jock looked around as if he wanted to confirm her presence.

"Hi," she said when his eyes landed on her. He'd swiveled a bit on the floor—and Ralf had grabbed Jock's clothes and dumped them on his lap, hiding a lot from view.

"Hi," he said. His expression was taunting, and it became even more challenging as he stood without putting on a stitch of his clothing first. Then, without rushing, he donned the outfit Ralf had tossed to him.

If he was trying to turn her on, he was succeeding, but Kathlene was not about to give him any indication of it. Keeping her tone cool and professional, she said, "Since you didn't see or hear anyone who shouldn't be here, there's no reason I can't head back to my place now."

"That's fine," Jock said. His acknowledgment should make her feel good, feel free—and yet she experienced a pang of sorrow. He obviously didn't care that they'd be parting for the night now that he'd done his duty and ensured her safe departure.

"Tomorrow is Friday, my day off," she continued, "so I won't be at the department. We should be able to get together early and also plan what happens next. My idea? We'll meet someplace private first, maybe my home. I want to hear everything you both saw and heard at that place."

"Yeah, you'll find it interesting," Ralf said. "I think we just reached the tip of the iceberg, but anarchists? I'd say so. They definitely appear to be looking at things their own way."

"And did you achieve what you wanted to—cozying up to them, showing them that you have attitudes in common?"

"We did," Jock acknowledged. He was fully dressed now but no longer wearing the jacket that had made him appear like a hunter. He'd donned only the white T-shirt and jeans. "And I think you were right, by the way, about the ones in that darkened car. We can tell you all about what we learned tomorrow, after we've all gotten some sleep. Your place is fine."

"After that," Kathlene said, "we should go out in public again since you're still supposedly my buddy, Jock, maybe for breakfast. But after we do whatever planning we decide on, let's have a very public argument so you can stomp back to the ranch and vent about your former friend and her nasty, official-government-loving approach to the world."

Jock laughed. "Good idea. In fact, that was also what I was going to suggest."

As they'd spoken, Ralf had gone to the bathroom door and let Click loose at last. Kathlene supposed that worked well now since there were no further canines around to confuse anyone who might be watching them.

Although, after the patrol by the man and wolf a while ago, it appeared unlikely that they were under observation by the anarchists—and therefore probably by no one.

Click jumped around, leaping first on Ralf and then on Jock, his two humans…at the moment. Then he came over to sniff Kathlene again, and she patted his head.

"Great," she told Jock. "I'll be up early, so let's talk first thing. Plan on being at my place at…let's say seven o'clock?"

"Okay," Jock said. As Kathlene headed for the door, he added, "Oh, and by the way. Don't be surprised if you see a vehicle following you on your way home."

"You don't need to do that." Kathlene let exasperation pour from her tone, even though she realized she felt a bit of relief. And more. Was she really starting to accept this man's too-protective ways? No. That couldn't happen.

"Maybe not," Jock said calmly. "But like I said, don't be surprised."

He didn't have to tell her he'd be right behind her, Jock thought as he followed Kathlene in his car while she headed back to her place. But she was a cautious person.

She might be…displeased if she just happened to see someone following her, even in a car she recognized.

But one way or another, he did have to follow her.

He hardly trusted anyone.

Fellow Alpha Forcers, yes. And Kathlene? Yes, partly because she had brought Alpha Force in to investigate a situation that could be highly dangerous to a lot of people if it was as she, and now he, believed.

Those guys at the ranch? The *sportsmen?* He trusted none of them. At all. And the fact that he had checked around in shifted form and found no indication that any of them was near his cabin was a good thing, but it didn't mean Kathlene was safe.

Now that Ralf and he were potential members of their group, they might even think it'd guarantee the newcomers' joining up if the gang did something to neutralize Jock's *friend,* who was now giving him a hard time.

But the ride was seamless. As alert as Jock was, he saw no indication that anyone else on the road had any interest in Kathlene—or him, for that matter.

This late, there was little traffic so it didn't take them much time to reach her home.

And of course Jock wasn't about to let Kathlene enter that house without an escort…just in case.

He parked on the street after watching her pull down her driveway and into her garage. She waved at him, as if she figured he would be on his way.

Eventually, he would. But first he had to make sure she got into her house okay.

He didn't see her go in. She shut her garage door, and presumably that was the way she entered.

Was she okay? He went to the front door and waited for a minute or so, listening with his enhanced hearing.

Scenting the air to ensure that there were no odors of intruders wafting through her home.

Even so, he had to make certain. He canvassed her neighborhood as he stood there. No cars creeping down the street, with or without their headlights on. No neighbors apparently peering out their windows at him, and that could be either a good thing or bad. No one was watching out for Kathlene or anyone else.

And no people out in the yards or street, even, at this hour, walking their dogs.

Safe? Maybe. Probably. But even so… He reached up to ring the doorbell.

And was startled as the outside light came on and the door opened.

Kathlene stood there, one hand holding the door and the other on her slender, sexy hip.

"What are you waiting for?" she asked. "Everything's fine in here, but come on in and see for yourself."

She'd have known he was following her even if he hadn't warned her.

She always watched her surroundings, but she was especially on alert tonight after her little jaunt once that car with no lights had headed down the road.

He should have known that.

But she also realized that this guy's protectiveness never quit.

She told him now that she would wait in the kitchen while he looked through her place and assured himself all was well. As he left her there, she opened her refrigerator door and brought out a couple of bottles of beer. He didn't have to come here, and she might as well reward him.

What she wanted to reward him—and herself—with wasn't beer, of course. But inviting him to make love to her—again—was beyond the realm of rationality. Been there, done that, and despite how enjoyable it had been, it had to be a one-time event. This was not a man—or whatever—that she dared to get any further involved with.

No matter how attracted she felt toward him.

While waiting, she opened her beer and took a swig, needing the kick to slow down her thoughts—and desires. But she knew better than to think that would work.

He was only gone for a few minutes, but she heard his footsteps here and there on her hardwood floors, including upstairs where her bedroom was.

When he returned, he just stood there at the kitchen door. Looking at her with those intense, erotically enticing hazel eyes.

"Everything okay?" she asked, forcing herself to stay cool.

"More or less."

"Do you want to stay for a few minutes? Have a beer?"

"Yes," he said, "and no. Here's what I want."

In less than a heartbeat he had joined her, taken her into his arms.

And lowered his hot, teasing lips to hers.

Chapter 17

Bad idea. But Jock wasn't about to stop. Not now. Not unless Kathlene pushed him away.

At least for the moment he would revel in the feel of her curvaceous, hot body against his, the taste of sweetness and heat in her mouth.

She apparently had reservations, too, since without backing up she said, "You should go." But her words didn't match her actions. Not at all. Her lips didn't stop exploring his, nor did her tongue, and her hands roved along his back and down into his jeans, pulling him closer where he grew and ached for her.

"Later," he said. "But now… Let's go upstairs." He had been up there while checking to make sure there was no one hiding in her house. Had glanced into her bedroom and sloughed off—sort of—his memories of being in it before with Kathlene.

That had been a few moments ago. And now…

"Okay," she whispered against him. She moved away and took his hand, leading him toward the stairway before he could scoop her up in his arms and carry her.

That was fine. It seemed more by mutual consent this

way rather than some demanding guy dragging her to her room.

And he knew too well that Kathlene preferred to stay in control. Maybe that was one of the things that he liked about her. No matter how frustrating…

She was almost running now, and he smiled as he kept up with her so she wouldn't have to drag him, either, to where he actually wanted to go.

Her stairway was wide, the steps bare and polished wood with a white railing. In only a minute they were upstairs, then a short distance down the hall and into her room.

She flicked on the overhead light, but only for a moment as if to gain perspective of where her bed was: still right in the middle. And then, lights out, they were on top of the fluffy floral-print cover. He didn't wait before pulling Kathlene's shirt over her head, then reaching down to remove her slacks.

Meantime, they nearly formed a knot as she, too, stripped him. Which was fine, but only the tiniest bit unfair since she had seen him nude that night—twice. It was his turn.

When he was finally finished getting her clothes off, he could see her thanks to the dim glow radiating from the hallway. She was beautiful, every bit as lovely as he remembered. He smiled before reaching toward her breasts, beginning to caress them softly, reveling in the feel of how the initial small contact caused her nipples to bud and grow. He had to taste them, and so he did, even as he continued to touch her, to stroke her, to ease his hands downward along her warm, smooth skin until he touched her buttocks, then moved so he could touch her hot, moist core and begin stroking her there.

He loved the sound of her gasp, then followed it with

one of his own as she gently grabbed his erection and began pumping it, driving him mad with need of her.

But his mind wasn't completely gone. He stopped long enough to feel around for his pants and reach into a pocket. He pulled out a condom and handed it to her. These days, he planned ahead, just in case....

"Would you care to do the honors?" he said in a tight, raspy voice he barely recognized.

"Yes," she rasped back, and he all but moaned as she pulled the taut rubber over him.

Kathlene refused to listen to the chiding voice in her head that still repeated how sorry she would be later. She wouldn't be sorry. No, this man wasn't the right person to form a long-lasting relationship with. One way or another he'd be out of her life soon.

But for now she might as well enjoy his sexy presence.

She cried out as he moved over her, touched her again down there where she was burning with desire, and then plunged his shaft into her. He began to drive into her, in and out, making her feel as if the wholeness of her being was centered on him and what he was doing and how he was making her feel—hot and excited and needy and wanting even more...

Until she screamed out when her orgasm surrounded her, and she heard Jock, too, groan as he apparently also reached his climax.

For a long moment he perched on his arms above her, connecting with her only down below where her thoughts and feelings were entirely centered.

And then he lowered himself gently on top of her, his breathing hard and irregular as hers.

"Wow," he said softly.

"Yes, wow," she agreed.

* * *

He hadn't intended to stay the night, but after his earlier shift to ensure Kathlene's safety, followed by his check of her house and, most exhausting and rewarding, their lovemaking, he had fallen asleep beside her on her bed.

She must have moved or made a small sound, since suddenly he was awake. He became aware immediately of where he was. Who he was with.

Why he was there.

He didn't move, not at first. It struck him that being here with Kathlene in her bed, both of them sated with lovemaking, felt right.

Right? Yeah, sure. He remained all too aware that the woman was a peace officer who threw herself into danger without a moment's thought. He still wanted to protect her, whether she wanted it or not—*not* being her usual scenario.

At the moment, they had to maintain a relationship while Ralf and he fulfilled the mission for Alpha Force. But he and his aide would be heading back to Ft. Lukman as soon as they dealt with the presumed anarchists, which he hoped would be soon.

The truth that he enjoyed being here with Kathlene, loved it, in fact, didn't make any difference.

Okay. He realized that, on top of his enjoyment of their incredible physical encounters, he was somehow being swayed by her apparent ability to accept who and what he was…and he actually wasn't sure what she thought about it.

Maybe he'd ask her. Tomorrow.

For now… "Are you awake?" he asked her.

"Yes," she said. "I guess you are, too."

He heard the smile in her voice—and that was enough.

He reached for her, smiled himself as he felt her warm, naked flesh, and began making love to her once more.

* * *

The next time Kathlene awoke in the middle of the night, she was the one to check on Jock. She woke him, too, but he didn't seem to mind.

Neither did she.

A little later, still lying there, out of breath and definitely happy, she realized she could get used to this kind of impulsive, immediate lovemaking.

She also realized she had better enjoy it while she could.

Tomorrow, who knew what would happen? After all, Jock and his buddy Ralf might be about to become anarchists. If they went deeper undercover in that capacity, they might even have to stay at the old ranch.

Where Kathlene would be absolutely unwelcome, even if she wanted to go there.

Which she didn't, except as an observer.

"You okay?" Jock asked, his voice hoarse. He was lying on his back beside her. She, too, remained on her back. But, heck, she might as well milk this one night for all she could get out of it.

She was too tired, too spent, to make love again—at this moment. But a snuggle wouldn't hurt.

"I'm fine," she responded, still a bit out of breath. She turned anyway to lie on her side, her arm over his irregularly rising and falling, and utterly warm, chest. He maneuvered his arm around her and she rested her cheek on his shoulder.

She must have fallen asleep, since she jumped sometime later when her cell phone pealed its musical ringtone. She'd left it on the nightstand and immediately turned on her back and reached for it.

The caller ID said that it was Myra Enager.

Kathlene turned and got out of bed. She felt Jock reach for her but needed to take this call.

"Hi, Myra," she said, then glanced again at the phone screen. It was barely six o'clock in the morning. Myra and she were friends, but this was the first time she'd ever called this early. "Everything okay?"

"I don't know," Myra said. "I need to talk to you and wanted to see you in person. I'm in my car, just down the block from your place. Could you let me in by the back door? I'll try to avoid being seen."

"What—?"

"I'll tell you in a minute," Myra interrupted. "Okay?"

"Of course."

Kathlene pushed the button to turn off her phone, then glanced back toward the bed.

Jock was sitting up, his back resting on pillows against the headboard. He'd pulled the sheet over him so she wasn't able to see much of his body. She felt a sigh of regret, but it was better that way. "What's going on?" he asked. "Who was that?"

"Myra Enager," Kathlene responded. "She's here, or will be in a minute. She needs to talk to me." Her mind somersaulted over whether she should kick Jock out, let him stay somewhere that Myra couldn't see him or let him in on whatever this meeting was about. He'd come to town in an undercover role, so would it be okay for Myra to know he was here now?

Myra had been told that Jock was a longtime friend who was here visiting Kathlene. Maybe she wouldn't be surprised that an old buddy from way back—especially one who looked like Jock—had stayed the night.

But part of the role Jock had undertaken here was to attempt to infiltrate the anarchists. Myra and the *sportsmen* were antagonistic. Maybe he should—

He took the decision away from her. "It'd probably be better if she didn't know I was hanging out here. With my new best friends acting out the way they did against the county commissioners, I'd probably have to snap at her to stay in character and that might mean she won't confide whatever's on her mind to you." He stared into her eyes from across the room. "Is that okay with you?"

"Definitely." Kathlene had moved toward her closet where she pulled out a plaid button-down shirt and dark jeans. "But she's coming to the back door, so something must be wrong. I'll let you out the front."

"No, why don't you make coffee for the two of you and join her in the kitchen? Your living room is fairly close, and I can sneak back in there after you're settled in to hear what she says. Okay?"

Kathlene had a feeling that if she objected he would spout a bunch of reasons why his way was the only way.

But she actually thought he was right. And so she said, "Okay."

After they both hurriedly dressed, Jock hid out in the bathroom near the closed door when Kathlene let Myra Enager into the house via her back entrance. Kathlene had already started some coffee brewing, and although it smelled inviting to him he held off sneaking some out, not wanting Myra to suspect there was someone else around.

"What's going on?" he heard Kathlene say. He used his enhanced senses just a little, since she'd raised her voice a bit as if to help him to hear.

Sweet of her, but he didn't need that kind of assistance— which she probably knew. Maybe she was just nervous.

"Something awful." The other woman's tone was high and shaky.

"Well, here," Kathlene said soothingly. "Come on into the kitchen. Sit down right here at the table, and I'll get you a cup of coffee. Then you tell me everything."

There was a little shuffling of feet and chairs and whatever Kathlene put on the table. Jock again inhaled the scent of good, strong coffee, plus some milk that Kathlene must have made available to the other woman.

He cracked the white wooden door open just a little. He didn't need help to hear, but it gave him a bit more freedom to sense what was happening and to determine what, if anything, he should do next.

What he heard Myra tell Kathlene didn't stun him. It didn't even surprise him. In fact, he was even a little pleased to hear it.

What was going on just might bring his mission here to a close very soon.

Kathlene considered giving her obviously terrified friend a reassuring hug.

But all she did was remain on one of the shallow calico pillows tied to a chair by her oval wooden table and lean forward, her hands around her white coffee mug.

Myra's age-textured hand remained on the handle of her mug, shaking a little. The older woman did not look as seasoned and professional and together as Kathlene was used to seeing the county commission's chairwoman. Instead, her salon-darkened hair was in disarray and the wrinkles on her face appeared deeper, as if she hadn't used whatever age-defying lotions and makeup she usually daubed on before leaving home.

Or maybe it was whatever was on her mind that made her appear ten years older.

"All right," Myra finally said, looking directly at Kathlene's face with stressed-looking brown eyes. "Here's what's happened. Yesterday, late in the afternoon, a couple of my colleagues on the commission asked for me to call a special session today. A special *public* session, where we'll go over the same issues we've been discussing, but they'll make a couple of additional motions for us to act on."

"Does that happen often?" Kathlene aimed a sympathetic glance toward her friend. She knew Myra loved being part of the government. Until recently, Kathlene had been interested in what Myra did but hadn't been involved professionally.

Yet she had a feeling that Myra had come here this morning not just because she needed a friend, but she also needed someone in law enforcement to hear what she had to say.

Would anything they discussed help to further Jock's investigation?

It might, so she kept her voice raised a bit to make sure he could hear—not that she doubted he could.

"Not really," Myra answered. "There have been some other local issues where the commission's factions were at loggerheads, but voting always seemed to resolve them." Myra shook her head, and her lips narrowed even further. "Not this time."

"When is your meeting, then?" Kathlene asked. This was her day off. She could possibly attend but she couldn't go there in any official capacity. Just as well. The sheriff had already made it clear that all gun control and wildlife-preservation issues around there were a whole lot less important than hunting abilities. He was hardly likely to send anyone off duty there, on overtime, to look official and stave off any physical altercations potentially resulting from the commission's consideration of preservation issues, even if they followed the state's latest guidelines.

But maybe she could find a way to get someone else who wasn't so eager to take sides to go there—Tommy X, maybe?

"It'll start around 10:00 a.m.," Myra said. "And—" Her sip of coffee seemed as much to give her time to think as it was to give her a caffeine lift.

"And?" Kathlene prompted.

"And I'm damned scared," Myra practically exploded. "Things around here are definitely not normal. I...I had a visitor last night at my home, at around nine-thirty at night. Or it may have been more than one person. I don't know. But someone unscrewed the bulb from the light on my porch. That could have been done earlier, I suppose. In any event, I didn't notice until the doorbell rang and I looked out the view hole in my door. I didn't see anyone, so I opened it. And...well, no one was there. But this was."

She bent down to where she had placed her small black leather handbag on the floor and pulled out a piece of paper. It had printing on it and looked as if it could have come from any generic computer.

Kathlene reached for it carefully, touching only the edges so she wouldn't smear any fingerprints. But she had a feeling that whoever might have done this knew how to avoid being identified.

The paper had large letters on it in a font that was not unusual.

Those letters said WE KNOW WHERE YOU LIVE.

Because she knew Jock was listening, she read it out loud. And then she said to Myra, "This isn't a threat in itself, but the time and way it was delivered...well, I'm glad you contacted me. Let me take this and have it checked for prints."

There had been threats before, of course, but not specific and not aimed directly at any individual commissioner.

This was different. And even more disquieting.

As Kathlene had figured, Myra also said, "Okay, but I'll

bet you don't find any. Or the computer this was printed on, or anything about the person who came to my house."

That was probably true. But the situation—and the time—certainly made Kathlene even more suspicious.

The vehicle that had driven down the main road near the cabins and ranch last night had arrived there not long after 9:30 p.m. with its lights out, indicating whoever was inside did not want to be recognized.

"That may be," Kathlene said slowly, "but I'll have it looked at, anyway."

"And that's not all," Myra said.

Kathlene's insides were already churning. Whatever was going on with those self-proclaimed sportsmen was polarizing, and damaging, the town she had come to love. Not to mention at least one person that she cared about: Myra.

"What else is there?" She made certain that her voice was strong, not only for Jock but for herself, too. If there was something worse, she might hate to hear it, but she needed to know.

"I was scared enough last night that I called not only Tommy X but also some of my colleagues on the commission—those allied with me on the wildlife protection and gun-control issues. Wendy Ingerton, for one. She told me the same thing had happened to her. I let Tommy X know that, too."

That was a good thing. Even if Sheriff Frawley wouldn't want to hear Kathlene's concerns, Tommy X remained on the sheriff's good side despite his relationship with Myra. Or at least he had till now.

"So where do things stand now?" Kathlene asked.

"I told Tommy X to protect Wendy. He didn't like it, but I told him I was coming here."

"Good. You can stay with me till the meeting." Kathlene would have to figure out a way to sneak Jock out, but he'd understand.

"No. I'm going home to get ready for the meeting. I'm nervous, of course, and I wanted to let someone else know what was going on. If something happens to me…"

"Stay with me," Kathlene said again. "We don't know who threatened you or, really, why."

"I think the *why* is fairly clear. The *who*…well, I've got some ideas, don't you?" Myra took a long swig of coffee, then stood. "I'd like for you to come to the meeting."

"I will, but I won't be on duty."

"Your position is clearer than most, so just having you there, a deputy sheriff not aligned with those terrorists—"

"But I am just that—a deputy. I don't have much authority, and—"

"But you do have integrity. I'll feel better having you there. I'd imagine that Wendy will, too. And we'll all be happy that Tommy X will also attend. I don't want this meeting to be a showdown, but that could happen. And I intend to vote my conscience—again."

"Okay, I'll be there, officially or not." Kathlene enunciated carefully and raised her voice a little. She suspected she'd get an argument from Jock, but so be it.

Whatever happened at the meeting might help—or hinder—the outcome of his determining what the *sportsmen* were up to, as well as preventing them from harming anyone.

She hoped.

Chapter 18

Jock had taken a seat on top of the closed toilet lid. With the keenness of his hearing, he didn't need to remain at the door to hear the ongoing conversation. He'd already checked out the size of the bathroom window along the wall beside him. It would be tight, but if necessary he could fit through it. Yet even though this was the first floor the window was high, and it would be a problem to reach the ground without injury, especially in human form.

Plus, if he tried it, he'd have to be careful not to be seen by anyone in the nearest house, of similar structure to Kathlene's, not far beyond the wooden fence separating the yards. No, it would be better not to leave via the window.

He wondered if, despite Myra's initial refusal, Kathlene would insist that Myra hang out here at her house until the commission meeting was scheduled to begin. Since she'd been threatened, it would be a good idea for Myra to remain in the company of a friendly law-enforcement officer.

But if she stayed here, he'd have to leave the bathroom, and he wasn't quite sure how to finesse his presence there—especially since it was so vital that he continue to develop his alliance with the sportsmen's group.

Under these circumstances, they might expect him to do something to the commissioner, or at least let them know she was here. That was presuming that whoever had threatened her was one of the group at the ranch.

The most obvious possibilities were those guys who had shown up late yesterday, the ones Kathlene had indicated were trying to hide their presence on the roads. Had they just come from leaving the threats at Myra's and other commissioners who maintained positions against the sportsmen's? And what about the hints they'd given regarding weapons in their car? He'd have to figure out a way to ask without making it sound accusatory, just interested.

In any event, he couldn't just stay in the bathroom. If nothing else, Myra might eventually want to use the facilities and come this way. Kathlene's only other bathroom was upstairs.

More important, inaction was not in his vocabulary. He had to do something that went with his undercover role—without, of course, embarrassing Kathlene about how she'd spent her night and who she'd spent it with.

He decided it was finally time for him to magically appear at Kathlene's doorstep, too. Even though this old friend of hers was now supposedly at odds with her about something going on in her town, they'd still see each other while he was here.

His decision was underscored even before he acted when Kathlene began to push Myra the way he'd anticipated.

"Myra, please. You really should stay here with me till you're ready to head to the meeting," she insisted.

Jock waited for the commissioner's concurrence, even if it was reluctant. She was wise enough to come here in the first place, so she'd clearly also be smart in this—having somewhere safe to hang out till she had to put herself in front of the county's citizens and visitors once more. Then, no matter which side they might be on personally, the sheriff's department officers on duty would have to protect everyone including the commissioners, at least during the meeting.

He was surprised, therefore, when Myra responded, "No. Really. I'll be okay. But I need to go home now, not only to change clothes but to go over my notes and computer files so I'll be fully prepared to counter any negative arguments at the meeting."

Jock was not surprised at Kathlene's response, but he wasn't happy about it. In fact, he was downright angry. "Then I'll come with you to make sure you're okay," she said.

Didn't the woman ever avoid putting herself into dangerous situations?

Hell, he knew the answer to that.

He also knew that he, too, would be heading to Myra Enager's home.

Kathlene checked the street to ensure that there were no strangers, no occupied cars, no other apparent dangers. Then she saw Myra out the door and into her car.

She hadn't spoken to Jock yet but felt certain he knew what she was doing. Myra and she hadn't been whispering—not that the sound level would likely make much difference to Jock.

She also figured he wasn't pleased about it. Right now Kathlene rode in the passenger's seat of Myra's hybrid car. For the moment she believed she was doing everything possible to keep her friend safe.

Jock would undoubtedly have a different opinion about the safety of what she was doing.

To be fair, she should give him the opportunity to bawl her out. Not that it would make any difference.

She told Myra she needed to make a phone call.

"Sure thing," Myra said. "I'd hold my ears if I didn't need my hands to drive."

Kathlene gave the laugh she figured was expected, then pushed numbers on her phone. "Hi, Jock," she said perkily when he answered.

"What the hell are you doing?"

"Yes, it's me," she responded as if he had said something friendly rather than argumentative. Myra should only be able to hear her end of the call. "I'm going to a friend's house now, since it's my day off work, and then I'll go watch the county commissioners' meeting. Maybe we could hook up there. Are you free for lunch?"

"I'm free to wring your neck," he muttered.

"Oh, I know you'd never do that. But I have a feeling that the meeting's going to be a bit wild. Even though I'm not on duty, maybe I can help out if there's any disturbance. You could watch me in action. Of course you have before, but it'll give you even more reason to understand why I became a deputy sheriff." She glanced over at Myra. "People don't always wind up doing what it looks like they're headed for in school, do they? My buddy Jock probably thought I'd go into journalism, since that was my field of study." It actually had been—until her parents had been killed....

"Did you figure he'd wind up doing what he did?"

"You mean insurance?" She talked back into the phone. "How about you, Jock? Did you think, in school, that you'd wind up where you are now?"

"Actually, not exactly. But—"

"So there. Anyway, we'll talk later." She pressed the button to hang up. She didn't really want to hear any more of his criticism. She might not be able to avoid it later, but for now she'd do as she wanted.

Help her friend.

And her town.

He followed them, of course. As unobtrusively as possible.

She should have at least allowed him to enter and check out the nice, huge house that was apparently Myra's, since they pulled up the driveway and into the garage. For now he remained in his car, listening for any disturbance. Presumably, Kathlene had brought her service weapon with her, just in case.

She didn't call out, didn't call him, and nothing sounded strange.

Consequently, he hung out for only a few more minutes. Then he knew where he had to go.

He called Ralf on the way. "I'd like for Click and you to go observe the street where Kathlene has gone to protect her friend on the county commission."

"Yes, sir," Ralf said.

"At ease, Sergeant." Jock couldn't help smiling, if only a little.

"Where are you off to?"

"I'm about to visit my newest best friends again. I have a feeling that, after the warnings handed out last night, this county commissioners' meeting might be the ignition for whatever they have in mind—unless, of course, everything turns around and the vote goes exactly as they want."

"Even then," Ralf began.

"Yeah, even then. I saw their attitude last night, and I don't think these guys are going to suddenly settle down and become nice, calm, law-abiding hunters and all-around citizens."

"Me, neither. You...you want to shift?"

"I will, but not now. Besides, I want Click to hang out with you for now, and you know what a bad idea having another dog around that looks like him, during daylight and with everything else going on, would be."

"Got it." Ralf paused. "Keep in touch, Jock."

Jock grinned. "Yes, sir."

As Jock had anticipated, the sportsmen weren't just sitting around drinking beer—or even, at this hour of the morning, coffee. He had no problem checking in with the guy at the gate, and when he parked and headed toward the ranch house he saw a lot of them around talking. They weren't even at the shooting range engaged in target practice.

What were they up to?

He was one of them now...kind of. He could just ask what was going on.

He saw tall Hal with the receding hairline almost immediately. The guy was decked out in a hunting jacket, as were most of the men around the house and parking area.

Jock approached and asked, "What's going on?"

"There's another of those damned public county commissioners' meetings today. Better than their private ones, but they're still trying to tell us what to do, and since it didn't work last time they're going at it again. We're heading there to...make a statement."

"Good idea," Jock said. "I'll come, too." He pretended to hesitate. "But what'll we do if the same damned thing happens and they enact more laws about our hunting the wildlife that was put on this earth for men to shoot and kill?" He hated even to say stuff like that, but it was necessary here for the role he was playing.

Hal smiled. It was the kind of smile that made Jock's skin crawl. "Oh, we've got some plans to take care of it."

"What kind of plans?" Jock pasted an eager grin on his face. "I want in."

"Good. We'll need all of our followers to get involved. But we're just in the planning stage right now. You'll be filled in at the appropriate time."

"Soon?" Jock asked.

"Yeah, real soon."

Jock stood there for a few minutes. The crowd seemed to ebb and flow, with men joining one group, and then some moved on to form another. With all the people, all the activity, Jock figured everyone would be too preoccupied to pay much attention to him. A good thing.

He began walking around the ranch, moving with the crowds as if he was part of them.

He grinned as he saw men massing together and working each other up into an angry frenzy. Who dared to tell them what to do? He was with them, shared their mindset. Or so he pretended.

He walked among them and between the buildings as if attempting to meet and support them all. How many were there? Dozens, yes. A hundred, maybe?

And finally, as most began moving toward the front of the property to prepare to go to the commissioners' meeting, he found his opportunity. He headed carefully, by himself, toward the shooting range.

There were a few remote buildings near the outdoor range area that intrigued him. Was that where the weapons brought by the guys who'd driven that SUV in the dark were stored? Were there more than what they had brought?

And were they regular hunting rifles, or something more?

Plus, where did they keep the C-4 explosives that he'd smelled?

For now it made sense to explore this property in human form. A canine would be way out of place. But an undercover military man worked out just fine…he hoped. And he'd been close enough to the main ranch building itself to pretty much rule it out as a storage area—no concentrated scent of gunpowder or anything else close by, although he could smell some near the sportsmen themselves when they were armed.

He kept his pace easy, as if he had nothing on his mind except perhaps finding a bathroom. Too bad it was morning, though. The cover of darkness would be preferable. At least the back of the property, near the shooting range, hadn't been cleared of all trees, so there was some cover available.

The double door to the first black metal shed Jock came to closest to the shooting range was open. That suggested all the sportsmen were welcome there. It wasn't what he was looking for. Nor was there any scent of interest.

He stopped and listened. Lots of voices were audible to his enhanced senses—near the front of the place. A pep rally of sorts was going on now.

That didn't mean he was alone here, though. He stopped and focused his enhanced senses. Without moving his head, he sniffed the air for any scents of people nearby but smelled none. He listened but heard no one around.

Even so, he would remain cautious.

He moved onward as if he hadn't a concern in the world, just a curious man checking out a place he'd hardly visited before. And of course he was interested in the shooting range and practicing there someday.

The next shed he reached was open, too. But there was also what appeared to be the ranch's old stable a short distance away, large and decrepit and hidden among tall bushes and trees, as if it had been allowed to fall into disrepair. And yet when he made his way there, its most visible doors that faced the interior area of the ranch were locked.

That made him all the more determined to get inside. This could be what he was looking for.

He edged his way around to the back and found another door, a single, sliding one. Carefully, he tried it... and it moved. Did that mean the stable contained nothing of interest, too? He believed he should check this one out—partly because of the sharper smells he sensed. Different kinds of gunpowder? He ducked inside and closed the door behind him.

No horses. Not now. But several of the stalls were filled with boxes. It was also dark inside. All windows had been boarded up, which was a good thing. He couldn't be seen.

He pulled his phone out of his pocket and turned on its light, shielding it to ensure that it remained dim as he checked the place out.

The closest boxes had rifles in them. Regular hunting rifles, the kinds that real sportsmen might use. Which frustrated Jock. He knew these guys weren't real sportsmen, but he needed proof.

A short while later, he found himself grinning as he checked through other boxes at the bottom of the piles of crates where the regular rifles were stored.

They were semiautomatic rifles, M-16s, like the military used, and there were a lot of them.

He wondered if they might even have been stolen from the military. He'd have to check.

Could they be used for hunting? Maybe. But why so many? And why were they hidden?

A couple of boxes also held handguns, Berettas and SIG Sauers.

Why would ordinary hunters need them?

Answer? They wouldn't.

Plus, he did, in fact, find some crates that were sealed, and yet he smelled the plastic scent that told him they contained C-4.

Jock had found what he needed. Maybe not all of the guns he'd found were illegal, but he'd no doubt that their collection was not for any law-abiding, neutral purpose.

And now it was time to go back to playing his role of supporting the anti-government position of these supposed sportsmen.

He cautiously edged his way back out of this shed, silently applauding Kathlene.

By contacting Alpha Force, she may have saved a lot of lives.

It was time now to head to the Clifford County Building. According to Myra, the meeting was scheduled to begin in about half an hour.

"Are you ready?" Kathlene asked. Myra had changed into a dark suit and white blouse, one that looked even more professional than the charcoal outfit she had worn to the last meeting. Kathlene wasn't sure whether Myra's attitude had shaved ten years off her appearance or if the makeup she had applied, along with her determined expression, had done the job, but at least for now Myra looked ready to face anything.

"I sure am," Myra responded.

"Then let's go."

Once again Myra drove, since Kathlene had left her car at her place.

"So tell me what the agenda is today," Kathlene said, although she had a pretty good idea.

"About the same as last time. We'll be talking about those gun-control laws that were passed in closed chambers after the last meeting. There've been some complaints, some challenges to the point of order, that claim statutes passed in private, without the opportunity of citizen comment and discussion, are not valid. Our county counsel will be talking about that, disputing it, but even so, we on the commission have decided to take that vote again. In front of everyone. After allowing the discussion, including any threats, tacit or explicit."

"Really?" Kathlene wished now that she was on duty that day. She would have much preferred being in uniform, acting officially to help control whatever issues were bound to come up with those discussions…like the threats. "Are you all nuts?"

Myra laughed. "No, but this is important around here—especially with that element that's come to town that argues against everything. They don't really have a say—but they were undoubtedly involved in the threats against me and the others. I appreciate your letting me stay with you before while I felt discombobulated, but I'm fine now. They can't hurt me—even if they wound or kill me."

"What?"

"I mean, it's more hurtful to me to cower and give in. And I think I'm not the only commissioner who feels that way. Wendy's said the same thing. Besides, Tommy X will be there officially. So will the sheriff himself, I've been promised."

"But…er, Sheriff Frawley…" Kathlene seldom was at a loss for words, but she knew her commanding officer at least favored the *sportsmen* and might actually be one of them.

Myra had stopped at a stop sign and glanced toward Kathlene. "If you're trying to say that your boss is as much of an outspoken creep in favor of guns and killing people and protected animals as well as breaking state laws as the rest of them, I'm not going to argue with you. But this has to be resolved. Now. So are you with me?"

Kathlene felt certain this was not going to lead to anything good—not until the anarchists were shown to be what they were and brought down.

But she had to answer the question the way she believed. "Yes," she said, "I'm with you. But Myra—"

"It'll all work out," Myra interrupted. "You'll see."

Kathlene knew her friend was right—but not for the reason Myra thought.

She wondered where Jock was at that moment.

And whether she would see him at the commissioners' meeting.

Jock had made some calls on his way to pick up Ralf.

The most important was to Major Drew Connell.

The others had been to fellow Alpha Force members, shifters like him.

It was time. He knew things were coming to a head around here. He would soon need backup.

It would be dangerous. He knew that, and he made it clear to Drew and the others.

This group of anarchists—and, yes, he felt certain now that was what they were—were out for blood. Maybe things would go their way in the upcoming session, but if they didn't, they would want to exact revenge on those who dared to oppose them.

Like Commission Chair Myra Enager.

And those who supported their opponents—like Deputy Kathlene Baylor.

Jock was not about to let anything happen to either of them.

Especially Kathlene.

Now he pulled into the area behind the cabins he shared with Ralf and Click, got out and went inside the first one.

His aide was there with his cover dog. "I just took Click for a walk," Ralf said. "I'm ready to go."

"Good. Let's hurry."

They got to downtown Cliffordsville in ten minutes, and Jock drove the city streets for a short while before finding a place to park.

By the time they got to the County Administration Building's main entrance, a huge crowd had gathered there. The sportsmen? Yes. But the town's entire population also seemed to be heading inside.

For genuine interest, or to witness a showdown?

It didn't matter. Nor did Jock give a damn whether they got seats in the assembly room.

They would be there.

He didn't see Kathlene at first as Ralf and he joined the crowd heading to the same location. But when they got inside, he noticed her right away. She sat at the end of a row in the middle of the room.

Two empty seats were beside her, and she appeared to be defending them.

Her gorgeous blue eyes met his nearly immediately, as if she'd been watching for him. She smiled and waved Ralf and him in her direction.

When they eased their way through the crowd to Kathlene's side, she stood, grabbed his hand for a quick squeeze, then motioned toward those chairs.

"I've been saving these for you," she said.

Kathlene pushed back a little as Jock and Ralf edged by her to the seats she'd kept empty, with effort, for them. Jock faced her as he slid by. His chest, in a navy T-shirt, just touched the tips of her breasts that were covered by the dressy blouse she had quickly donned over slacks for this outing. His quick, meaningless touch made her insides tingle—with relief, she told herself. She was glad he was here. Ralf, too.

She hadn't been positive they would come because it wasn't exactly within their cover here to observe the local government. Since they'd attended the previous meeting, maybe being here today would feel like too much.

On the other hand, Jock had apparently been doing fairly well in establishing himself as a potential member of the sportsmen, and a whole bunch of them were here. The guys who'd mostly come dressed in hunting jackets like Nate Tisal, and who hung out with him, were part of that group.

Sitting near her might not be Jock's best choice. On the other hand, ostensibly knowing her was what had brought him to town in the first place. He could always hold a public argument with her if that turned out to be in the best interests of their investigation.

Even if she'd hate it.

Ralf took the vacant seat farthest from her. Jock sat beside her.

"Hi," she said. "Good to see you."

"Likewise." But his tone wasn't especially friendly. She understood. In the role he had taken on, he was now supposed to be pulling away from her as part of the sportsmen's group.

But despite recognizing, and even admiring, his acting ability, she couldn't quite keep a pang of hurt from stabbing her.

She considered how she'd react if who he was pretending to be was real, what someone in her position—what *she*—would say to her soon-to-be-former friend.

Before she figured it out, she heard a stirring through

the audience and looked up. The seven county commissioners were taking their places at the table facing the onlookers. With them was Mayor Laurence Davonne.

The show was about to begin.

She hazarded a glance toward Jock. He was looking at her, his stare hard and challenging and unfriendly.

She knew now how someone in her position, how she, would feel when the person she had presumably thought of as a longtime friend had backed away. Maybe even turned on her.

"Jock," she began.

But she got no further. "Hello, everyone, and welcome," said the mayor. "Let's get started."

Jock gave a decisive nod in the direction of the front as if commanding Kathlene to pay attention.

Feeling irrationally hurt at his attitude, Kathlene nevertheless obeyed.

Chapter 19

Under other circumstances, Jock would have reached over and taken his *friend* Kathlene's hand.

The tension in the room was almost palpable. Everyone stared at the people in front, and the undercurrent of grumbling, especially loud to Jock but clearly discernible to everyone else, made the mayor speak even more directly into the microphone in his hand.

Even though Kathlene wasn't on duty, two people in uniforms similar to hers stood at the doors, arms crossed. One Jock recognized as her friend, Senior Deputy Tommy X. He didn't know the other one, a young woman. Would they be able to keep the peace?

Surely this crowd wasn't going to get out of hand right here and now…he hoped.

Jock shot a look toward Ralf. His aide's face was placid, as if all was fine.

And in fact, if Jock had really been recruited into the sportsmen and in turn convinced his friend to join, all would, in fact, have seemed fine.

Even with a buddy like Kathlene. He knew he had to act as if their friendship was fraying. It was damned hard to put on an act like that, when what he wanted to do was to wrap his arms around her and usher her from this room and all of the controversy and potential for danger being initiated here.

But he had a role to maintain.

He hadn't had a chance to tell her what he'd found yet. Maybe that was just as well—for now. He'd let her in on it when he could, but for the moment, for her protection, it might be better if she wasn't aware that additional evidence supported her theory.

The mayor, standing near the end of the table with the commissioners mostly behind him, had started to explain the reason for this assembly of the county commissioners so soon after the last one. "I requested the meeting," Mayor Davonne said, "because of how important I think it is for all aspects of our government to be transparent, to be open and aboveboard." He turned slightly as if trying to solicit the commissioners' opinions.

Kathlene's friend Myra had pasted a completely blank expression on her face. A couple of the others were nodding, including the man whose name card on the table in front of him reminded Jock he was Commissioner Grabling.

Not Commissioner Ingerton, though. She sat right beside Myra Enager. From this distance, her face seemed pale, her expression stoic yet scared, as if she expected someone to hit her. With all of the people present in this room, Jock could not be certain he'd picked out her scent from the rest, but he'd little doubt that, if he were closer, he would distinguish the smell of her fear.

"Now you all know," the mayor said, "that things were rather out of order at the last meeting. It was dissolved, and the commissioners went off by themselves and voted on some of the matters before them. Before *us*."

"Now, just a minute, Mr. Mayor." Myra had stood and moved to speak into the microphone without taking it.

Davonne pulled it away, turning his back as he continued to talk. "Point of order," he said. "I have the floor."

"But this is a meeting of the commissioners of Clifford County," Myra shouted so she could be heard. "You are an official of the City of Cliffordsville."

The mayor ignored her. "All sessions where matters of public importance are to be voted on should be held in front of our citizens. That didn't happen, and so I requested—no, demanded—that this new meeting be held. The commission should vacate whatever was decided in private chambers before. We need to ensure that laws enacted that affect all, or a significant part of our citizenry, be discussed and voted on in public."

"Mr. Mayor," Myra said. "We acted in good faith. And—"

"Excuse me, Madam Chairwoman," the mayor said smoothly. "Let me continue."

Interesting, Jock thought. Maybe he had a point.

Or would this situation be different if the laws to be discussed in private and potentially enacted did not affect those who might be prone to violence?

If all that happened was to keep hunting laws as they were, Jock might not like it personally but it wouldn't necessarily be inappropriate.

Even failing to enact stricter gun-control laws might be acceptable. That was definitely a sore subject in many places in this country.

But the county commissioners had acted in what Jock—and he assumed others, too—considered to be good faith to adopt local laws that followed and clarified for local enforcement those their state had recently passed to affect everyone who lived within its borders.

Feeling a stirring beside him, Jock glanced toward Kathlene. She was biting her lower lip. She looked ready to spring up and chew out the mayor, too.

Maybe it was out of character—or maybe not. He reached over and took her hand.

She looked shocked as she glanced back at him. And then she seemed to relax, if just a little.

She nodded slightly, as if he had offered her an explanation of his actions. And then she sat still once more.

This was such a travesty, Kathlene thought. This place, Cliffordsville, Clifford County, was her home now. And yet the mayor was acting as if he wasn't an elected official but a dictator.

But Jock was right. If nothing else, what was happening here this morning might cause a reaction in the people she believed to be anarchists. She could be proven correct. Vindicated.

But more important, it would then be time for Jock and Ralf to fix things around here. And she would help.

Somehow, whether he liked it or not, she would remain on Jock's team for that.

To the extent possible—and she realized how difficult it might be—she would stay by his side.

The mayor continued to speak for a while. Was this a kind of local equivalent of a filibuster? He didn't seem inclined to cede the floor for anything.

Not until Myra faded back and Commissioner Grabling stood and walked up beside him.

"We very much appreciate your position, Mr. Mayor," the thin, nearly bald guy in the plaid suit said. "In fact, let me be the first on the commission to say that I, too, believe that our vote in secrecy is not effective. We can all vote the same way as we did then, of course, but we need public comment first. Anyone?"

He looked out over the sea of people.

Kathlene looked around, too, and noticed that her boss, Sheriff Melton Frawley, had arrived, and so had Undersheriff George Kerringston. They remained near the door where Deputy Betsy Alvers stood, one of those on duty today.

Still, Kathlene was glad. The more law-enforcement personnel who were here and obvious, the less this place was likely to get out of hand. She hoped.

Although she wasn't certain what Sheriff Frawley's position would be on that, or on what was being discussed.

Kathlene wasn't surprised when the first person to stand was Tisal. The tall, hefty man had come in his hunter's jacket, as had many of his friends. He hurried onto the stage and took the microphone from Grabling.

Kathlene hazarded a glance at Jock. His expression, as he stared toward the man, looked pleased. Until he looked back at her, and for an instant she could read anger in his gaze, and she knew that, despite what other people who might catch it might think, it wasn't really aimed at her.

She didn't allow herself to smile.

"Thank you, Commissioner Grabling. And Mayor Davonne. My name is Nate Tisal. I'd just like to say that I, and some of my friends, came here to Clifford County temporarily at first, just to meet up and engage in some sporting activities like target practice and hunting. We've found we really like it here and want to stay. But I have to say that what's going on here, at this meeting, is important to us. We've discussed it as a group. We're very concerned not only about where and how new laws are passed, but also the fact that there are new laws at all. Any laws can be too much if they restrict citizens' rights. Yes, we understand that the mayor's in charge of the city, and the commissioners are in charge of the larger county, but none of them, no one, should be in charge of the populace. And so, having this open forum, ensuring that any vote that's taken is in front of all of us—well, we really appreciate it."

Kathlene again looked swiftly toward Jock. Tisal had done it—nearly. He had all but admitted that he and his group were anarchists, against any kind of laws or government.

That in itself didn't make them dangerous. And yet their engaging in target practice—and in setting off the explosives she had heard—seemed to vindicate her, show that her position was correct.

Were they dangerous, though? She believed so, but so far they hadn't demonstrated it.

Unless, of course, some of them were behind the threats sent to Myra and at least one of her fellow commissioners—and Kathlene felt sure that was the case.

Myra must have thought so, too. She rose suddenly once more and placed herself firmly beside the man who now held the microphone. She grabbed his arm, apparently startling him, since he didn't yank it away.

"Thank you, Mr. Tisal," she said, and somehow managed to take the microphone into her own hand. "And thank you, Mr. Mayor. As I mentioned before, this is a meeting of the Clifford County Commissioners, and I am its chairperson. We do appreciate the opinions of our citizens, and our potential citizens like you, Mr. Tisal. We normally do like to hold all of our meetings in public to get citizens' comments. This time, though, considering how our last meeting fell apart, we decided to act in private. We regret that some of our county's citizens are unhappy about that, and we will be glad to take a new vote—although I don't think that the results will change. I can see why some people might think otherwise. You see, a few of us, myself included, have received some very frightening threats that make us fear for our lives. Now, I'm not accusing anyone in particular, but considering the timing and what went on at the last meeting—and what's gone on so far here—I believe that anyone who is uncomfortable with our local government and how we enact laws or anything else, doesn't need to come to our meeting or even stay here." She turned to glance at the mayor, then at Tisal and then at Sheriff Melton Frawley. "So who here, in this room, is ready to admit they issued those threats?" She looked down into the audience, and her gaze stopped in the area populated by men in hunting jackets. And then she again looked at Tisal. "Who's first?" she goaded.

Tisal was not at all polite as he wrested the microphone back into his possession. "I think you are accusing us, Commissioner. Without any proof. You represent the government here in Clifford County. Do you think it's any wonder that I, and my friends, are not fond of the government—or you?"

His turn to look down at his gang, who all stood and started leaving the room.

"We like it here, even if we don't like you," Tisal continued. "You can be sure that we will stay here, at least for a while. On our own terms. And you can certainly expect some changes around here very soon—to your government and otherwise."

The sportsmen were gone quickly. And among them were Jock and Ralf, who hadn't even bothered to excuse themselves as they edged out of their seats around her.

Which was only appropriate under the circumstances, Kathlene thought. Even though she wanted to talk to Jock. Maybe even receive a hug of reassurance that all would be well.

But he was doing as he must in his undercover role.

He would remain safe. He had to. But she felt almost desperate to talk to him. Surely they would find a way to stay in touch.

The citizens who were still there were mostly familiar-looking to Kathlene. Myra, again in charge of the microphone, told her fellow commissioners that it was finally time to discuss in public the measures they had passed in private before.

She looked pale to Kathlene, and scared.

Kathlene looked toward the door where Sheriff Frawley, Undersheriff Kerringston and Deputy Alvers stood. Most of the sportsmen had exited that way, and none of the officers had followed.

Was that a good thing?

No one else in the audience seemed inclined to speak. There was obvious tension on the stage where the commissioners remained, particularly when they took their vote.

The matters before them passed. Again. In public.

Unsurprisingly, no one looked thrilled.

And as they finally followed the crowd out of the assembly room, Kathlene felt her phone in her pocket.

Did she dare call Jock?

No. That might only increase the danger to him. But he had assets, methods his new allies couldn't possibly know about.

He would be safe.

He would come back to her—temporarily, of course. But despite his dangerous undercover role, he would stay alive.

Wouldn't he...?

Ralf drove Jock to the ranch. On the way the two of them mostly discussed their strategy.

"I'm not sure how long it'll take for the rest of the Alpha Force team assigned to this situation to get here," Jock said. "They've been on alert, so I doubt it'll take long, especially since they can get a military jet to fly them into Billings or a closer small airport."

"Meantime, we're sportsmen, all in a huff because the county commissioners ignored what our leader, Tisal, had to say." Ralf jutted out his lower jaw and nodded his head. "We'll join up with our fellow sportsmen and grumble and...well, whatever."

"Exactly," Jock said. "Whatever. Or at least we'll get to see what their *whatever* is, hopefully in time to give a heads-up to the rest of the Alpha Force team before they arrive so we can plan in advance how to handle the sportsmen. We may not be able to stall them from starting their *whatever,* but we'll be able to keep our eyes on that weapons cache to make sure no one gets into them, at least not before Alpha Force can take over."

"Maybe we can lock the stable down," Ralf said, "and even, if necessary, destroy it. It's in bad enough condition that it shouldn't be hard to set it on fire."

"Maybe," Jock agreed, "but I'd rather have its contents available as evidence—and not destroy any people along with it, either."

"You're right, of course, sir." Ralf smiled. And then he grew more serious. "Too bad we don't really know what they're up to."

"Yeah. And it'd sure be easier for our Alpha Force members to deal with if those sportsmen stay on the ranch till nightfall. And that might make sense if they intend attacks on civilians. Why not do it under cover of darkness?"

"Exactly," said Ralf.

"Let's hope that's what they have in mind," Jock said. "That would make it a whole lot easier for shifted Alpha

Force members to shut them down." He intended to take
on Tisal himself. But in any event, no matter what precau-
tions the sportsmen were taking, no matter what kind of
opposition they anticipated, an attack by a pack of wolves
would not likely be what they prepared for.

Once again, Ralf and Jock were admitted onto the ranch
grounds with hardly a glance by the guard. They were now
accepted members, which could only help.

They immediately parked and began mingling among
the crowd on the grounds of the ranch house and around
the firing range. Jock heard a lot of angry grumbles, in-
termixed with mention of the talk Tisal was about to give.

Jock's mind seldom left Kathlene and what she was
up to. She had come to this area nearly every time he had
gone undercover here.

He understood that she believed she was doing the right
thing to keep civilians safe.

Even as she endangered herself.

Just in case, he had called her briefly before, while they
drove. She had sounded happy to hear from him but he cut
her off quickly. "You need to go home," he'd said.

"But—"

"Please, just do it. I promise you'll be included in our
handling of the situation. But I can't explain everything.
Not now. Just know that I've found some evidence that I'll
try to fill you in on later."

There had been a silence. And then she'd said, "Okay.
I'm heading home...for now."

That, at least, was something. Once he learned what the
plans were around here, he would figure out a good excuse
to leave temporarily, go and find her—and take her along
when he met up with the Alpha Force unit as they arrived.
Kathlene could definitely provide good background information to his teammates. She could work with their aides,

do as they did, mostly observing and being ready to assist their shifted superior officers.

Stay with them—and remain safe.

It was midafternoon by the time Tisal had his sportsmen all assemble in the courtyard behind the ranch house where barbecues had previously been set up. Now chips and beer made the rounds but nothing more substantial.

Except what the crowd heard.

They still mostly wore hunting jackets over jeans. There were a lot of them—around sixty, if Jock's count was correct. He'd overestimated before thanks to their moving around the property so much, which was probably a good thing. He was sure the guys he had overheard talking about how much they despised government were here, and so, undoubtedly, were the ones who'd arrived at this ranch with a dark SUV containing weapons, even if he couldn't pick any of them out of the crowd.

But there certainly were enough of them present to wreak a whole lot of damage if they used the weapons of terrorists.

Tisal stood on top of a picnic table, and everyone quieted down and watched him expectantly.

"Did you hear what those damned county commissioners said today, my friends?" Tisal shouted.

"Yeah!" came the response that was nearly in unison.

"Wasn't it bad enough that there were already laws in place that supposedly told us what to do with our guns and hunting and other things important to us?"

"Yeah!"

"And now they're imposing even more governmental restrictions on us. Saying that we are even more limited in our ability to shoot game that should be available to us. Thinking that they have rights to tell us what to do, when we're the ones who should have rights."

"Yeah!"

"Well, that's not gonna happen. Not more restrictions. No laws should apply to us, anyway, and no one should attempt to foist any more on us, right, my friends?"

"Yeah!"

It wasn't as if Jock hadn't seen other maniacs get crowds stirred up by using their dynamics, the psychology of groups aroused by outspoken individuals. Even though he attempted to be low-key in nearly all he did to keep the secret part of his identity completely hidden, as a college student years ago, and even once he had joined the military, he had observed how crowds worked now and then. Plus, there had been enough in the media about revolutions throughout the world to underscore how groups of people working together fed off one another to get riled into action.

But here, on this small ranch in the middle of nowhere, the dynamics seemed as potent as some huge crowds with common goals.

Something was going to happen in little Clifford County. Something dangerous to its populace. Something in which those dangerous weapons would be used.

Unless Alpha Force could stop it.

"You think we're going to be allowed to leave here easily?" Ralf whispered into his ear as Tisal continued his cheered-on rant.

"Of course," Jock whispered back. "Just play along."

They stayed until Tisal had finished. The man's plans were not explicit, but he did make it clear that they would show these miserable locals tonight that they could not mess with men who had absolute rights to freedom.

The crowd started to disperse. It was time for Jock to make his play.

He couldn't reach Tisal, who was surrounded by his admirers and laughing along with their enthusiasm.

But Tisal's peon Hal was at the fringe of the crowd. Jock, motioning to Ralf, approached him.

"That was so outstanding!" Jock exclaimed to Hal. "I never thought there were others who hated restrictions as much as I did—except for my friend Ralf, here." He nudged his aide. "But I always figured I might get so mad someday that I'd take a stand. Fight, no matter what the consequences." He paused. "You know, to prepare for it I've been collecting some pretty special weaponry, though I have to dismantle and disguise it if I fly or otherwise get subject to some government jerks looking over my things. We left what we've got in the cabins where we're staying here. I'm not sure what Tisal has in mind, but a couple of AK-47s and an Uzi won't hurt."

"Really? Well, yeah, go get them," Hal said. "I'm not sure if we need them or if there'll be any questions if you leave right now, but extra stuff might come in handy."

Extra? That did imply the existence of what Jock had found but wasn't exactly an admission. Not that it mattered.

"Just tell the guard to call me if there's any problem," Hal finished.

"Sure thing," Jock said. "We'll be back soon. Looking forward to being part of whatever happens tonight."

Sure enough, they were permitted to leave.

Only when Ralf drove them through the gate and they got on the road away from the ranch did Jock breathe a sigh of relief.

"To the cabins first," he told Ralf. "To get Click."

"Not our collection of imaginary weapons?"

"Well, those, too." Jock grinned. And then he grew more somber again. "Next stop will be Kathlene's. We'll go pick her up. By then we should have an update about the progress of our Alpha Force teammates—and where we'll need to go pick them up, too."

It was going to be a long—and eventful—night.

Chapter 20

At home, alone and waiting, Kathlene entered the kitchen she had fallen in love with when she had first bought this house yet had hardly ever used for cooking large meals and entertaining. It contained a stove with two ovens, an island in the center for food preparation, a state-of-the-art microwave and a side-by-side metallic refrigerator, all synchronized by the pale wood of the cabinets that matched the oval table, and the yellow tile counters and floor.

She had most recently cooked breakfast for Jock and her here, and then had brewed coffee when Myra was visiting. But the room definitely wasn't used as much as she had initially planned.

She employed the fridge and microwave the most, depending on fruit and veggies and prepackaged meals for herself. She had no time for fussing over food.

Deputy sheriffs had very little time of their own, since even when off duty they could be called in for emergencies. And despite how small Clifford County was, it seemed to have more than its share of car accidents and vandalism and even thefts and robberies.

Now she sat on a stool at the island in that kitchen,

staring around the room as if it belonged to a stranger. She had made herself a cup of herbal tea after heating the water in the microwave. She'd considered something stronger, something with alcohol, but she needed all her wits about her.

Tonight was key in the potential showdown that had started months ago, that had haunted her, frightened her. Made her stronger, even as she had reached out for help.

She sat still, using all of her strength to remain there, sipping tea while wanting to scream. To act.

To be with Jock, one of the men who had come here because of her quest for assistance in dealing with this potentially horrible situation.

The man, yet more than a man.

Was he learning anything now that would help in the upcoming fight? For she felt certain there would be a fight. The anarchists seemed to be spoiling for one. Maybe they had come to small, remote Clifford County because they thought they could win here, could use it as a hopping-off place to take over the state. The country. The world.

Or maybe her imagination was just working overtime in her fear for her friends and her adopted hometown.

She thought about her parents, and how she had lost them to those hoodlums who had robbed their convenience store and shot them.

No, she would not allow the bad guys to win, no matter who they were, or how many, or—

Her phone rang. She snatched it from her pocket. Was Jock checking in?

But no, the caller ID said it was Myra.

"Hi," Kathlene said. "Are you okay?"

A short, ironic laugh was the response. "That's exactly what I was going to ask you."

Kathlene's turn to laugh, but only a little. "I'm fine, but

really concerned about what's going on. I was just considering a drive to the sheriff's station to check out how things are around there."

"No need," Myra said. "I happen to have a senior deputy here who just left the department a little while ago. He wanted to check on me, too."

"Tommy X? Let me speak with him."

She heard a mumbling away from the phone, and then, "Kathlene? You okay?"

Once again Kathlene smiled. "That's a pretty common question tonight. I'm glad you're keeping watch over Myra."

"Me, too. I'm also heading to Wendy's soon to check on her. I really didn't like how things went at the meeting earlier. Combined with those written threats—well, I tried to get Melton's attention while I was still on duty but he didn't seem concerned."

No, he wouldn't. But Kathlene didn't want to tell Tommy X her suspicions about the sheriff and his leanings and the possible confirmation she'd learned about from Jock. And Kathlene also didn't want him asking questions about her visiting friends that she wouldn't want to answer.

Instead, she said, "I wondered about that. I get the impression that Sheriff Frawley may have some sympathy for the positions those sportsmen have taken against additional hunting laws."

"Maybe, but I think there's more to those sportsmen than simply wanting to go shoot some animals."

"It sure sounded like it tonight," Kathlene agreed. "We'll just all have to be on our guard, especially our county commissioners. I'm glad to hear that you're checking on them." She hesitated, trying to figure out what to say next. "My friends are going to be leaving town soon,

I think, and once they're gone I'll be able to help out even more."

At least that told Tommy X, her true long-term friend in this area, that she was on his side, the county's side, but had some distractions at the moment.

If he only knew what those distractions were...

Her doorbell rang, and her heart leaped into her throat. She made herself calm down just a little as she got off her stool and started walking from the kitchen to the hall toward the front door. "I've got to run now, Tommy X. I'm really glad Myra and you called and that everyone's okay." For now. "My friends just arrived." She hoped. Oh, did she hope. Who else could be at her door?

The anarchists?

As she finished saying goodbye, she stopped at the small bureau near the entryway that had a tall mirror on top and reached into the back of the top drawer. She pulled out the Glock she used on the job, checked it quickly to ensure that it was loaded, then walked up to the door. She looked out the peephole.

And almost melted in relief.

She had told Tommy X the truth. Jock and Ralf had arrived.

She returned the gun to its drawer, pulled open the door and smiled. "Hi. Come in," she said loudly. But in case any neighbors—or sportsmen—were around listening, she said more softly, "I want to hear everything you did tonight."

They both entered. If Kathlene hadn't known better, she could have assumed they truly were part of the sportsmen-anarchists. They wore hunting jackets over their casual outfits.

Before she shut the door, Jock said loudly, "We just have a few minutes. Some errands to run, including heading back to our cabins soon."

When they were all inside and the door had been closed and locked, Jock said, "There's a lot going down tonight. I want you with us. We're heading back to the cabins, ostensibly to pick up the wonderful weapons I promised our fearless leaders at the ranch. But we're not going to be alone there, and I want you to be with us when we meet the people who're showing up."

"Who's there?" Kathlene asked.

"Alpha Force."

Without moving from the doorway, Jock explained to Kathlene that he'd found some pretty major, potentially lethal weapons at the ranch. After that, anticipating the tone, if not the results, of the meeting before, he had already called in his special unit, and the plane containing his backup would be landing soon if it hadn't already.

"We communicated with them with phones no one'll be able to hack," Ralf confirmed, leaning his back against the nearest wall in the house's entry, arms folded across his chest.

Ralf was definitely acting the role of a good aide. He looked and sounded calm in the face of what could be total chaos if they were unsuccessful tonight. But that wouldn't happen.

"We've got them scheduled to meet us at the cabins," Ralf continued. "There's a rental car I reserved for them and I provided them with GPS coordinates."

"I'd really like for you to come with us and meet them," Jock emphasized to Kathlene. He stood just in front of her, looking down into those skeptical blue eyes in her lovely, pale face. He wanted to take her into his arms, kiss the sternness from her lips. Reassure her that he was telling the truth. Which he was.

But what he wasn't telling her was that he simply did not want to leave her alone tonight.

He wasn't sure how things would go down, but he expected some major confrontations. The anarchists—no more euphemisms from him about their nature, either in his mind or spoken—had issued their threats. No matter what else they had planned to make their point, they had threatened several important people, including county commissioners.

And they had the means to really make good on their threats.

The sheriff's department did not look primed to protect them, so Alpha Force would take that on as well as controlling whatever other damage the anarchists intended to do.

Jock had wanted to pick his fellow Alpha Force members up at the Billings Logan International Airport, where the decision had been made for them to land to maintain better anonymity around here.

But after discussions with them, Jock had figured it would be better, in case Ralf and he were being followed, to have his backup team members meet them at the motel, where they had already booked cabins in names that couldn't be traced.

"That's why we're here now." Jock reached out to touch Kathlene's arm, very gently. She had changed from the dressy outfit she'd worn to the meeting to jeans and a royal blue knit shirt that hugged her curves. "I'll tell you a bit about what happened at the ranch tonight, but for now let's just say things are coming to a head, fast. We said we'd hidden some very special weapons of our own at the cabins that we'll bring back for our fellow anarchists to use, too, if necessary, since we're not supposed to know, at least not yet, about what the group already has. That's how we got away easily. My coming here to see you shouldn't be too suspicious if we're being followed, but I'd like for you to pretend that I'm coercing you to come with us—as if we want to keep an eye on my old buddy the deputy sheriff, rather than leaving you loose to do something against our interests."

"I guess that's okay, but why do they think you'd have been in communication with me again if you're supposedly part of their team?"

"Oh, we're just being wonderful sportsmen," Ralf said with a laugh. "We all saw you at the commissioners' meeting and knew you weren't happy. Jock's your old buddy, so to show how much he's wanting things to go well for the anarchists he offered to give them those really fun weapons, and if they ask we'll both say we didn't like your attitude so, while we were out and about anyway, we decided to take you into our control."

Kathlene's eyes widened and she took several deep breaths, seemingly to calm herself. "This is all just an act, right? I mean, the fun weapons—and your supposedly taking control of me."

"Right. No actual Uzis or AK-47s in our possession at the moment," Jock assured her, "although I've warned my Alpha Force team and they're bringing along some heavy-duty military gear. And, yes, you're our team member." His wanting to keep an eye on her, to protect her, was part of that teamwork, but he wasn't going to mention that to her and rile her all the more. "Now, we'd better get on our way. Please come, Kathlene."

He wasn't sure what he would do if she dug in her heels to stay, as unlikely as that might be. She'd always wanted to be included as part of their team.

But despite his not saying so, if she realized he wanted her along mostly for her protection there was a chance that she'd balk.

If she did, forcing her would not be a good idea—even though that was the show he wanted to put on as they left here. He wanted her genuine cooperation.

He wanted…more. Whatever it might be. He wasn't sure. But he might need to convince her that, like it or not, he recognized she could help Alpha Force succeed if she chose to.

She certainly could deter it from succeeding, at least for a short time, if she didn't go along.

He looked directly into her eyes, wanting to read her thoughts.

Thinking he saw…lust? Oh, yeah. Or was that just wishful thinking? Even if he was right, they couldn't do anything about it, but just maybe, if it was true, it would encourage her to go along with them.

"All right," she said. "Let's go."

Kathlene hated playing games. Always had. She much preferred directness, especially on the job.

She'd rather arrest someone, a robber or whoever, rather than pretend he was simply a person who'd had a tough life and made some bad decisions and now had to suffer needlessly for them.

Ha. But this situation could be a matter of life or death. Not for her, but for her friend Myra and other commissioners who thought like her.

Not to mention Jock. And Ralf. And even innocent civilians.

And so, as she left her house with the two men, a substantial-sized handbag over her shoulder, she pretended to hesitate as she shut her front door behind them. She wasn't surprised when Jock took her arm beneath the elbow and tugged on it not so gently. Not enough to hurt her, of course, but enough to show he meant business to anyone who might be watching.

She appreciated his touch. Even liked knowing he was this close.

But this was playing a game, one she could not avoid going along with.

She didn't have to pretend much to show some resentment. And when he opened the rear car door for her she stumbled as she resisted getting in.

"No tricks!" Jock shouted. In a lower voice he asked, "Are you okay?"

"Yes," she whispered. Aloud she said, "Shove it, Jock. Some old friend you are." She slid onto the seat, tossed her bag onto the floor, and yanked at the seat belt. He got into the passenger's seat in front of her and let Ralf drive.

Okay. She was playing along.

She also felt excited. They were going to meet up with some other members of the military unit to which Jock and Ralf belonged.

"Can you tell if we're being followed?" she asked. With her own skills as an officer of the law she had been keeping watch but did not see any vehicle or person that appeared to be spying on them.

Perhaps Alpha Force members had better skills in figuring that out, although she didn't know how, on the road.

"Doesn't look like it," Ralf confirmed. "Jock?"

"Nothing that I see, either."

"But then sight isn't your best sense," Ralf said, shooting a glance across the front seat to his superior officer.

Jock gave him the finger, obviously in jest, and then turned back toward Kathlene. "You okay back there?"

"Fine, except that I've just been kidnapped by a shape-shifter pretending to be an anarchist." If they could jest in this time of stress, so could she—although what she had said wasn't exactly a joke.

"You got it."

A phone rang in the front, and Kathlene saw Jock check the screen before answering. "It's Drew," he said to Ralf, then glanced back toward Kathlene. "Our commanding officer."

For the next few minutes Jock talked about logistics. The rest of the Alpha Force team was apparently nearing Cliffordsville. From what Jock relayed to Ralf, they'd check into their cabins and then happen to be out walking their dogs when Jock and Ralf walked Click. And yes, they'd brought some military weaponry, although they didn't expect to have to resort to that.

"Sounds good."

A short while later, Ralf turned onto the road that led first to the cabins and, farther on, to the ranch. Kathlene opened her eyes even wider. Even if they hadn't been followed, they were much more likely to be seen by the anarchists now.

Assuming that they all hadn't gathered already at the ranch to prepare for whatever mayhem they were planning.

A lot of cars were parked at the motel complex so the place appeared busy, but Jock said that, fortunately, there had been enough empty rooms to reserve some for the people they were expecting. Ralf parked in the same space as he had before, and they all got out of the car.

"Do you need to arm wrestle me or aim a gun at me?" Kathlene asked Jock.

"You tell me. But it would be better if you appeared angry but accepting of whatever's going on."

"I'm not much of an actress," Kathlene said, but she pasted a scowl on her face, grabbed her bag and stalked irritably up to the door of the main cabin they'd rented.

"You two have fun arguing," Ralf said. "I'll go take care of Click, then bring him over to our cabin to wait for the walk you and I take later, when anyone watching will assume I'm accompanying Click again."

"Right." Jock edged past Kathlene and used a key card to open the door. He motioned for her to enter.

She shot him a mock-furious glare, then stomped in. He followed and shut the door behind them.

When they were inside, Kathlene faced Jock. He looked wound up. Edgy. And damned handsome.

Never mind that they were likely to encounter danger from the anarchists sooner rather than later that night.

Never mind that she was supposed to be angry with him for controlling her.

He had, in fact, sought and received her cooperation. In effect asked for her help, to the extent she could provide it to him and the rest of his team that night.

Had, in effect, treated her as a genuine member of his team.

"Kathlene," he began, "I want you to know—"

She didn't let him finish. Instead, impulsively—or maybe she had planned it all along—she put down her bag, threw herself against his hard, hot body, pulled his face down and met his lips with a provocative, needy, suggestive, and entirely inappropriate, kiss.

Chapter 21

Kathlene was tired of telling herself what a bad idea this was. It was a good idea. A damned good idea. Her active, eager mouth told her so. And her whole body… Oh, yes!

She pressed herself even closer as her entire being concentrated on the feel of his lips on hers, his tongue playing taunting games, his arms locked around her so his body pressed against hers even more.

Did he taste her more than she could taste him? He was human now, yes, but he'd said he had enhanced senses even while not shifted. He was both sweet and salty, addictive and enticing. Really enticing.

What did she taste like to him?

She wished he would tear off her clothes and make love to her right there, on the cabin floor. At least her hair was free, not pulled back the way it had to be when she was on duty. Somehow that made her feel sexier and want more in the way of physical contact. Real, deep, urgent physical contact.

But notwithstanding the urgency, the ecstatic pleasure of that kiss, enjoying sex right now with this man was impossible.

Any moment now, Ralf could come in with Click, and they could even be accompanied by whichever of their Alpha Force coworkers had come to town.

Jock knew that as well as she did. Those who could burst in were people he knew. He should be the one to call this off. Now.

And yet his mouth only pressed on hers with even more urgency. Continuing to kiss and taste and experience the rush of being near him, she knew her sensibility was about to dive out of her brain, maybe causing her to start tearing her own clothes off.

No. She was too smart for that. Too well grounded.

She enjoyed being with Jock, that was all, even while knowing there was no future in it. She might as well take advantage of—

A sound. A song. A cell phone. Jock's.

It broke the spell. He pulled away, leaving her wanting more. Wondering if that was the last time they would ever get to be that close.

He glanced at it, then, with a regretful look toward her, he lifted the phone to his ear. "Yes, Ralf? Where?" A pause. "Good. We'll be right there." Lowering the phone, he pushed a button. "Ralf has run into the rest of the gang from Alpha Force. We need to go meet them."

"Of course." Kathlene tried to even her breathing and make her voice sound calm and cheerful.

"This isn't over." Jock's shining hazel eyes locked on hers. His chin rose, and his handsome, chiseled features seemed to grow even stronger in apparent resolve. As if, by his saying so, they owed each other a time to finish what they had begun. Again.

Kathlene wished it were true.

She smiled. "I think we have a busy night ahead of us. After that...well, we'll see."

"Yes," Jock responded forcefully. "We will." He took her hand, and the feel of its strength protecting hers somehow made her believe that whatever might come that night, it would end well.

And maybe, just maybe, she could hope for one more night with Jock.

Ralf had told Jock that the gang had met up in the parking lot outside the reception cabin where the new arrivals had just checked in.

How amazing. They were a bunch of strangers with similar dogs who happened to run into each other and connect because of their pets—or so they all intended it to appear.

That was the scenario Jock described to Kathlene as they left the cabin and strode in that direction in the shadows of late afternoon. "We're all going to become great buddies, thanks to the coincidence of the three dogs, including Click, looking so much alike. Of course the other guys already knew one another and came here together to do a little hunting, but it was a real kick to see another dog so similar that Ralf got to talking to them…et cetera."

"Et cetera," Kathlene repeated, smiling at him. She kept pace with him along both the lawns and paved areas of the motel as they headed toward the front. He had an urge to take her hand, ostensibly to make sure she kept her balance on the shifting ground, but actually because he regretted, would continue to regret, that they'd had to cut that amazing, hot kiss so short.

But no need to give the guys they were meeting up with any indication of something between Kathlene and him besides their cover story of prior friendship and their actual alliance to check out, and bring down, the anarchists.

Plus, just in case those anarchists had eyes on them

somehow, Kathlene and he needed to continue to appear as if their former friendship was fraying.

Of course he'd seen no evidence of their being observed, but he knew better than to trust anyone around these cabins as being as innocent as they seemed.

Besides, the anarchists might be watching him to try to get hold of the imaginary weapons he claimed to have brought here. And might also be wondering why he was taking so long to bring those weapons to their compound.

So instead of taking Kathlene's hand, he put one of his at the back of her neck as if controlling where she was going.

She glanced at him quizzically, and then, obviously getting it, looked down as if upset.

"I have a pretty good idea which Alpha Force members will be here, but I'll wait and introduce you to them as we see them, okay?"

"Sure." Her stride seemed to break for just an instant before she continued walking, and when he glanced at her gorgeous face it looked actually, and not artificially, troubled.

"What's wrong?" he demanded.

Her smile appeared rueful. "I'm somewhat aware of what makes your Alpha Force so special. I assume that some of its other members are like you—shifters, right?"

"Right." He kept his tone light despite his continued scowl for effect. "And one of the good things is that we all get the advantages I've told you about from the elixir you've seen me take."

"I get it. But…well, are all the people who've come here shifters like you? And do they all shift into wolves?"

"I'll have to confirm who all is here," he responded. "I know at least one aide was being sent, and aides are like Ralf: nonshifters. I think I mentioned that some Alpha

Force members can shift into other types of animals, but as far as I know only wolf shifters were coming here— for ease of blending into the background, for one thing."

"The wild wolf population around here isn't huge," Kathlene said. "But there are some."

"Which makes those potential changes to wildlife protection laws of great interest to us." He stopped as they reached the front parking lot. "Here we are. And there they are." He gestured toward the left where a small group of people were hanging out with some dogs—three dogs that resembled wolves, in fact, including Click. "And it looks like we have two more shifters here, brothers—although I only see one aide. Come on and I'll introduce you."

Their names were Simon and Quinn Parran and Noel Chuma. Kathlene knew she would have no trouble remembering who was who—even though all her questions hadn't yet been answered. Which were shapeshifters? The brothers, right? And Noel was their aide?

And why on earth did that fascinate her so much?

The men stood with Ralf and Click at the edge of the parking lot, with the three dogs on long leashes availing themselves of the nearby lawn that led to the reception cabin on one side and several of the motel cabins beyond. The dogs did look similar and, if she'd guessed, might have assumed they were all at least part wolf, with otherwise varying canine lines that probably included some German shepherd or deep brown, furry Labradors—all good-sized for dogs, and all in breeds considered smart.

Even if Kathlene hadn't known, she would probably have guessed that the three newcomers might be in the military or law enforcement. Not that they were in uniform. And their hair wasn't military short. But they all appeared muscular and sure of themselves. They seemed to be having a great time talking together. That probably wasn't just part of their cover stories.

The guy introduced as Noel was shorter than the others but looked just as strong. His complexion was dark, and he seemed just the slightest bit deferential to the others.

The Parran brothers did look related. Both had black hair and eyebrows and a light trace of beard. Their eyes were golden, their bone structure sharp. Quinn was the taller and seemed more inclined to talk than his brother, Simon.

Ralf was the one to introduce the newcomers. There weren't many other people coming and going in the parking lot, but Kathlene noted that all the men maintained their cover—despite stolen, brief words between Jock and Ralf and these men. Serious words, judging by their facial expressions.

She didn't join in the exchanges. Wasn't invited to. But she did try to maintain her cover.

"Hey, Jock, these guys came here to do a little hunting, too. They're from South Dakota."

"As awesome as this area is," Jock said, "you need to know that there's some politics going on that could affect how fun it is to hunt. Look, why don't we all meet for dinner and we can tell you about it, okay?"

"Fine with me." Quinn turned toward the dog he had on a long leash and gave a slight tug to get his attention. The dog came trotting over. "Good boy, Saber." He looked back at the people around him. "If we can't hunt around here, we'll probably move on."

"Yeah," Noel said. The other two dogs had accompanied Saber, and Noel bent to give Click a pat on the top of his head. The other dog—Simon's cover dog?—was called Diesel.

Time for Kathlene to interject her role. "It's not that

hunting is going to be outlawed around here or anything like that," she said. "Our county commissioners have been debating whether our local laws comply with some changes made in state statutes. The laws they're passing are to make sure everything's conformed."

"Deputy Baylor is with the local sheriff's department," Jock said. "She's an old friend of mine, and we came here for a visit because I hadn't seen her in ages. But we don't see eye to eye on a lot of things going on around here."

"I get it." Simon's gaze moved from Jock to Kathlene and back again. "I like this area but yeah, let's get together to chat tonight. I've got a feeling we're not going to stay long, but maybe you can convince us otherwise, Deputy."

"I'll try," she said.

That appeared to be the cue for Jock to go off a short distance with Simon. To talk about dinner plans? Maybe, but Kathlene figured they'd go into more detail than they had before, would be all wrapped up in their strategizing about how to handle the rest of this evening, too.

And the night.

The two men looked very serious as they conversed, not surprising considering the circumstances. When they were likely to be overheard, they'd have to keep things light.

But what was likely to transpire was anything but light.

In a minute, they returned to the rest of the group. Kathlene, trying to maintain the cover of friends and new acquaintances meeting without a care in the world, barely had time to make over all three dogs and tell the two newcomers how beautiful they were as she patted them and knelt to give them hugs. She noticed the approving look Quinn shot her way, and Noel, too.

"Here's the plan," Jock said. "We're all going to my cabin first to toast the evening before it gets here. Later on, we'll head downtown and see if we can find a bar worth trying out. Maybe a couple. Grab some pizza then. Sound okay to you?"

"Sure does," said Simon. "What kind of beer do you have?"

They were in the main cabin rented by Jock and Ralf, all of them plus the dogs.

"Here's the actual plan," Jock said, standing and facing the rest, his expression solemn. The other humans were all leaning on the sides of the two beds. "It's not nighttime yet, but it's still getting late enough that I'm concerned those guys are already starting whatever they're up to. We'll first go on the prowl in the two cars we have here. Just an initial drive through town to make sure all looks well, and we'll pretend to give a tour to you guys. As long as we don't get a hint of anything starting yet, we'll head to that run-down house past the turnoff for the old ranch—and then start our strategy. But we need to be cautious and assume some of the weapons are now in hands that are more than ready to use them." He paused, then continued, "Oh, and by the way, even though it's not in our plans, if I run into any of our new buddies without being shifted, I'll have to tell them I'm mad as hell that I forgot to pack some strategic parts of the weapons I told them I'd brought along. I already said I carry them in pieces to avoid detection while traveling."

"They won't like that," Ralf said.

"No, but I'll beg to borrow some of their wonderful stuff if the occasion arises. I suspect it won't, though, considering what else will be going on."

Kathlene figured that, as part of their plan, there'd be shapeshifting involved. But she had something else important to ask. "What if you're being observed, Jock? Maybe heading downtown won't look suspicious, but if you come back this way and wind up at that old house—"

"Not a problem," Ralf interjected. "Jock and I came partly prepared for what could be going on here, but these guys are really ready. They brought some amazing satellite surveillance equipment that'll shadow us and let us know if anyone's peeking at what we're up to, following us or otherwise using electronics to snoop into our gear. If there's anyone or anything out there that shouldn't be, they'll jam it. And it contains metal-detecting equipment, too, so we'll be forewarned about who's carrying what."

"Really?" Kathlene couldn't help glancing at Jock, who'd taken a seat beside her at the edge of his bed, for confirmation.

"Really," he said. "Plus, just so you know in advance, they're not the only Alpha Force members around here now besides us. The others have come into the area in smaller groups so they won't be as obvious. But this way there should be enough military—and other—strength to bring those anarchists down if they try anything or otherwise reveal themselves more." He glanced, as if for confirmation, toward the three men who'd just arrived. Simon must have been the one with the highest military rank since the others looked toward him. He nodded decisively.

"Before we go," Ralf said, "we actually do have some beer here, but I'd suggest that we forgo it for now."

"Agreed," said Simon. "But since we're not likely to stop for drinks of any kind, or even food, do you have any snacks?"

"Yeah," Quinn said. "Some of us in particular are going to need a whole lot of energy to accomplish what we're up to tonight. Especially—" He stopped and looked first at Kathlene, then Jock.

Kathlene knew what he was driving at. He wanted to

know how much she knew. She should have remained serious, but instead of responding directly she said, "Oh, you mean Click, Diesel and Saber?"

The three men who'd just arrived shared pointed glances with Jock and Ralf. Jock laughed.

"Don't worry, guys. Kathlene's the one who wound up bringing in Alpha Force. She's been working closely with Ralf and me—and yes, me shifted. She knows what's going on. In fact, she's part of our team."

Which made Kathlene beam and feel warm and fuzzy inside.

Until he added, "Of course we have to ensure that every member of our team stays safe. And that includes our favorite deputy sheriff."

She tried to hide her nervousness in anticipating what was to come by offering a half smile. "Just make sure I remain part of your team, Jock. As you well know, I can take care of myself." Maybe she was being repetitious but then, so was he with his attempts to keep her out of harm's way. Nice, but no thanks. Especially not now.

"Yes, I do know," he said, not sounding thrilled about it. "And in fact, I've a feeling you might get an opportunity tonight to prove it."

It was time to get started. Jock had confirmed it with Quinn Parran, commanding officer of the small visiting group, who'd been designated as the one to keep in closest touch with the rest of the Alpha Force team in the area—for now. Until Quinn, like Jock and his brother Simon, shifted into wolf form.

And then? Well, it would be one of their aides—even though it would be safest for all of them to have as many nonshifted personnel as possible watching their backs as the mission ramped up.

The newcomers, along with their cover dogs, headed back to the cabins they had rented, but only for a minute. They were to pick up their supplies, stick them in their vehicle and then head out to the old house.

Ralf had provided them with directions to get there. Jock knew that the other Alpha Force members in the area would be notified that this group was on the move—and how they intended their operation to proceed.

Jock, tense yet eager to get started, waited for about two minutes then nodded to Ralf. "Go ahead and get things ready for our departure." Ralf nodded and strode to where he'd left his backpack against the wall farthest from the door. He started going through the contents, undoubtedly checking to make sure the light and elixir, the most important objects they would need that night, were there. Then Jock said to Kathlene, who was kneeling on the floor petting Click, "It's our turn to leave. You still okay with that?"

She looked up at him, suspicion marring her lovely face. "Why? You want me to head back home and stay out of trouble?"

Yes, was what he thought—but not what he said. "Actually, no. I've a feeling we're going to need your presence tonight for things to go as smoothly as possible."

Her dark eyebrows arched even more than usual as she rose to her feet. "Really? Or are you just saying that so I'll be more receptive when you tell me to run into town for a bottle of water or some other simple time filler?"

"I don't think that even driving down the side road here for some water will be simple tonight."

Her face froze. "It's going to be bad, right?"

"We'd better anticipate things'll be rough. But you can still opt out. We'll make do without you if we have to." And that would be his preference, given a choice.

"Forget it, Larabey. I'm in." She was standing straight

now. "Just tell me what you want me to do to help. If nothing else, I'll have your back." Turning away from him, she stalked past Click, who appeared mournful about no longer being petted. She grabbed her large pocketbook up from the space along the wall where she'd dropped it and reached inside. She pulled out the Glock she kept at her hip while on duty. "I've come prepared."

It wasn't a humorous situation or a humorous evening, but he gave a brief laugh nevertheless. "Why am I not surprised? Okay, Deputy. We'll talk on the way about some of the possibilities, but I think I'm about to deputize you myself—as my aide for tonight. I've got other things for Ralf to do, like act as our main liaison between our group and the other Alpha Force members who're still outside of town." He glanced toward Ralf, who had hefted the backpack up and was jutting his arms through the straps.

Ralf nodded. "Sounds good to me, sir."

Jock shook his head in mock irritation. "Stop calling me sir, Sergeant."

"Yes, sir."

Jock shot a glance at Kathlene, who was looking from one man to the other and shaking her head. "Levity at a time like this?" she scolded, but then she smiled. "It can only help us succeed, guys, so keep it up." She walked to the door then turned back. "Are we bringing Click along?"

"Yes," Jock said. "We'll most likely leave him, along with Diesel and Saber, at the old house, but at least we'll have them close by if we need a little canine cover tonight."

"Got it. You two ready to head to the car?"

"Go ahead," Jock said. "For the moment, I have *your* back."

Chapter 22

Kathlene observed how the three of them walked out to the car, all in their casual jeans and shirts, as if nothing in particular was happening or expected that night, chatting about the weather and how Click was, as usual, sniffing everything in his path—a prepared team pretending to be independent and friendly individuals.

Jock walked beside her, and she appreciated his presence. He bolstered her optimism. Things were going to be fine in Clifford County very soon. Alpha Force was here.

He was here.

Good actors all, in their undercover roles.

But it was nearly evening. Who knew what might still occur tonight?

Despite Jock's presence, she realized that she anticipated some pretty bad stuff to take place before everything was over—especially considering those weapons Jock had found—but surely things would end up well.

After all, hadn't she brought in the military's most elite and covert unit?

She didn't feel like laughing at herself or anything else as she again slid into the backseat of the car, this time with Click. She might have been the catalyst for getting Alpha Force sent here, but she'd hardly asked for their help, not specifically. Who knew what Alpha Force was about—before?

And how would they deal with such nasty weaponry?

Jock was the driver this time. That was probably because Ralf had donned some kind of communications device and had unobtrusive plugs in his ears as well as a tiny microphone attached almost invisibly at the neck of his shirt.

"Are you in touch with them?" Jock asked Ralf as he started the engine and began to drive away.

"Yep," Ralf said. "They followed our directions and found the house. They've parked under the cover of some nearby trees and have gotten inside." He paused, then said, apparently into the microphone, "I was just bringing my team up to date, Alpha One."

"They're Alpha One?" Kathlene asked. "The guys who were just with us?"

"That's right," Jock agreed over his shoulder. "We're Alpha Two. And the ones out there in the ether—our nearby backup—they're Alpha Zero."

"How many of them are there?"

"As many as we'll need," he responded cryptically.

"I'm in touch with them, too," Ralf said. And then, toward the microphone, he asked, "Alpha Zero, do you have us in your scope?" He paused. "Good. And what about the tangos?" Once again, he seemed to listen.

"Isn't *tango* the term for terrorists?" Kathlene asked Jock.

"Sure is," he acknowledged. "And that's what we believe our buddies the sportsmen are, above all else. People who don't like the government but don't act on it are one thing. These guys appear primed to do something to make some kind of statement—or worse."

They'd pulled out of the motel complex and started down the road toward the ranch. Kathlene kept watch for any vehicles or signs of life around but saw nothing. "Do we know what they're doing right now? Are they all hanging out on the ranch?" She doubted her companions could know that with any certainty, though.

Even so, she was pleased when Ralf said, "That's what Alpha Zero's been talking about in my ear—and Alpha One's ears, too. They've got surveillance on them from some pretty clever satellites. At the moment it appears there's a bunch of activity on the ranch, at the shooting range and the old stables. It's not clear what the guys there are doing but heat patterns apparently indicate they're teaming together. Possibly assembling some explosives."

Kathlene drew in her breath. "Getting ready to pull some bad stuff."

"Tonight," Jock said in apparent agreement. "Looks like we're right on time and on target."

They passed the turnoff to the ranch. "And no one's following us?" Kathlene asked Ralf. She couldn't help looking out the car windows nervously.

"According to our overhead resources, the answer's no. That doesn't mean we shouldn't be cautious, though."

"Of course." Kathlene wished she could call in some reinforcements of her own—but at the moment, considering the sheriff's shrugging off what the sportsmen were doing and even what they said in public, that would probably be a bad idea.

On the other hand, she still completely trusted Tommy X. If she got an opportunity later, she would at least notify him. Maybe even find a way to meet up with him and get his backup when—and not if—she jumped in to help with this operation.

After a couple more bends in the road, they reached the area where the old house was back behind some trees. Jock slowed down and looked into the rearview mirror. "We still okay?" he asked Ralf, who murmured something into his microphone.

"No indication of anyone paying attention to us at all," he said.

"Good." Jock quickly made a turn that took them behind the old house. Kathlene glimpsed the rental car the other Alpha Force guys had been driving behind a bunch of trees, and Jock pulled behind another stand of growth.

Ralf held on to a metallic briefcase as they went inside. Jock carried Ralf's backpack, which left her in charge of Click. Quickly, they all headed up the rickety back steps and inside.

Kathlene noted how well trained all three dogs were. Neither Diesel nor Saber barked at the intrusion by Jock, Ralf, Click or her, and Click, too, remained silent as he traded sniffs with the other two wolflike canines inside the shell of a house.

She wondered, not for the first time, what this place smelled like to men with enhanced senses. It stank of rot and mold and unidentified bad odors even to her.

And for the time being, it was headquarters.

"Glad you could make it." Quinn Parran grinned at them as he stood in the middle of the dogs, his arms crossed. The other two men were just beyond him, engaged in a conversation near the rotting wood visible behind the cracked plaster that formed the wall of what had once been the living room. "We're nearly ready to rumble. You?" He aimed his gaze toward Jock.

"I take it that we're handling preliminary recon." Jock glanced toward Ralf, who nodded.

"That's what these guys say. Looks like the sportsmen need to be invaded by only a few highly trained K9s who look like wolves at first to check out what they're up to."

"K9s?" Kathlene asked.

"It'll be more easily explained without giving away Alpha Force's true status if we appear to be our cover dogs while shifted," Jock explained.

Kathlene nodded. That did make sense.

"That should work well," Ralf continued. "And if it's like we think, there's backup galore nearby. In fact—" he paused as if to listen "—I need to head back to town real fast. They can tell by the GPS where to go and I'll be able to tell them when, but they want a little face-to-face dialogue first, more about who's who and what we anticipate." He aimed a stare toward Jock. "That's my job. Yours is to shift, sniff and obey the orders of your ostensible trainers."

Jock laughed. Even Kathlene smiled, despite feeling suddenly quite nervous.

But she couldn't afford to let it show. Especially when Jock said to her, "Confirming that you're my aide for tonight, Deputy. You up for that?"

"Yes, sir," she said and made herself grin.

Simon and Noel joined Quinn beside the dogs. "What's the plan?" Simon asked Jock.

"It's close enough to dusk to give us some cover, especially in the forest. Time for the three of us to shift. Ralf's meeting up with Alpha Zero. That'll leave Noel to act as shifting aide for you two, and Kathlene'll assist me." He glanced at her, even as she realized that the other men were studying her skeptically.

"Hey, I can handle it," she said. "I've observed what Ralf does before, and Noel can always act as my adviser."

"If you three are good with it," Simon said, "then so are we. And afterward, you'll also work with Noel to have our backs and communicate further with Alpha Zero?"

"I—" Kathlene was ready to say yes, but she realized she didn't have proper equipment to do so. "If Noel will advise me on that, too, then sure."

"You got your phone with you?" Jock asked.

"Of course."

"Good. You can always use it to communicate with Ralf. Program your number into her phone," he told Ralf. "And if you can get one for our C.O., Major Drew Connell, that wouldn't hurt, either. I assume that Drew's one of our Alpha Zero team, isn't he?"

"Yeah, but in case he's shifting, too, I'll get her Jonas's number." He looked toward Kathlene. "That's Captain Jonas Truro. He's a medical doctor like Drew and he's also essentially Drew's aide. All us aides will stick together to help our shifters, right?" He winked at Kathlene, who laughed.

"Count me in," she said. She realized that all the repartee was calming her nerves a bit, even as she anticipated some nasty stuff going down tonight. But she'd act as backup—and she would have backup, too, even if it wasn't her standard sheriff's-department gang.

"Okay, then," Ralf said. "I'm out of here. Oh, and it looks like it's pretty much dusk here, partly thanks to the forest. It's dark enough that you shifters can do your thing anytime now and go check out the place."

"Once they're shifted," Noel added, looking at Kathlene, "we'll go with them to the fence outside the ranch. We won't be able to see everything that happens, but we're equipping all three of them with cameras that'll let us see what they do. They're hooked up to my phone and I'll add the app to yours after we get these guys shifted. We'll be able to report to Ralf and the Alpha Zero folks if we need immediate action or if we can just let these shifters take care of things and record them. Under orders as well-trained K9s, of course."

"Sounds like a plan," Kathlene said, smiling gamely. She just hoped it was a *good* plan.

But she couldn't help feeling impressed by all the technological backup that seemed to be in effect. Who would ever have thought there would not only be an army unit comprised partly of shapeshifters—a pretty ancient myth—but that they would also have ultra-modern cameras and cell phones and satellite equipment working in their favor?

"Okay, Ralf, you can get on your way," Jock said.

"Yes, sir." He grinned then added, "Hey, we'll reconvene later and outline everything we did when this is all behind us. See you later." And then, after giving all three dogs quick pats on the head, Ralf went out the house's back door.

"Okay," Jock said, "the rest of you—ready to get started?"

The three Alpha One guys said yes. Kathlene didn't feel as if she had much choice. But, heck, she was ready, too.

She was going to help Jock shift.

And then he would sneak onto the ranch in wolf form, where there were dozens of anarchists who liked to hunt—and most likely worse.

Her feelings about Jock might be indecipherable even to her, but she cared about him and who he was and what he did—not to mention how much she enjoyed sex with him.

Even though that part was now a thing of the past, she would be damned worried about him this night.

You've got to be okay, she thought, looking at him as the other men moved toward the far side of the room where they'd left a couple of backpacks similar to Ralf's.

Her thoughts must have been legible on her face, since the look Jock gave her seemed to blend certainty and sympathy. "Like Ralf said, we'll all talk about our roles in this and how everything went later, when this is all over and we've rounded up the anarchists. Okay?"

"Okay," Kathlene said, as forcefully as if she was convinced that there couldn't be anything but success before them.

"Then let's do it." Jock retrieved Ralf's backpack and knelt on the floor near Kathlene. The other men had gone into another room, so Jock would have some privacy as he shifted. He pulled out a glass vial filled with liquid. "I'll start with this," he said and downed the elixir as Kathlene dug into the pack and pulled out the special battery-operated light. That meant she wasn't looking directly at Jock as he started to pull off his clothes. "Hey," he said. "You're supposed to be watching."

Kathlene couldn't help but oblige, even as Jock started to strip as though he was an entertainer on stage, pulling his T-shirt over his head first, flexing his perfect, buff chest, then reaching to remove his jeans and underwear.

Kathlene felt her breathing become uneven as she stared at his perfect body—and his long, hard shaft that seemed to grow as she watched.

Too bad this moment would be wasted, at least to her. "Looks good," she said as lightly as she could manage, but heard the aroused catch in her voice. "Here we go." She turned on the light and aimed it at him, then watched, enthralled, as his shift from gorgeous human male to wild wolf took place.

* * *

*He waited for a collar to be fastened about his neck by
Noel so he would have a camera to record all he experienced. Then he waited for his packmates, also with cameras attached, to join him before he left the house where
they had shifted.*

*Kathlene was there, observing. He knew she would con-
tinue to be there for him. She would also help to watch the
dogs that provided cover for the shifters.*

*Soon, all three of them in wolf form loped through the
forest toward the fence that surrounded the ranch hous-
ing the anarchists. Jock showed the others the holes in
that fence through which they could enter the compound,
careful to listen to be sure that no humans were nearby,
that no humans would spot them.*

*When they were inside the fence and in the deepening
shadows around trees and bushes on the old ranch, he
nodded toward the firing range to get the others to head
carefully in that direction.*

*Him, too—but beyond. He walked slowly, with caution,
using all his senses to ensure no human was following, toward the crumbling stable where weapons more powerful
than mere guns were being collected.*

*He hoped that the cameras on him and his packmates
were working well. He intended to demonstrate to all members of Alpha Force who were watching now, or who later
observed what was being recorded, what these anarchists
were really about.*

*There. He sensed a large contingent of humans near
where he was going—that stable. He smelled a heavy scent
of gunpowder and other explosives.*

*He heard laughter and swearing and men discussing
with one another in hushed yet ecstatic tones the idea of
blowing up anyone trying to tell them what to do.*

Time to get closer. Allow the camera to take pictures and record voices.

And ensure there was enough to bring in the rest of Alpha Force to handle this ugly but anticipated situation.

Jock was gone. He had shifted in front of her eyes again, and she had watched, enthralled. Wanted to touch him, to understand better the change that had overtaken him.

Instead, Kathlene had done nothing.

And now Jock had left, stalking his way with the others like him onto the grounds of the ranch, to observe and, if necessary, to act. Perhaps to attack. To put himself in imminent danger.

Now it was her turn to feel protective without being able to do anything about it. She wanted to help him. To keep him from harm. To ensure that the bad guys were brought to justice, but not at Jock's expense.

Yet here she was. She couldn't help him…could she?

Wait. That wasn't true.

She was still with Noel inside the old house. "I gather that we're to lock the cover dogs inside here," she said to him, "so anyone spotting Jock and the rest will assume they're real dogs who happen to have gotten loose—those belonging to Jock and the guys who've just arrived here, right?"

"That's right, although depending on the circumstances we might admit that they're K9s trained to move around an area for recon, taking pictures from their collars." Noel seemed to study her with his deep brown eyes. He was a nice-enough-looking guy, young, serious, dark-toned skin and maybe even a little bit deferential to her. Because she was a civilian—or at least nonmilitary? Because she was a woman?

Because she was a deputy sheriff?

Heck, none of that mattered. The fact that he was at least listening to her was a good thing.

"Can we go to the area outside the ranch?" she asked. "We can stay beyond the fence but keep an eye on what's happening inside the best we can. Show me how to use the app you added to my phone to its best advantage. I want to see what Jock's looking at."

"Sure." He complied, and she got to see, as if through Jock's eyes, what the inner grounds of the ranch looked like at his level.

He appeared to have stopped near the stable, and she heard loud, boisterous, menacing voices without, at the moment, observing the speaker.

"Let's head toward the ranch to observe better," she said to Noel.

"Okay. I was already about to do that. Ralf and I are in contact and he'll keep in touch with our shifters via their cameras, too, and with the rest of the Alpha Force team sent here to help. He's coordinating."

"Then let him also coordinate with me."

"Okay."

"You can talk to them on the way. Let's start our walk toward the ranch."

Phone to his ear, he followed her.

It didn't take them long to reach the outer area of the ranch. For now they remained in the seclusion of the surrounding woods.

"Here," she whispered, handing Noel her phone. "I also want to see what the guys in Alpha One are up to."

He tweaked her phone, and she then was able to look at the pictures on a split screen. Using her fingers, she was able to enlarge one picture, then the other. For now it appeared that Simon and Quinn were near the ranch's shooting range. They must have been hiding in the shadows near the old stable or maybe the ranch house itself, but they faced a whole bunch of men who looked high on alcohol or maybe testosterone. They were laughing, goading each other. Sounded as if they were telling each other that it was nearly time, and no one would ignore them ever again.

Jock appeared to have stopped to continue listening at the stable.

She decided to call Ralf. They were still a distance from the ranch so she didn't have to maintain total silence.

"Yes, I'm with the Alpha Zero guys now," Jock's aide told her. "They're ready to move in whenever the order's given—and that'll be up to Jock or the other shifters."

"How long will it take them to get here?" she asked.

"Not long. No more than ten minutes. We're close by."

But ten minutes could be an eternity if Jock or the others got into trouble.

She didn't say anything to Ralf, though. He was military. He knew how critical even seconds could be if someone was in trouble.

Was Jock in trouble? She enlarged his camera picture again, listening only to what he heard around the stable.

Men continued to rant and laugh there, too.

And then a voice could be heard that was distinguished from the rest. It sounded familiar. Tisal's?

It said, "Which of you wants to be the first one to detonate one of these babies near that county building where they thought they could ignore us?"

A lot more voices rang out, volunteering for the assignment. Kathlene froze. It was time for Ralf to call in the rest of his team.

It was also time for her to let her own team, the sheriff's department, in on what was happening, even if she couldn't explain how she knew.

But before she could, another voice yelled, "Hey, what's

that? Is that the dog that was prowling here the other day? It looks like a wolf, and in my book wolves are fair game. Time to start our fun."

The next thing Kathlene heard was a volley of gunshots. The picture she was viewing started bouncing. At least Jock must still be alive, but he was in trouble.

And she definitely had to help.

Immediately.

Chapter 23

"Jock's in trouble!" Kathlene yelled to Noel as she started running. "Maybe Simon and Quinn, too." Had they been spotted? She didn't know, but she felt sure they would also go to Jock's rescue and put themselves into this horrible situation. "Get the rest of your guys in there." She knew it was time to call in her own reinforcements, as well. It might be too late. But she had to try.

She pressed the numbers into her phone to call Tommy X.

"I'm near the old ranch," she said, keeping her voice somewhat low. They were almost there, and she didn't want to be heard in case any of the anarchists were out patrolling. "There's trouble brewing. They may be planning on using explosive devices on buildings downtown." She'd heard that, and it was more likely to get the sheriff's department moving than mentioning that a wolf or three might be the sportsmen's current target.

"A bunch of us are already on our way," Tommy X told her. "Sheriff Frawley got a call from some of the sportsmen and they've said something's wrong, like they're under some kind of attack."

By wolves? Or did they somehow know more?

"I'll see you there, then," Kathlene said. "And hurry."

"Who'd you call?" Noel demanded as she pressed more buttons on her phone and concentrated fully on what Jock must be seeing. Trees and bushes and undergrowth along with edges of buildings, and the view was bouncing and veering first one way, then the other. He must be running sideways to evade the shooters. At least they weren't all shooting at once in his direction, but Kathlene did hear the sound of erratic gunshots.

Fortunately, Noel and she had nearly arrived at the fence. She started running toward the front gate.

"Where are you going?" Noel demanded from behind her.

"We need to get onto the ranch. I'm not sure they'll let either of us in. They won't like my badge, and I doubt they'll respect military ID any more than they do mine."

"Then we've got to get in another way. Do you know how Jock got himself and the others inside? Are there vulnerable parts of the fence?"

"I'm sure there are, but he didn't tell me where they are. Look, let's head to the front gate first and see if we can bully our way in."

"I don't like it, but—"

"Neither do I," Kathlene snapped, "but there are already a bunch of mad terrorists inside shooting guns at what they think are wild wolves. Do you think they'll be nicer to a couple of humans if they catch us trying to sneak in?"

"No," Noel admitted. "Let's give it a try."

Hurrying through the woods toward the front gate, Kathlene kept watching the phone screen. The picture continued to move. That meant so did Jock.

She still heard gunfire in the background.

As they reached the front, she saw a couple of official sheriff's-department vehicles arriving at the same time.

Sheriff Frawley was in the first one. Good. Surely even he would have to respond to what she had to tell him.

"Sir," she said as the tall man in his uniform with all its medals showing what a bigwig he was strode toward the front gate. She met him there. "I'm so glad to see you. There's a lot going on here. The men inside are not just sportsmen, they're terrorists. They plan to blow up the County Administration Building, and that may not be all."

The sheriff stopped moving and stared down at her with cold eyes. "I got a call that something was going on here that shouldn't be. We're here to find out what and protect the citizens who've chosen to reside here for a while."

"What!" Kathlene's mind fought for a way to try to give a better explanation without revealing the existence, nature or presence of Alpha Force. "They don't need protection. The rest of our citizens need protection from them."

"Get out of the way, Deputy, or I'll have your badge for insubordination. You're not even on duty, are you?"

"Not right now, sir, but—"

The sheriff strode right by her. So did Undersheriff Kerringston and a couple of deputies.

Tommy X emerged from the second car and approached her. "I tried to get Sheriff Frawley to see reason about the sportsmen, told him there was good reason to arrest them, not defend them." He paused, looking at Kathlene. "There is, isn't there?"

"Yes, absolutely." She watched in horror as the sheriff high-fived the guard who opened the gate to let them in.

She'd known the sheriff was okay with having the sportsmen around, maybe even liked the idea, but had hoped he'd been wise enough to change his mind about them after they showed their true colors and spoke out at the last meeting against any kind of government control.

But he hadn't reacted at all to her report that they were intending to blow up public property—presumably with people inside.

Sheriff Frawley must not only accept them. He must be one of them.

What was she going to do?

And where was Jock? How was Jock? She looked frantically toward Tommy X. "We'll go inside, too. We need to help." She didn't explain who she intended to help, but she figured Tommy X would know it wasn't the sheriff or the terrorists.

"Not a good idea, Deputy," he said. "We don't have any evidence about what you're alleging, and—"

"But we do! Video recordings." She couldn't tell him how they were being collected, although the cover dogs would come in handy for the explanation later.

And then she saw several large black vans barreling down the driveway from the main road.

"Reinforcements have arrived," Noel Chuma told her. He was grinning. "I'll introduce you later, but right now they've work to do."

Kathlene watched as humans in military fatigues, carrying weapons, poured out of the vehicles—along with half a dozen other wolves. They'd already done their shifting.

And now they were going to take over this terrorist installation.

Kathlene grinned briefly toward Tommy X, who looked confused.

"Military?" he asked.

Kathlene nodded. "I'll fill you in later." But not about everything.

One guy with lots of stripes on his camo uniform confronted the guard, who quickly backed down.

Kathlene smiled. "We've got work to do, too," she said to Sgt. Chuma. "Let's follow them inside."

People who called themselves sportsmen...hunters. Those hunters seeing wolves—or what they believed were true wolves. Of course they chased the three canines, shot at them. Perhaps allowed them to be a distraction from their own intent to destroy property and kill more than wildlife, at least for a short while.

Fortunately, there were a lot of shadows at this hour, thanks to buildings and trees. Places where Jock could veer in and out for protection. His shifted companions, Simon and Quinn, were equally adept at staying hidden or out of range, splitting up to make themselves more difficult targets.

But it couldn't last much longer.

Jock stopped behind a large vehicle in the ranch's main parking lot to catch his breath, and to use his senses to learn what was happening. Had Ralf and Noel and Kathlene sent for any reinforcements? If not, it was time.

There were loud, continuous sounds behind him, those chasing him, those firing shots from automatic weapons each time they believed they saw a moving wolf.

They were drunk. They were human and could not see well in the growing darkness.

Eventually, though, they might get lucky.

But then, he heard sounds before him, toward the main entrance to this encampment. Voices, raised and angry and menacing, and they included that sheriff's, but not only his. Kathlene's. And Major Drew Connell's. Yes! And there were also vehicles, large and military.

His additional backup was here.

That meant he could change things where he was. Fast. And relatively safely.

His shifting companions would not be quite so aware, but he nevertheless lifted his muzzle in the air and howled. The sound was echoed by two more voices—and then several more toward the entry.

Gunshots sounded. One bullet even hit the side of a vehicle near him.

He bared his teeth, wishing he could bite the wrist of whoever dared to raise a weapon and aim it at him.

Not now, though. Not yet.

He carefully lowered himself to the ground, moved forward while crouched on his wolfen legs, veered around one vehicle, then another, using his nose to smell and identify those anarchists who were nearest him.

As he had hoped, expected, one was the out-of-control human in charge who obviously wanted to make an example of what he deemed to be a stupid wolf creature who had dared to enter the property he controlled.

The man named Tisal.

Instead, Jock would make an example of him.

He moved slowly, quietly, around the vehicles, on cooling, rough concrete that scratched at his stomach, smelled of oil and of vehicles and more, circling back in the direction from which he had come, all the while knowing the camera about his neck continued to record all that occurred.

All the while hearing the noises of allies, both human and wolfen, as well as vehicles, drawing closer.

Not all were allies, though. Yet he believed they, too, were under control since at the moment the voices he heard were curt, giving orders, but without arguing.

And then—yes! He scented Tisal nearby, just beyond a

large van. Not far from other human smells, yet not sur-rounded by them. Jock maneuvered around the vehicle.

And saw Tisal. Alone.

Jock prepared to leap, even as the large, rounded human in his hunting jacket raised his weapon and aimed it at him.

"Don't you dare," shouted an angry female human voice. Kathlene's voice. She was off to the side, and she aimed her own service weapon at the offending anarchist. "Drop it, Tisal. You're under arrest."

The anarchist pivoted, aiming his gun toward Kath-lene. She fired, even as Jock leaped onto the man, knock-ing him to the ground, planting his teeth around the beefy, vulnerable neck, growling, and forcing himself not to bite down and kill the creature who had dared to fire toward Kathlene.

"It's okay, J—er, Click," she said, as if talking to Jock's cover dog. Smart lady. "Good boy. You've done a good job, and I'll be glad to tell your trainer, Ralf. Not that you understand what I'm saying, but I'm fine, and I've got this jackass's weapon. I'll cuff him and then you can go help the others like you. There are a bunch, and with all the other military backup that's here I have a feeling we've got a really productive bust of these anarchists underway."

Jock moved back, out of the way, his hackles still raised and his teeth still bared, ready to attack again. But the man remained docile as Kathlene rolled him onto his belly and cuffed him.

"Where's your boss, bitch?" Tisal demanded. "The sheriff will fire you for this. Maybe even arrest you for interfering with citizens' rights. And—"

"That's enough, Mr. Tisal. I'm sorry to say that your friend and my boss, Sheriff Frawley, isn't going to be able to help you."

That was when Jock scented the sheriff barreling in their direction. He stood up and barked.

"What is it, Click?" Kathlene knew Jock was warning her about something but she didn't know what.

But she wasn't overly worried. The Alpha Force contingent who'd come here as backup was now fanning out all over the place. They looked damned official in their uniforms, accompanied by what appeared to be a whole group of trained attack dogs—probably all shifters who were apparently using their own special senses and abilities to help round up every one of the anarchists.

The recordings Jock and the other shifters had made would provide all the evidence necessary to convict every one of them for breaking all sorts of terrorism and conspiracy laws, at a minimum.

"I'm sure everything's okay," she continued, addressing the wolf who clearly remained in protective mode. "Go ahead and look around. You'll see that your fellow—er, anyway, there are a lot of these guys being taken into custody now."

"Who the hell you talking to?" Tisal demanded.

"Everyone watching the recording that's being made thanks to the camera around that dog's neck," she said, tugging on the head anarchist, making him rise to his feet with his hands now cuffed behind his back. He leaned on the nearest car, and Kathlene assisted him a bit by manipulating his arms.

But Jock didn't move. Which worried Kathlene. She decided it was time to drag Tisal off to where the others were being taken into custody.

"Let him go, bitch."

Kathlene turned in the direction of the voice. Nearly under the cover of growing darkness, Sheriff Frawley strode out from between two parked sedans. He held a gun, and it was pointed at her.

"No, sir," she said. "We have evidence that this man intends to commit terrorist acts in Clifford County." She gave Tisal a gentle nudge in the back with her elbow.

"So you brought in the military? Are you the reason those jerks confronted me at the gate? Well, I got away and I'm going to make sure that all of the law-abiding sportsmen who have been living here are released by the feds and allowed to go about their business. Right now you're going to come with me and tell them you made a mistake, that you recognize now that these gentlemen are just that—gentlemen. They're sportsmen and hunt legally within the laws, even if they don't want those damned laws made any more onerous."

"And you, sir? Are you willing to obey the laws, whatever they are, and enforce them in your role of sheriff of Clifford County? And arrest people for possession and use of illegal weapons and explosives?" Kathlene had met Jock's eyes. His were more feral than she had ever seen them. He again looked ready to attack.

But she knew he recognized what she was doing and he stood still, at least for now—and allowed the security camera around his neck to do its job.

"What am I willing to do?" the sheriff snapped. "I'm willing to fight for the rights of people who don't want to be weighed down by stupid laws that make them give up their natural-born rights, like those to protect and feed themselves and shoot anyone or anything they damned well please." He suddenly dashed toward Kathlene and put his service weapon to her head. "And you're going to agree with me, Deputy, or you'll be damned sorry."

The angle was bad. She couldn't trip him or otherwise grab control.

Turned out she didn't need to. In seconds, she was released. The gun went off but it fired uselessly into the air as Jock pounced onto the sheriff and weighed him down, his teeth at the anarchistic lawman's throat.

"Get him off me!" The sheriff's voice sounded strangled. Kathlene was angry enough that she considered encouraging Jock to bite down—just a little.

But she got control of herself—a good thing, too. A whole group of Alpha Force members suddenly appeared in the parking lot—humans and wolves. With them was Tommy X, as well as Undersheriff Kerringston, who looked confused but hung back, just watching.

"These folks say they're friends of yours, Deputy Baylor," Tommy X said to her. "There are more of them around here, too, and they're taking a lot of the guys from the ranch into custody."

One of them, a tall guy in a camo uniform with black hair flecked with silver and shining amber eyes—a nonshifted shifter?—approached with his hand extended toward Kathlene. "Deputy Baylor? I'm Major Drew Connell of Alpha Force. I hear you were instrumental in bringing us here to stave off some potentially pretty nasty terrorist attacks."

"I did ask for help, sir," she acknowledged, shaking his hand.

"Well, we've been more than happy to provide it." He glanced down toward where Jock sat at attention near Kathlene's feet. This soldier must be Jock's commanding officer.

"Well, I thank you, sir. And so will the rest of this town when they fully realize what's been going on."

"I think we'll be informing them about it very soon." That was Tommy X. "Interesting group, this Alpha Force. I'm sure we'll all be interested, too, in how you've trained all those dogs you've brought along who look like wolves to act as your canine backup. They've been wonderful in helping to herd the anarchists together and get them rounded up and into custody."

"Yes," Kathlene said wryly, "I'll be very interested, too, in what explanation Alpha Force provides our citizenry. Will you be taking these guys into your custody?" She gestured toward Frawley and Tisal.

"Yes, we will," said Major Connell.

"Great. Then I'm going to walk around and observe the rest of what's going on around here." She glanced down toward Jock. "And I wouldn't mind at all having a canine companion."

Chapter 24

They walked the perimeter of the fence around the ranch in the darkness, this time on the inside. "That's all so amazing," Kathlene remarked more than once, and Jock, still in glorious wolf form, looked up at her often. She sometimes believed he was smiling and when she knelt and hugged him he licked her cheek.

She was fascinated to watch the teamwork of soldiers and wolves pretending to be trained K9s while they rounded up the dozens of anarchists, disarmed them, herded them into the outdoor assembly area where they had previously plotted against the Clifford County commissioners and government in general, and ensured they remained there.

Jock seemed quite pleased with himself, assuming Kathlene could read wolf body language accurately. He almost pranced at her side, sometimes growling if one of the anarchists appeared at all willing to protest what was going on.

It all seemed so surreal, and yet it was wonderful. What she had feared had been proven true—that these men had intended to harm innocent people as well as the government. And what she had tried so hard to accomplish—getting an appropriate law-enforcement group here to take control—had also come true.

Alpha Force was outstanding.

She was also amazed—well, maybe not so much—when Jock led her to the front gate and walked through, looking back at her with his glistening hazel wolf eyes as if he wanted her to follow. She complied, and they headed for the old house.

Once again, Kathlene assisted him in a shift, this time back to human form.

Once again, she got to aim the light at him and observe his wolfen body morph into his gorgeous human form.

And when he was fully shifted and had caught his breath, still nude, he took her into his arms.

"Kathlene," he said. "Thank you for all you did tonight."

"You're the one who deserves thanks," she whispered to him, and he lowered his mouth to hers.

She knew she would never forget that sexy, sincere and wonderful kiss....

Especially because she feared it would be their last.

He eventually pulled back, if only a little. "You know," he said, looking down at her with an expression she couldn't read—lustful? worried? "you still drive me nuts, putting yourself in danger that way, even when it's to help me."

She pulled back a little, too. "I still don't understand why you're so overprotective. I can take care of myself."

"I know you can. And maybe that's why...I do trust you, Kathlene. But—well, maybe you should know that there was once another woman in my life, a shifter like me. She joined a police department even before I ever thought about getting involved in any kind of military life or law enforcement. She was killed in the line of duty."

Oh. That explained so much. He'd obviously cared about that woman. And now he wanted to protect everyone.

"I'm not her, Jock," she said softly.

"I know," he said, and kissed her again.

Kathlene was glad to see the number of Clifford County residents piling into the assembly room for the ad hoc commissioners' meeting that was convened on the afternoon after the confrontations and arrests at the old ranch, even though it was a Saturday.

She was on duty, guarding the doors while in uniform. Her partner, Jimmy Korling, stood at the other door. He'd been less than friendly with her that day. He had obviously heard of her involvement in what had occurred the night before. Had he wanted to be brought into it?

Maybe Kathlene would have considered that if she'd thought she could trust him. He'd seemed, at least before, like a favorite of Sheriff Frawley's, and that made him less than an ideal cohort to work with her, especially as it had become completely clear whose side the sheriff had been on.

For the moment, Senior Deputy Tommy X was in charge of the sheriff's department, since Sheriff Frawley was unsurprisingly being investigated for his alleged roles as part of the anarchist team, and Undersheriff Kerringston, thanks to his close alliance with the sheriff, was also being scrutinized to determine if he had any role in what had occurred.

First thing that morning, Commissioners Myra Enager, Wendy Ingerton and the others had been briefed—or at least as much as wasn't classified under the control of the federal government. Kathlene had been the one to call Myra, who'd sounded thrilled and relieved.

Unsurprisingly, Tommy X had spoken to Myra, too,

and the three of them had gone out to breakfast together to discuss the situation.

By then, Kathlene was alone, since Jock and the others had joined the rest of Alpha Force for the law enforcement events that would occur that day. Kathlene hoped to see him later but wasn't sure when...or even *if*. She figured the members of Alpha Force would leave as soon as they confirmed that all was under control, and that would probably include Jock.

After breakfast, Myra had spoken with the other commissioners, and this afternoon's meeting had been planned nearly immediately. They wanted to inform their constituency about what was going on, even if they didn't know the details.

Unsurprisingly to her, Kathlene hadn't been informed of all that was happening, either. All she knew—and all she needed to know—was that a specialized FBI crime scene team had been flown in from D.C. to the nearest air force base, Malmstrom, in Cascade County, which wasn't too far away. As soon as they arrived, they started collecting evidence, which would be used to charge the anarchists, or at least the leaders of the group, with plotting some pretty major terrorist crimes—like potentially blowing up the County Administration Building. And although the collection of weapons Jock had discovered might not be fully illegal, how they were intended to be used probably was, especially after the threats made to the county commissioners.

And Jock had also learned that a cache of weapons of the type he'd found had been stolen from an army base in Michigan. Serial numbers were being checked to see if they matched.

The recordings made by Jock and the others would also help in the investigation and prosecution, but the more evidence they collected, the more likelihood there was of convictions.

Last Kathlene heard, all the members of Alpha Force who had come here, including Jock and Ralf, were meeting and debriefing themselves and the FBI team.

The commissioners' meeting had started. Myra was the first to explain what had gone down the night before. "A local citizen had believed there was more going on at the old ranch than target practice by a bunch of sportsmen." Meaning *her,* Kathlene knew. "In fact, for those of you who were present yesterday at our most recent commission meeting, some of the sportsmen had spoken out and sounded somewhat threatening. That was followed up by several commissioners, including me, receiving written threats that were delivered anonymously and circuitously to our homes. We suspected who had sent them but couldn't prove it—and yet a series of events not even we know about occurred where evidence was gathered at the ranch, and now a full federal investigation is progressing into prosecuting all of the sportsmen as anarchists and terrorists, or at least those in charge."

"What about Sheriff Frawley and Undersheriff Kerringston?" came a question shouted from the audience.

Myra paused and exchanged a brief glance with Kathlene. "There is some reason to suspect that they might have known what was going on. We don't know that for sure, however. Just in case, the investigation will include them, too."

Before heading to the meeting that afternoon, Kathlene had called Jock, just for an update, she had told him. If there was anything that Alpha Force or the feds had found out, or at least suspected, that the public should know about, she requested that he let her know.

Her mind had been circling a lot around what he had told her about the woman he had lost....

But he'd sounded pretty formal when he responded, and she suspected that she had caught him in the middle of a meeting. What he told her surprised her, but only a little. "Part of what is being looked into," he said, "is some allegations made by several of the top anarchists who said they were invited here by Sheriff Frawley, who promised them a perfect venue to meet and make their plans for doing whatever was necessary to let the world know who they are and why they were a major power to be reckoned with. That's for your information only, for now, Kathlene. Just let the people at the assembly know that a full-out investigation is in the works and that justice will be served."

"Against Sheriff Frawley as well as the others?" she asked, and he agreed.

She had hung up feeling all the more vindicated—and lonely. Whatever she had imagined to be growing between Jock and her was clearly something that had ended with the night's final raid on the terrorist encampment.

She had not told Myra any details before the meeting, but she had confirmed, as Jock had told her, that the investigation was continuing but that there appeared to be sufficient evidence to arrest and put at least some of the anarchists on trial. And that the investigation would also continue to include Sheriff Frawley and Undersheriff Kerringston, but it was premature to assert that they would also be prosecuted. Myra's description at the meeting of their suspected involvement had gone far enough...for now.

That meeting continued for just over an hour. And when it was over, Kathlene stayed as long as she felt she must in her role as one of the deputies protecting the room. She ducked questions, deferring to the commissioners.

When she finally could, she hurried back to the sheriff's

department, stayed in the background as much as possible
and was relieved when she was once more finally off duty.

Jock loved being a shapeshifter. He always had, always
would. He particularly loved being a member of Alpha
Force, with all its shifting perks and camaraderie with
other shifters and military members.

But right now, it was Sunday, the second day after the
invasion of the old ranch and the taking of so many anarchists into custody for further evaluation and, in most in-
stances, prosecution for planned acts of terrorism.

He was in the cabin he still shared with Ralf—for now.
Most of the other cabins in this motel had also been taken
over by Alpha Force members for at least one more night.
They'd all been meeting and debriefing one another and
sharing thoughts about what should come next—all of
which was presented to their commanding officer, Major
Drew Connell. He was their liaison with the FBI and other
feds who were now involved with this situation.

Although they'd spoken on the phone, Jock hadn't seen
Kathlene since late on the night when the raid on the ranch
had been conducted, which had been the day before yesterday. And he was probably leaving Clifford County tomorrow. Forever.

There was a lot of cleanup work awaiting him at Ft.
Lukman. Debriefing and planning for whatever his next
assignment would be, and who knew what else?

Yet another meeting was scheduled to begin in half
an hour at Drew's cabin. Jock would go there. He had to.

Ralf had already strolled over there so he could touch
base with all the other shifting aides who'd come to this
area, not just Noel Chuma but about half a dozen others
who'd helped their shifters change into wolves and invade

the camp en masse, the best way of handling it safely for Alpha Force.

Before heading to Drew's cabin, Jock grabbed a bottle of beer from the fridge. Then he picked up his laptop computer.

He was going to say goodbye to Kathlene tomorrow—maybe.

But he also had an idea, and he had to flesh it out now to determine if it might work.

"You've got to be joking," Kathlene said to Myra.

Her friend had called her first thing on that Monday morning and asked her to come to see her at the County Building. She'd had her secretary serve both of them coffee, and now they sat in the tiny conversation area in Myra's office.

"No, although I'm not sure what all it'll take to get approvals for you to be named sheriff. But the other most likely person to be named acting sheriff of Clifford County, Senior Deputy Tommy X Jones, has already told me, his closest contact on the commission, that he likes things as is. He doesn't want to be promoted, at least not now." Myra had taken her navy suit jacket off, but otherwise she looked every bit the official County Commissioner that she was. Her dark hair was arranged perfectly around a face with just enough makeup to hide her wrinkles and underscore the attractiveness of her large brown eyes.

Kathlene felt underdressed, even though she was wearing exactly what she was supposed to, since she was on duty that day. Her uniform looked as good as it always did, and she'd pulled her hair back into a clip at the base of her neck, as was required.

"I'm not sure I do, either." On the other hand, this might be a perfect time to take on more responsibility like that.

Despite all her self-chiding, she already missed Jock, and as far as she knew he remained in town. She'd checked around and learned that the Alpha Force contingent that had arrived on Friday was still present, as were some of the feds who continued to collect evidence. Others had taken the alleged anarchists somewhere for preliminary incarceration and arraignments or whatever the system required.

She'd last talked to Jock yesterday. She figured he wouldn't be here much longer.

She just hoped he would call to say goodbye. At least that way she'd get some closure.

She realized how odd it was that she had accepted who and what he was and had nevertheless, despite all good sense, fallen for him. It was probably a good thing that he had backed off like this. Her interest was clearly one-sided.

Maybe he could only fall for another shifter, like that woman he had lost.

That should make it easier to forget him...shouldn't it?

Feeling sorrow welling inside her, she took another sip of coffee without looking at Myra. "Tell you what," she said. "Right now I'm against the idea, but I'll think about it. Meantime, there are surely others with more seniority than me who would make a better sheriff. Tell Tommy X my feelings about this, and I'm sure he'll help you figure it out."

"But—"

"I'll think about it, too, Myra. I promise." Her mind wrapped momentarily around her partner, Jimmy Korling, then unwrapped him immediately. Not only was he more junior within the department than she was, but he'd seemed much too accepting of Sheriff Frawley's position. Plus, he wasn't wild about having women as equals, let alone superior officers.

But there were others in the department who'd work out a lot better than he would.

She would start making a list.

"I'll talk to you later," she told Myra. "Right now, I need to head for the department. I'll be officially on duty soon."

Not for another hour, but she didn't need to tell her friend that.

What she'd do for that hour she wasn't sure, but—

No sooner had she exited the County Administration Building and walked out onto the sidewalk than a car pulled up to the curb beside her. She glanced inside.

It was Jock.

She ignored how her heart started racing, how her mouth almost curved up into an automatic smile, and just nodded. "Hi," she said. "Are you leaving today?"

"Yes, we are." He'd stopped and opened the window. Lord, did he look handsome in his white knit shirt, with a hint of dark shadow at his cheeks and chin.

"So everything's in order. That's good."

"Nothing's final till the prosecutions finish successfully, but it looks good for now. My commanding officers will be in touch to thank you again. And I want to talk to you about that."

"No need to thank me. Stopping those miserable anarchists before they hurt anyone is all I wanted."

All she started out wanting. Now, if she was honest with herself, she knew she wanted some kind of ongoing relationship with Jock.

But that wasn't going to happen.

Even so, she felt a warm glow inside when he said, "Look, this isn't the place for us to talk. Grab some coffee with me, please?" He looked serious, and she figured he, too, just wanted to thank her—but she should probably give him the courtesy of letting him say goodbye gracefully.

"All right. Where—"

"How about your house?"

Interesting. Did he want to indulge in one last love-making session for the road?

Well, if so, maybe that would be the best goodbye she could get. "All right."

"Get in and I'll drive us there. No need for you to make the coffee. We'll stop for some on the way."

Their conversation in the car was all about the case. Everything was coming together well.

"And all of the other shifters who came," she said at one point as if she was discussing a standard form of weapon that was used that night. "I assume they really helped to make all this successful. It looked that way."

"That's for sure."

They stopped at the town's only chain coffee shop and used the drive-through. She ordered a mocha, figuring she deserved the sweet chocolate considering the sourness she was about to experience. A short while later, they were at her house.

This was probably a very bad idea. On the other hand, here they were and she might as well enjoy what she could of this goodbye session, however it occurred.

She didn't wait for him to open the door before getting out of the car and striding up the front walk to her home. She opened the front door and waved for him to go in first.

And closed her eyes briefly as the tall, muscular, amazingly good-looking guy brushed by her, undoubtedly for the last time.

She showed him into her living room and sat down herself at one end of her fluffy, familiar sofa. She put her mocha down on the coffee table in front of them and waited for him to begin.

She expected thanks and congrats and all sorts of standard stuff people would say to strangers they would never see again.

And was shocked to hear him say, "Kathlene, I've got a proposition for you."

She had raised her chin expecting a blow, but now she cocked her head and stared at him. "Like what?"

"Let me preface this by saying that I've run this by some of my superiors at Alpha Force. They're all impressed by how you saw things that other people didn't, or chose not to see. How you put yourself in jeopardy of losing your job and worse by taking a stand to protect the public and never backing down."

They were impressed. What about him?

It was as if he heard her. "Of course I was sure to make that clear to them quite a bit as we were discussing what I'm about to tell you. I'm the first to admit how impressed I've been—even though you've driven me nuts at times by putting yourself in dangerous situations to make your points. They've all been good points, by the way."

At least now she knew why her putting herself in peril bothered him so much. But— "Stop buttering me up and tell me what you're up to." Now she was filled with suspicion, even though her heart felt like it would burst from his compliments.

"Sure. Here it is. Why don't you come to Ft. Lukman and join Alpha Force—as a nonshifting member, of course. You'd be ideal, as a former deputy sheriff, for training members—both shifters and not—in measures to protect themselves and others, and ensuring that justice is served. Oh, and looking for problems and speaking up when they find them."

Ft. Lukman. That was where Alpha Force was head-quartered. She would see more of Jock. A lot more.

But he hadn't mentioned that. Not at all. Maybe he didn't really want to see her again. "Why are you suggesting this?" she asked. "Do you and your fellow Alpha Forcers just want to make sure I keep my mouth shut about what I know about the unit?"

"Nope. I already trust you not to announce to the world that we're a bunch of shapeshifters. That could really harm the unit, and I don't think you'd want to do that. Besides, if you did, everyone would consider you a nut case."

She laughed. "I think a lot of people already do, and I've never even mentioned shapeshifters." But then she grew serious. "I...I don't know, Jock. I'm surprised that I'd even like to consider the offer. I just turned down an offer that might have made me sheriff here, and that's more appropriate."

"Maybe. But...well, okay, let me fill you in on my ulterior motive. The thing is, I've fallen in love with you, Kathlene. And if you might care for me at all, it'd be a good thing for you to see more of Alpha Force in action. We've a lot of shifters married to nonshifters, and those relationships work well, believe it or not."

She felt her eyes widen. "Are you asking me to marry you?"

"Not yet, but that's in my plans if things go as well as I think they will. And I know now very well how you'd handle yourself if any of our assignments wound up putting you in danger. You'd protect me."

She didn't recall rising to her feet or seeing him rise, but she was suddenly in his arms. His kiss was soft and exploratory and still caused waves of heat to pulse through her.

She soon pulled away and looked up into his eyes. "Let's

discuss this later, okay? Right here. Can you stay here one more night?"

"I think so," he said softly, "but—"

"I want to give you a night to convince me." She grinned. "And, by the way, I don't think it'll be hard to do. I've fallen in love with you, too, Jock Larabey. You and the sweet wolf inside you. And—"

She couldn't finish since his mouth was on hers again.

But she had a feeling that she would soon be moving to Ft. Lukman…and a whole new, wonderful life.

* * * * *

 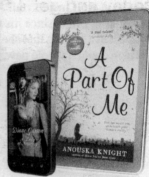